THE FURIES OF WINTER

A DELAFIELD & MALLOY INVESTIGATION

BOOK 6

TRISH MacENULTY

For the furious women,
then and now

"Blood avengers, always in pursuit,
we chase them to the end."— the Furies.
—Aeschylus
The Eumenides,
translated by Ian Johnston

Contents

Chapter 1

Louisa

Snowflakes swirled outside the window of the silk shop. Louisa checked her watch. Almost closing time. She'd been working every afternoon for two weeks now and still no sign of the thieves. She closed the *Delineator* fashion magazine she'd been reading, stood, and meandered among the bolts of silk stacked on tables in the center of the cavernous room, losing herself in the piles of cloth — the bright jewel tones, the brocades, the gold-threaded flower patterns. With travel to Paris canceled due to the war in Europe, America's silk trade was at a peak. Some of the bolts were worth upwards of ten thousand dollars. She unrolled a bolt of turquoise silk and held the cloth up in the pale light, eking through the windows. She envisioned a dress, swirling around her calves as she danced in Francis' arms at the Paradise Club.

The bell above the door tinkled, and a blast of cold air barged in, raising goosebumps on the back of her neck. The silk slid from her fingers. Louisa turned to see a stout, middle-aged woman bundled in a dark wool coat and a black rolled-brim hat, snow dusting her shoulders, with a boy about seven years old at her side. The woman smiled as she approached. She was missing a front tooth.

"May I help you?" Louisa asked.

"I believe youse have a package of ribbons for me."

"Your name?" Louisa walked over to the counter where the packages were kept.

"Mrs. Smith," she said.

Louisa looked through the small packages under the counter. "Ah, yes, here it is." She brought the package to the counter.

"Coldest winter I ever remember," the woman commented.

"At least the snow seems to be letting up," Louisa said, glancing at the window. "That will be one dollar and forty-five cents."

The woman handed her an envelope. "Keep the change, dearie," she said.

Louisa peered inside the envelope, swallowed when she saw the sum, and then looked up at the woman. This kind-looking lady and child were the thieves? Her heart rate accelerated. "Th-thank you."

"And would you mind looking after the boy for me? Just for a while?" The woman nodded at the child, a sullen-faced boy in knickers and a jacket with a tweed cap on his head.

"The boy? You want to leave him here?" Louisa asked, dumbfounded.

Even though there was no one else in the shop, the woman leaned forward and said in a tight whisper, "That's the way it works, sweetie."

"I see." Louisa eyed the child once more.

The boy came around the counter, and sat down on an overturned crate.

The woman leaned over the counter and pointed her finger at the boy. "You be good for the nice lady."

"Wait," Louisa said as the woman turned to leave. "What do I do?"

"Close up shop like always. The kid'll be fine." She strode out of the store, clutching her package of ribbons.

Louisa looked at the boy hunkered down on the crate.

"Do try not to touch the silk," Louisa whispered, then realized that was a stupid thing to say as he was part of a gang planning to haul as much of the valuable fabric out of the shop as they could.

The boy ignored her. He propped his elbow on his knee and put his chin on his fist, posed like the statue of *The Thinker*. He was awfully young to be a criminal. She wondered what would happen to him.

Of course, the silk thieves had to be stopped, Louisa thought. Recently, they had killed a night watchman. Then after months of robbing shops, train cars, and designers' lofts, the gang finally made a mistake and approached an honest clerk to see if she'd be willing to take a bribe. She said she would be, then promptly told the owner what had happened, and quit her job. The police had been no help as a crime had not yet been committed. Hence, the owner turned to Louisa Delafield's "Discreet Investigations."

At five o'clock, Louisa looked outside. The snow had stopped falling. She donned her coat, her fleece cloche, and wool scarf and locked up the shop. The boy hadn't moved from the crate where he sat. It was an ingenious plan. Train a child to hide in the store and then unlock the door when the thieves arrived later that night. He would probably have to wait for hours. She wished she'd had some food to leave him.

Louisa walked briskly along Park Avenue, checking her reflection in the store windows to see if anyone was following. Three inches of snow had settled onto the sidewalk, but her boots were sturdy and warm. At the Belmont Hotel on 42nd Street, she entered the massive lobby and glanced around. No one had followed her inside. She found the concierge and asked to use the telephone. He showed her to a desk in an alcove.

"Operator, please connect me with police Captain Tom Tunney. He's at the Centre Street location in the fifth precinct."

When Captain Tunney's gruff voice came on the line, she informed him of the bribe and the forthcoming burglary. "Do be careful," she said. "There's a child involved."

Fifteen minutes later she dashed up a flight of steps inside a building on Broadway and opened the door to the offices of Francis Holland, Esquire & Associates. Over the past few months, Francis had steered several investigations her way. Working together, consulting on cases, dining in restaurants to discuss the details—they'd grown close. The dinners had turned into dancing, and dancing had turned into kissing and touching. Which is where their relationship lingered for the moment.

The secretary was gone for the day, and since Louisa was the only "associate," she hung up her coat in the reception area and walked directly into Francis' office, where she found him bent over a contract. He looked up at her and smiled, broad smile that reached all the way up to his warm hazel eyes. He had perfect teeth and an adorable cleft chin.

"The discreet investigator returns," he said.

"The owner of the store was right. An older woman came in with a bribe just before closing time." Louisa dropped the envelope with the money on his desk.

He straightened up—tall, lanky, and boyish in his gabardine suit—and came around the desk. "So how do they do the heist?"

She pulled her gloves off finger by finger as she spoke. "You'll never guess. They leave a child hidden in the store to let the thieves in later."

"Starting them young, I suppose." He picked up the envelope, looked inside and whistled.

"We can paint the town with this."

"No, we can't. You're taking it straight to your uncle at the precinct. He's expecting you."

"Too bad. I was going to let you buy me a steak at Delmonico's," he teased, pulling her close to him. The warmth of his body made her tingle.

"Delmonico's is too stuffy." She gazed up at him. This close she could see the end-of-day stubble. She rubbed her index finger across his sandpapery jawline.

"How about I take you to Cafe Montmartre instead. Friday night?" he asked. "I want to celebrate."

"Solving this crime?" she asked.

"Maybe," he said. "Maybe something else."

She looked into his eyes and saw a yearning that surprised her. Her breath caught. Did he intend to propose? She lowered her gaze. "I'm not sure I'm available Friday night."

"Is that right? Just how many suitors do you have, Miss Delafield?"

"Only a dozen or so."

His lips landed warm and soft on hers. She kissed him back and felt a fire at the back of her throat. What if he did plan to propose? What was she so afraid of?

"Of course, I'm available Friday night," she said.

He smiled. "Then it's a date. In the meantime, I'll run this bribe to the precinct station and make sure the police do their job."

"Who would have imagined silk houses would lose so much money to thieves?" she wondered. "The stuff is worth as much as gold."

"And now it will stop thanks to you."

The next day, when Louisa returned home from the Silk House with several yards of the turquoise fabric the owner had given her in return for her services in addition to her fee, she found Martin Malloy sitting on the sofa in the parlor with Carlotta. Martin usually came by about once a month to find out if she'd heard anything about his sister, Ellen. This time he'd brought Paula O'Neil's older boy, Sean, with him. At least something good had come out of it all, Louisa thought. Paula had been left a widow much too young. How surprised Ellen would be that one of the first things Martin did when he got to New York was to join the police force and second, to marry Detective Paddy O'Neil's widow. The Irish lawbreaker was now a law enforcer.

"There she is," Carlotta said as Louisa set down her package. "Martin's been telling me all about his latest arrest. Plenty of excitement. They nabbed that gang of silk thieves."

"Bang. Bang!" Sean said, startling the cat from her perch on the windowsill.

"A whole family of crime stoppers, aren't you?" She tousled Sean's dark hair, black like his dead father's.

"Thanks to you," Martin said. "We caught the thieves red-handed – or silk-handed."

Sean piped up. "Pops is still a rookie, but they let him arrest the old lady!"

"And she seemed like such a sweet old thing," Louisa said. "What will happen to the little boy?"

"Reformatory, I s'pose. Thievin' is no life for a wee lad."

"Louisa didn't even take me on the job," Carlotta said, piqued. Since Ellen had left them to go to Ireland last April, Carlotta had been Louisa's right hand on her "discreet" investigations, but the silk house had been a one-woman job.

"You would have been bored," Louisa said to mollify her.

Carlotta scoffed and turned to Sean. "Say, Sean, let's go down to the park and chase some pigeons so's your Papa and Miss Louisa can talk."

After Carlotta left with the boy, Louisa poured herself a cup of tea from the silver service on the coffee table, sat down in the overstuffed armchair, and gazed at Martin. Gingin the cat jumped on her lap and settled down.

"Are you enjoying married life?" she asked.

"Aye, Paula's the best. And I love the two boys as if they were my own. They were mighty young when Paddy was killed, so they don't remember him well. You knew Paddy, didn't ya?" Martin's lilting Irish cadence reminded Louisa so much of Ellen.

"I did," she said. "He was a good detective. His death was horrid." Paddy had died when a pallet "accidentally" fell on him at the docks where he'd been investigating German saboteurs. "Marrying you is a decidedly better outcome for Paddy's widow and his two boys than if you..."

"Than if I'd been shot by a firing squad in Dublin. I know what you're thinking," he said. "You're thinking of the sacrifice my sister made to save me."

Louisa sipped her tea, set down the cup, and ran her fingers over Gingin's soft fur. "Ellen made that choice of her own free will."

"Did she? What sort of choice is that? Her brother's life in exchange for losing all she'd managed to accomplish, even giving up her baby to go back to Germany and be a spy?"

Louisa understood the guilt he felt. If he had not been a member of the Irish Brotherhood, if he had not been hellbent on casting off the British yoke during a time of war and gotten arrested in the Easter uprising last year, Ellen would still be in New York, publishing *The Ladies' Lantern* and raising her child. But Ellen had given it all up so the British would commute her brother's sentence and send him and their mother and her youngest brother to America.

Louisa was loath to admit how bereft she'd been since Ellen's departure. Not to mention the baby. Even with three women living in the small Harlem townhouse, the rooms felt empty without Ellen, publishing a magazine in the parlor, the baby sleeping in her little swing. At the time it had seemed a nuisance, and she'd told Ellen in no uncertain terms she should find another office space. Was that part of the reason Ellen gave up the baby and left? Louisa understood Martin's guilt because she had so much of her own.

"Something occurred to me," she said. "Ultimately, Ellen would never have been satisfied simply publishing a magazine. She's the sort of person who has to do things. Publishing stories about women's rights, the plight of children, and the troubles of workers — that would never have been enough for her. Ellen has a drive to change the world. And the magazine, for all the good it did, was simply not enough. That's why she left to go to Ireland as soon as she knew about the uprising.

And that's why she went to Germany to be a double agent when the British told her to go." Louisa wasn't sure if she was trying to make Martin or herself feel better.

Martin rubbed his cheek and frowned. With his trim blond mustache, his face had acquired a distinguished, handsome look. "And what about the baby?"

"Ellen loves Hester, but..." Louisa hesitated. Ellen *had* loved the child, but there was an enormous wall of grief in the way of her expression of that love. Not to mention the circumstances behind Hester's very existence. "Did you ever meet the man who...fathered the child?"

"No, he was someone she met in Germany. I wasn't there." He pounded his knee with his fist. "I never shoulda let her go there. I encouraged her. I thought she could help the Brotherhood get weapons from the Germans for the uprising. Dammit to hell."

"Young man!" Anna Delafield stood in the doorway of the parlor, leaning on her cane.

"Pardon me, Mrs. Delafield," Martin said, rising.

"Oh, sit down. I assume you two are discussing the whereabouts of Ellen Malloy." Anna headed over to her favorite armchair by the window. "Well, don't let me interfere."

Martin stayed standing. "Thank you, but I must be off at any rate. Miss Delafield, if you run into your British friend, that Grant fella, you might ask him the whereabouts of my sister. At least, let us know she's alive. For poor Ma's sake."

"I will." Louisa walked him to the door. "You'll find Carlotta and Sean down the street at Morningside Park."

After she shut the door, she turned and leaned against it. She felt it again, that yawning chasm in her chest whenever she thought of Ellen. Europe was in the throes of a war that seemed it would never end, and her friend was somewhere in the thick of it. She imagined mustard gas seeping across a continent, the slaughter in its wake. A roaring sound filled her head.

Stop, she told herself. Do not think of it. She strode into the parlor and put a record on the phonograph. Beethoven's Fifth Symphony. She lay down on the sofa and let the music drown out the clamor in her head.

Chapter 2
Ellen

Ellen double-checked her watch. Four o'clock in the afternoon, and yet the sky had turned inky. Sleet streamed past the train window as it barreled east toward Petrograd. Her stomach fluttered in anticipation. She'd been traveling for nearly a week. First, by train through shell-shocked Europe, then by ferry on tossing waves, and then by train again, past burned villages, scorched fields, rotting carcasses of farm animals and caravans of refugees. She had left everything behind — Ireland, New York, and then Germany for this snow-bound world of Russia.

Captain Boehm, her German handler, had told her there was no time to lose. The mad monk, Rasputin, had been murdered in December and the situation in Petrograd was explosive. "Secure a position with a British or even an American family with political connections. Keep your ears and eyes open. Send cables to your cousin, Olga. Food shortages. Unrest. Morale. At some point, you will need to search out the Bolsheviks to work with them. Help them get their message to the

Americans. Anything to discourage them from entering the war."

"Why the Bolsheviks?" she said. "And why me? I figured you for sending me to Ireland." She knew the Germans hoped that the troubles in Ireland would continue to be a thorn in the side of the British.

Captain Boehm had taken off his spectacles and gazed at her with watery blue eyes. "The Bolsheviks under Vladimir Lenin will take Russia out of the war. And Lenin wants a worldwide revolution. With your experiences as a rabble-rouser in both America and Ireland, they will expect you to be most useful."

"But Lenin is in exile."

"Not for long."

A heavy woman lumbered onto the train in Helsinki and stopped in the aisle next to Ellen's seat while she took off her hat and a ratty fur coat to reveal white hair and a dark cotton dress with buttoned cuffs. She stuffed her coat and hat in the compartment above and sank down in the seat beside Ellen with a heavy sigh.

Ellen shifted her attention back to the white landscape outside. The train wheels on the track made a rhythmic chunka-chunk sound. The whistle screamed as the locomotive picked up speed. The rocking of the train car lulled her as she thought of the past four months living in a chateau outside Berlin, away from the signs of the war. Captain Boehm kept her sequestered from the horror, immersed in the countryside, learning the Russian language, target shooting, running and doing calisthenics to build muscle. A restless spirit, she welcomed the challenges ahead.

The woman pulled a greasy sauerkraut-and-ham sandwich out of her bag. She ate loudly, smacking her lips. She said something in a language that Ellen didn't understand, so Ellen just nodded and looked away, hoping the woman would stop talking to her. Ellen spoke German and Russian, but not whatever language this woman had uttered. She wondered if the woman was a refugee from the front like so many of the other passengers, a motley bunch of Lithuanians, Ukrainians, and Poles as well as Russian Jews. The Great War had been going on for three years now with no end in sight.

The old woman beside her finished her sandwich and opened a tin of cookies. She offered one to Ellen, who shook her head "no." But the woman insisted, shaking the tin of cookies at her. So, Ellen took a cookie and bit into it. It was dry and flavorless. The woman shook the tin again and Ellen waved it away. The woman sighed.

They must be getting close to Russia, Ellen thought. She looked at the itinerary. One more stop in Finland coming up. As the train wheels squealed, the woman next to her got up and offered Ellen the cookie tin. El-len smiled but shook her head. The woman then put the tin on Ellen's lap and said, in perfect English, "From Parvus. You know what to do with it."

Ellen stared at the cookie tin. When she looked up, the woman was trundling down the aisle, her coat and hat in her arms, her bag knocking into the other pas-sengers. Ellen looked once again at the cookie tin with its picture of children skating. From Parvus? She re-called meeting a portly man with a neat beard who called himself Parvus during her training in Germany. Captain Boehm told her it was this man's idea to sup-port the Bolsheviks. What sort of support came in a cookie tin?

As the train pulled away from the station, she gazed around to make sure no one was watching and then cracked open the tin. She slid the paper under the cookies aside and saw official-looking papers trimmed in gold borders with a picture of King George. British treasury bonds! She closed the tin and leaned back. How much were they worth, she wondered, and what was she s'posed to do with them?

The conductor came through, announcing first in Russian and then in French that they had crossed the border from Finland and would soon be in Petrograd, the imperial capital of Russia. Passengers gathered their belongings and crowded the aisle. With a metallic screech and plumes of steam blowing past the windows, the train pulled to a stop. Ellen gazed out at the people waiting in front of a greyish stucco building. Each person was bundled up so thoroughly, all that showed were their eyes and reddened noses.

She jammed the cookie tin into her carry-all and followed the others out of the train car. As the passengers on the platform gathered their bags and dispersed, the protective layer of body heat surrounding her dissipated and she discovered the meaning of "bone-chilling cold."

"Christ on the cross," she muttered as she gathered her suitcases and went to look for some sort of transportation.

When she came around to the front of the station, she didn't see a single motorcar. Instead, a sleigh pulled by a sturdy horse stood in front of her. She had seen sleighs like this in New York on occasion. Rich people rode in them for fun at Christmas time.

"Is this a cab?" she asked the *izvozchik*.

He nodded and indicated she should get in the back.

She shoved her suitcases inside and climbed aboard, then asked him to take her to a hotel. He spit a wad of brown tobacco juice onto the white snow and said, "You will not find anything."

"Why not?"

"All the hotels are full."

"Why is that?"

"Look around you. Refugees infest the city like fleas on a starving rat. The poor ones sleep in rail stations. The rich ones try to find hotels."

She took a deep breath. She hadn't expected to sleep in a rail station. He shrugged and tossed the reins, bells jingling, signaling the beast to get moving. "But we will try."

She huddled under a thick wool rug behind the driver as the horse trotted along the streets of the city, spewing a white fan of snow behind them. Ellen was too busy trying to stay warm to get a look at Petrograd, not that she could have seen much under the dark, moonless sky. They stopped at one hotel after another from the dingiest hovels to glittering palaces. At each stop she heard the same thing.

"No rooms here. We have guests sleeping in the dining rooms, bathrooms, and on the billiard tables," or "our guests are already sharing rooms," or "we turned away a duke and a duchess, what makes you think we have room for you?"

A scream of frustration stirred inside her chest, but she kept it tamped down. She leaned forward, willing her vocal cords to stay calm and steady. "What will I do?"

The driver had a long, scraggly beard, flecked with snow. His eyes looked as though they'd seen the dawn of time. He sent another long arc of tobacco juice through the air and onto the ground. Then he turned toward her. "A lady in the Vyborg district will give you a place on her floor for two rubles."

"On the floor?"

He shrugged. "You will be out of the cold."

It would only be for one night. How bad could it be? The wind screeched, and the horse stomped its foot. She nodded. The man drove over a bridge across an ice-coated river through a maze of factories and tenements. Men, she judged to be factory workers by their coarse clothes and their trudging gait, streamed along the side of the road.

The driver pulled the reins and stopped the horses. He pointed with his chin at a brick building. "Top floor."

"Thank you," she said and paid him. She gazed up at the brick building. The wind nipped at her ankles, and she hurried inside, climbed to the top floor with her two suitcases, stopping between flights to catch her breath, and finally knocked on the door. A woman with a face like a codfish opened the door. She didn't have a single tooth that Ellen could see. Ellen wanted to turn around and run, but the thought of the bitter wind stayed her.

"Would you have a spot for me?" Ellen asked, holding out the rubles.

The woman took the money and beckoned her inside. The tart odor of kerosene and flatulence nearly knocked her over. Ellen followed the woman past sprawled men and boys into a second room, where five women, one with a baby and another with twin toddlers, huddled under blankets. The twins chattered to each other in their own private language. A pisspot occupied one corner, its odor mixing with the earthy scent of the women and their children. The woman with the codfish face pointed to a blanket and a space next to the wall.

Ellen had seen poverty. She'd grown up in the Claddagh, a poor fishing village in Ireland. She'd visited the tenements of New York's Bowery. But never had she imagined such squalor. She didn't hope for a wink of sleep, but at least she was out of the wind, which whined like a wolf at the windows.

The women were hollow-eyed, skin stretched taut. Scarves covered hair that hadn't been washed in ages. They muttered among themselves. After Ellen sank onto an inch-thick mattress in the corner, the mother of the twins struck up a conversation with her. She told Ellen that she and her two children had nowhere to go after her husband had driven them out of their house.

"He stuffed the chimney and lit the stove." She peered at Ellen. "Why would he do that?"

Ellen understood what the woman seemed not to. The husband had intentionally killed himself. How hungry, how desperate he must have been.

"What will we do? What will we do?" A lament rather than a question.

Ellen could find no words of comfort to offer. The other women cast glances at her as they talked of hunger.

"The bakers save the bread for the restaurants," one of them said, "but for us, nothing but mold."

"Even soldiers at the front don't get enough food," another said, "while the Tsarina's children eat cakes."

They grumbled a bit more, but one by one they fell asleep. Ellen heard the suckling sound of the nursing baby. Her breasts tingled. Against her will she remembered her own baby's mouth on her nipple before walling off the memory. She must not think of either Hester — not Hester French, the woman she had once loved, and not Hester Murphy, the child she had borne and given up to be raised by others. *What you must do, Ellen Malloy," she told herself, "is stuff your memories, your feelings, in a lockbox in your head, and consider the here and now.*"

Even though suffering was all around, she was glad to be out of that German chateau where she'd been as useful as a one-string mop. Here in Russia she might do something meaningful. Not for her German or British spymasters but for regular people. Something that might make all her sacrifices worth the cost. She had no idea what that something would be, but she imagined a world of possibility opening before her. Three years of war had crippled this country, and the people here had nothing to lose. What would happen when they'd had enough? Captain Boehm believed there would be a revolution, starting right here in Petrograd. He only cared because he wanted Russia out of the war. Ellen, however, cared for other reasons. Might the time have finally come for the poor and oppressed to rise up? Might this war just be the world's birthing pains?

It was still dark when she awoke. The codfish woman who ran the flat slept on a cot near the door, snoring like a bull. Ellen shook her awake and asked if she knew where someone might get a wee bite of food. The woman shook her head. "Nyet."

Ellen grabbed her two suitcases, squeezed out of the door, trundled down the five flights, and stepped into the bitter cold.

Chapter 3

Louisa

Suzie examined the turquoise silk in the light streaming through her brownstone windows.

"What do you think?" Louisa asked.

"I think this will make a gorgeous dress." Suzie took off her spectacles. Her hair was going gray, but her brown skin looked as smooth as it had when Louisa was a child. "Is it for a special occasion?"

"I don't know," Louisa said.

"You don't know?" Suzie gave her a look of disbelief.

Louisa tilted her head. "Perhaps, there may be a special occasion soon."

Suzie leaned in close. "A proposal?"

"I don't know, Suzie. Francis did say something mysterious about having dinner to celebrate something."

"Let me get my measuring tape." Suzie rummaged in the old sewing basket she'd had for as long as Louisa could remember. "If Francis does propose, what will you say?"

"I'm not sure. I really don't want to be a spinster when I turn 30, and that's only two years away."

Suzie wrapped the tape around Louisa's waistline. "Louisa, do you love Francis?"

Louisa pondered the question before answering. "I enjoy his company. He's fun to be with and he's kind. How did you know it was right with Mr. Sweet?"

"I suppose it was one of those love-at-first-sight situations. I was an old woman by then, but just being around him, I felt like a girl."

Louisa knew Mr. Sweet had been smitten from the moment he saw Suzie. "I was in love with Forrest Calloway, and I lost him to another woman because I didn't see what I had right there in front of me. I'm afraid if I don't say yes to Francis, I might not get another chance at happiness."

Suzie lowered the measuring tape, dark eyes searching Louisa's. "You've suffered a lot of loss, child, including your father, but before you say yes, you best know what's in your heart."

No one knew Louisa the way Suzie did. Not even her own mother.

The door knocker sounded.

"I wonder who that is." Suzie laid the silk on her sewing table and went to answer the door.

Louisa heard voices in the hallway and was pleasantly surprised when Pansy, Suzie's grandniece, came in. Pansy had lived with Louisa, Suzie, and her mother for a short while before going to nursing school. It seemed a lifetime ago, but it had only been a couple of years.

"Miss Louisa, how are you?" Pansy asked. She wore a nurse's outfit, and her dark hair was curled into a neat roll from one ear around the back of her head to the other. She'd always been lovely, but recently she'd filled out and looked more like a young woman than a gangly girl.

Louisa opened her arms and embraced her.

"I have news for you." Pansy looked from Louisa to Suzie. "I'm going to France."

"France!" Suzie exclaimed. "Why would you do that? There's a war going on over there, in case you didn't know."

"I do know it. I also know that America won't stay neutral much longer. There will be Negro soldiers. And I'm afraid that white doctors and nurses won't treat them. I'm going ahead of time so I can be ready when they come."

Louisa had been holding her breath. Now she exhaled. "That's incredibly brave of you, Pansy."

"Brave or foolish." Suzie shook her head. "I don't like it."

Suzie went to the kitchen and came back with a pot of tea and a plate of applesauce cake on a silver tray. The three women sat in comfortable, chintz-covered chairs around the coffee table while Pansy talked about her plans — all the while Suzie frowned.

"Why can't you just stay where you are? Plenty of people need your help right here," Suzie said. Suzie had been so long without a family of her own before finding her brother and his children in Florida, Louisa understood her fear of losing Pansy.

"But, Suzie, what she'll be doing is so important," Louisa said. "It makes me feel rather useless."

Suzie scoffed. "You and Ellen foiled German plots on American soil. You have done your part. And Ellen's still out there somewhere, risking her life..."

They were silent for a moment, all wondering where Ellen was and what sort of danger she might be courting.

Pansy changed the subject, turning the conversation to Louisa. "Are you still writing for newspapers and magazines?"

"I write freelance articles, but my investigative work is more fun and pays better," Louisa said. "When I can get it."

"I always did think you liked the investigating most of all," Pansy commented. She wasn't wrong.

They finished their tea, and Louisa told them she had to leave. Suzie promised to have the dress ready by Friday afternoon.

"You must let me pay you," Louisa said.

"You can pay me in leftover fabric," Suzie said. "I can make some nice little geegaws with that silk."

Louisa took a taxicab to Francis' office. As the motorcar puttered along Broadway, dodging horse-drawn carts, roadsters and trolleys, she thought about Pansy's plans and the terrible cost the war was exacting even though America was still officially neutral. She wondered if she ought to help with the war effort somehow, but the thought depressed her. Suzie was right. Louisa had already sacrificed enough for the wretched war. Her best friend, Ellen, was gone. Ellen's baby, Hester, now lived with the Murphys. And two years earlier, Louisa had broken off her engagement with Forrest Calloway in order to devote herself to exposing German spies and saboteurs. She had wept at his wedding the next year and not from joy. Now, Forrest was happy, she reminded herself. It was time for her to seize her own happiness. The blasted war could take care of itself.

Chapter 4

Ellen

There were no taxis or sleighs about, so Ellen trudged in the biting cold under a sky so low she might scrape the top of her head on the clouds. In the streets men huddled around bin fires, and soldiers loitered on corners. She passed a line of women and children stretching far down the block. The line didn't move.

"What do you wait for?" she asked one of the women in her rudimentary Russian.

"Bread," was the answer.

As she crossed the bridge into the city proper, the sun crept over the horizon, sending golden shafts across the belly of the clouds. From her geography lessons in Germany, she knew the frozen water below was the Neva River.

The Russians called boulevards "Prospekts." A metal plate on a corner building informed her she was on the Nevsky Prospekt. What a magnificent vista of stupendous buildings of pink granite and colorful stucco with domes, arches, pillars and statues on every side. Restaurants and theaters lined the streets. Ellen patted the purse she kept tucked in the pocket of her skirt. Surely, there was food to be had for a price, she thought.

Finding an open cafe, she went inside. The aroma of tea from a samovar greeted her. She sat at a table and looked at the menu. Most of the items had been scratched off. She knew enough about Russian currency to know that the prices were extravagant for such limited fare.

"Might I have some bread with butter and a cup of hot tea?" she asked a red-nosed waiter.

"No white bread," the waiter said. "Only black. No butter, but we do have cheese."

So the shortages were everywhere, but people with money would not starve. Not yet. She ate the chewy black bread along with a slice of cheese.

"Why so little food?" she asked the waiter.

He bent close and whispered, "There's food out in the country, but we cannot get it. The problem is the rails. Meat rots in the provinces. Fish are thrown back into the sea. We have the most inefficient transport system in the entire world. Not to mention this is the worst winter in years. Between the blizzards and the breakdowns, the country is paralyzed. If you have petrol you can drive to the country to get milk and eggs from the peasants, but petrol is only for the rich. There is still food for the rich. Always food for the rich."

He stared down at her, his eyebrows raised, inviting her to share his outrage — but quietly. It was most likely dangerous for him to speak so frankly.

"What about the wheat fields?"

"There's no one to harvest wheat. All the men have been sent to the front. The women can only do so much on their own. Whatever they do harvest must feed the soldiers."

Must the whole world starve whenever kings and emperors decided to squabble, Ellen wondered. She paid her bill, making note of a sign that said in French and German: "Just because a man must make his living as a waiter, do not insult him by offering a tip."

When she emerged from the cafe, the sun had climbed high enough to be obscured by the gray clouds pressing down on the scurrying populace. All around her, the roofs heaved with piled snow. She pulled her scarf around her face, but her skin already felt cracked as a china dish hit with a hammer.

The city, carved up by canals and streets lined with palaces, spires and domes reaching toward the sky, gave off the air of an old queen, robbed of her throne. Sidewalks teemed with tattered refugees, eyes hollow with old hunger. All the while fancy motorcars tooled along, stopping in front of French clothing shops or flower shops, and women draped in furs dashed from their cars to the warmth of the stores.

As Ellen walked alongside an ice-covered canal, a church bell tolled. She needed to find employment and a place to stay, and she had no time to waste. Her body still ached from the hard tenement floor. When Captain Boehm told her to find domestic work with a British family, he didn't know that would work in her favor as well. She needed to get in touch with London somehow. Sir Basil Thomson would be wondering where the Germans sent her. He thought they would place her back in Ireland. She worried if she did not get in touch with him soon, he might think she'd crossed over to the Germans, and Christ only knew what trouble he'd cause for her family then.

After nearly an hour roaming the streets, she passed a building that looked promising: The New English Club. But when she went to the back door, an officious man said they did not hire women except as scullery maids, and they didn't need English speakers for that.

"Do you know where I might find some English families? Someone who might need a governess or a lady's maid?" She held out some rubles.

He sniffed, took the money, and said in an English accent, dripping in disdain, "Lady Buchanan runs a soup kitchen for refugees at Warsaw Station. If anyone will know of any employment, it will be she."

It was about a forty-minute walk to the Warsaw Station, a much larger and more impressive railroad building than the Finland Station where she had disembarked. She had lugged along her suitcases, hoping she might find a staffed cloakroom in the station to store them, but when she went inside the terminal, she stopped and stared, stupefied. Everywhere she looked were men, women, and children, slumped against walls or sprawled on the floor, some of them shoeless, wearing nothing but rags. The stench of poverty and desperation wrapped around her like a poisonous gas.

At the far end of the room, tables held large pots of what was probably porridge. A group of bustling English ladies tried to herd the hordes of hungry refugees into orderly queues. She approached one of the English women, who was ladling porridge into tin bowls.

"Excuse me," Ellen said to the woman over the din of crying children.

"You'll need to get in line," the woman said.

"I'm not a refugee," Ellen responded in English. "I'm looking for work."

The woman looked up at Ellen. "Do you wish to volunteer?"

"No. I need a job. I have experience as a lady's maid."

"A lady's maid? Ha! Do you know how many lady's maids are currently unemployed? With so many British having fled back to England, countless servants have been left behind."

"What about governesses?"

"I'm sorry I can't help you."

"Well, there must be something."

Another woman, who was handing out chunks of bread, leaned over and said, "Go ask Lady Buchanan. She's over there distributing clothes."

Ellen looked in the direction the woman pointed and headed over to another table where mothers picked over stylish and impractical English hand-me-downs.

An elegant woman with a soft chin, a beaked nose, and imperious eyes glanced at her.

"Are you Lady Buchanan?" Ellen asked.

"I am," she said as if she were a general addressing a foot soldier. "My husband is the Ambassador to Russia, and this is *my* refugee station. Who are you?"

"My name is Ellen Malloy."

"Where are you from, Ellen Malloy?" she asked.

"Ireland," Ellen answered, "by way of New York."

"What in heaven's name are you doing here?"

"I had a job offer but it seems the family has left."

Lady Buchanan looked her up and down.

"Do you speak any Russian?"

Ellen's Russian tutor had been satisfied she could manage well enough to get by. "Yes, ma'am. *Я немного говорю по-русски.*"

"So, you speak a little Russian, if I understand what you just said. I happen to have a friend who is looking for someone with just your qualifications."

Lady Buchanan gave Ellen an address for a Lady Greystone's house in the English district. Ellen thanked her and then zigzagged through the crowds of families occupying every bit of floor or bench. She tripped over a woman combing lice out of a little girl's hair. She hurried outside and away from the squalid rail station and took a horse-drawn cab to the address in the Sergievskaia district.

The *izvoschik* pointed out a majestic building of red stone with an imperial crest on the top as the Palace of the Grand Duchess Olga. The difference between this opulence and the chaotic scene of degradation, hunger, and desperation she had just left was staggering. He turned on a side street and deposited her in front of a large granite house that would have been right at home on Fifth Avenue.

"Lady Buchanan sent me to apply for a position with Lady Greystone," she told the English butler.

He advised her to leave her suitcases in the hallway and took her into a room that could have passed for a parlor in Hampstead except for the bearskin rug on the floor, which she took care to avoid.

The mistress, a woman of about 35 years, sat close to a fire, reading a book, and barely took notice of her. Instead of logs, a pile of what looked like pieces of broken fencing sat in the woodbin. She listened with a bored expression as Ellen described her qualifications.

"I do need someone, as it turns out." Lady Greystone blew her nose into a handkerchief. "Show her to her room, Myers."

The butler took Ellen to a back stairwell and up to a small room with two beds in it.

"You will share quarters with the scullery maid," he said.

Better than a floor in a tenement with five other women and their children, Ellen thought. "What will my duties be, Mr. Myers? I do have experience as a lady's maid. I am happy to be a nurse or governess if there are any children in the house."

"No, no. Those positions are already filled."

"Then am I to do scullery work or general cleaning?"

"No, we have a Russian girl for scullery and two Ukrainian housemaids."

"Then what?"

"You're to wait in the bread lines."

Ellen pictured those unending lines of desperate-looking women she had passed earlier that day.

"Do you mean to tell me that in these fine houses they don't have flour to make their own bread?" When she had worked as a domestic in New York, the smell of baking bread had been a constant in the kitchen.

"There is no flour to be had. Sometimes we get pickled herring, caviar, jam and even sugar in the mail packets, but it's harder and harder for anything to get through. And flour or meat — impossible. So, you shall wait in the lines because the cook doesn't have the time. Are you hungry now?"

"Famished, as a matter of fact," Ellen said.

"Then after you get settled, come down to the kitchen. Supper is in one hour, and cook does manage to put together a decent English meal in spite of the shortages."

After he left, she unpacked her suitcase. She placed her underclothes, a nightgown, her two plain dresses, and a few toiletries in the dresser. The rubles Captain Boehm had given her would be safe hidden in the secret pocket in the lining of her suitcase. But what about the British treasury bonds the old woman on the train had given her? For the first time she was able to look them over and count their worth. Christ on the cross! A million pounds. The man Parvus must be serious about helping the Bolsheviks.

She took the ivory-handled pen knife from her purse and made an incision at the end of her mattress. Just wide enough to slip the bonds into the stuffing. She'd sew it up later for safety. As she folded the blade back into the pen knife, she noticed an eiderdown comforter at the end of the bed. She couldn't wait to crawl under it and get a good night's sleep. Then she remembered she'd be getting up in just a few hours to begin her new job.

Chapter 5

Louisa

Friday evening, Louisa adjusted the turquoise dress so that it didn't show too much decolletage — just enough. Her gray eyes picked up the color of the dress and she couldn't help but admire her reflection. Glowing skin. Long, smooth neck. She was not normally vain, but this dress made her feel positively captivating. She still did not know how she would answer Francis if he made a proposal. A voice in her head whispered, *Tempus fugit.* Yes, time flies. She was not getting younger.

"Wow. You look like a million bucks," Francis said when she opened the door of the brownstone.

He led her to his Ford Model A, his hand cupping her elbow, and they drove down Broadway to the Montmartre Café on the corner of 50th Street.

"Penny for your thoughts," he said.

"I'm remembering it was exactly four years ago when the Grand Central Terminal opened. What a night. I covered the story for *The Ledger*," she said.

"The doors opened at midnight. All of New York was there."

"That must have been exciting," he said.

"Oh, it was. And I was desperate to write about something other than debutante balls." How innocent she'd been back then. It may have only been four years but it felt like a lifetime. What a difference between 24 and 28. Since then she'd had two lovers, been briefly engaged, lost her job, gained another job, lost that, changed careers, and had the blinders unceremoniously ripped from her eyes when it came to high society. She had believed the upper classes to be superior to other people. Now she knew that many of them were no better than those silk thieves and, in some instances, a good deal worse.

They arrived at the restaurant a little before 10 o'clock, and were seated at a table on one of the upper levels. Francis, who spoke perfect French, ordered lobster for both of them.

"That's a stunning dress." He gazed across the table at her in the candlelight. "It brings out the blue in your eyes."

"My eyes are gray," she said.

"Not in that dress."

The lobster arrived. About halfway through the meal, Francis said, "My best friend from Harvard, Paul, and his wife, Rosalind, are visiting from Connecticut in a couple of weeks. They want to meet you."

Louisa was surprised to hear this. "You told them about me?"

"Well, sure. I had to let Paul know I'd met the woman I planned to spend the rest of my life with. That is, if you..." He dug into his jacket pocket. "I mean to say, I would be honored if you wore this ring when you meet them."

"Francis, what...?"

Before she knew what was happening, he was down on one knee with a ring in his hand, a brilliant sapphire flanked by tiny diamonds in a gold setting. She felt the blood rushing to her face. Even though she'd known a proposal was possible, even likely, she was still surprised when it actually happened.

"Oh, Francis, no..."

"No?"

She caught herself. Was she turning him down? *Tempus fugit.* "I mean, no, don't dirty your trousers. Please."

But he didn't rise. He knelt before her, his eyes questioning. She still wasn't sure of her answer until it slipped over her tongue and out into the light.

"Yes?" she said. It came out like a question.

"Yes?" he asked.

"Yes." The word rushed through her body with a shiver. A couple at the next table watched, smiling as he slipped the ring onto her finger. A perfect fit.

"The stone belonged to my grandmother," he said as he sat back in the chair. "I had it reset for you. Do you like it?"

"The art deco setting is perfect," she gushed. "Were you close to your grandmother?"

"She died when I was five so I barely remember her, but Mother tells me she loved to read and she made sure all her girls received an education. And as you are an educated woman, I believe she would approve."

Louisa gazed down at the ring. She had said yes. Was this what she truly wanted?

Francis rubbed his chin. "I know I should have approached your mother first, but frankly she terrifies me."

"Darling, I'm a modern woman. No one else can give permission for me to marry. You did exactly the right thing," she reassured him.

"I wasn't sure you would say yes. You've got your work. Writing articles, investigating crimes. I was afraid you wouldn't want to give that up," he said. "I mean, you don't have to, of course, but if..."

She took a deep breath and placed a hand on his. She had been pondering this very question.

"A modern marriage is a partnership, and I will do everything in my power to help you climb the ladder of success. If I happen to investigate something along the way or write an article here or there, so much the better. After all, Nixola Greeley-Smith is married, and she still writes for *The Evening World.*"

"Yes, of course," he said. "I would never want you to feel useless. That's the worst feeling."

She wondered what he meant by that, but didn't dwell on it.

"Let's have dinner at my house soon, and we'll tell my mother and Carlotta the news. In fact, I'll invite Suzie and Mr. Sweet, too."

He leaned forward. "Are you happy?"

"Deliriously," she said. "Let's dance."

They danced the one-step and the tango and the fox-trot. She twirled in her turquoise silk dress. On her finger the sapphire engagement ring glittered. For this moment the Great War was but a whisper in the distance. She still wasn't sure that she was in love with Francis, but she could think of no reason not to marry him. At least with his heart murmur, he wouldn't leave her to get killed somewhere in Europe. She simply couldn't take another loss.

The house was quiet as she made her way upstairs. Her thumb rubbed the inside band of the ring. She had gotten engaged for the second time. This time she would not throw the opportunity for happiness away. She entered her room and quietly shut the door, only to find someone asleep on her bed. She gasped in shock, which almost immediately turned into outrage.

Chapter 6

Ellen

Ellen sat in the warm kitchen with the servants as they ate their dinner. The family had already been fed upstairs, and the dining table cleared. The children had been put to bed. For an hour or so, the servants could relax while the lord and lady of the house were off at the opera. The conversation revolved around a "coming catastrophe" and what might happen to the English population of the city when it did.

"Thank heavens that Rasputin fellow is gone," Lady Greystone's personal maid, Jones, said. "Imagine what it took to murder him! Poison, shooting, stabbing, drowning."

"I'm surprised he didn't rise out of the icy river and take revenge on his killers," the cook commented. "What a ghoul!"

"What of Lady Greystone? What's she like?" Ellen asked.

"She volunteers at a hospital, taking care of the Russian soldiers, as almost all of the English ladies do. Of course, they're all in competition to see who is the most compassionate. Unfortunately, Lady Greystone caught a cold and that's why she was home when you came," Jones said. "Not that it stops her from going to the opera."

"And Lord Greystone?"

"He spends his days at the embassy doing important work," Mr. Myers said.

"Playing poker," the housekeeper added with a wink.

The cook gave Ellen an extra helping of soup.

"I'm mighty glad you're here," she said. "On Mondays, Wednesdays, and Fridays you'll wait in line for bread. Tuesdays, Thursdays and Saturdays you'll go to the vegetable line. This is the winter of the turnip, the Russians say. Nasty yellow turnips and old cabbage."

Ellen went to bed at an early hour, for she would have to go to the bread line at five the next morning. She put on her flannel gown and got under the eiderdown comforter. The room was cold, but the housekeeper had given her a hot water bottle to take to bed with her. As she settled into bed, she thought of all the hunger in this vast city and those poor lice-covered refugees. Then she thought of her own child safe and sound and warm in a beautiful apartment with loving parents in New York. As long as Hester was safe, Ellen could do whatever she had to do. She would provide information to the Germans as well as to their enemies, the British. They could slaughter each other and dance in Hell for all she cared. But with the "coming catastrophe," which terrified the servants, perhaps she could make herself helpful in other ways. The old, slow ways of reform weren't working.

As soon as she closed her eyes, a voice in her head piped up. She'd given up religion years ago, and yet, since leaving her child behind, she found comfort in the traditions ingrained in childhood, though she adjusted the wording a bit. "Mother of God, watch over little Hester this night. Keep her body and soul safe from harm. Amen."

Only then could she fall asleep.

For a moment, Ellen had no idea where she was. Then she heard soft, snoring sounds coming from the other bed. She sat up and wondered how long before she needed to get up and go to the breadline. She'd forgotten to wind her watch but she remembered seeing a grandfather clock in the hallway downstairs. Might as well go check. She got out of bed, put on some woolen socks, wrapped her shawl around her shoulders, then quietly slipped out of the room.

She made her way down the servants' stairwell, through the kitchen and into the hallway of the house. She heard voices. A light was on in the same room where she had met Lady Greystone. The door was open. She padded softly across the floor and stood just out of sight.

"I am sick and tired of freezing all the time."

"You have a bit of a cold, dear. That's all. You'll feel better soon."

"No, I won't. I hate this beastly place. I hate it with every fiber of my being. I hate the weather. I hate the lack of decent food. I hate the people, their smell, their laziness. Why can't we go home?"

"Because we are needed here. At least, I am."

"Any lowly clerk from Liverpool could do what you're doing, for crying out loud." Her voice simmered with bitterness.

"As you know, *dear*," he said, "in addition to helping my countrymen get home, I'm also in charge of our propaganda office."

"For all the good it's doing. Trying to convince the Russian people they are winning the war. Come meet the soldiers in the hospital. They tell a different story."

"They're wounded. Of course, they tell a different story. I'm afraid your so-called duties at the hospital have warped your thinking, love."

"So-called duties? And what about my so-called duties to keep our children safe? And fed. Do you know I had to hire a new maid to stand in line for bread? I was lucky enough to find an Irish woman who knows Russian."

"Irish? Dear God, the most untrustworthy people on God's green Earth! She's probably a spy."

A long pause.

"Now you doubt my abilities to run my own household. Good night. My door shall be locked, so do not bother visiting."

Ellen backed into the shadows. Lady Greystone stalked out of the parlor and then stood still as if she sensed someone watching her. The grandfather clock chimed twice, breaking the spell, and she stalked up the grand staircase.

Two o'clock. Ellen could get three more hours of sleep if she got in bed quick as a wink. Assuming she could get any sleep after Lord Greystone accused her of being a spy. Lucky guess, that one.

Chapter 7
Louisa

Louisa marched over to the bed and yanked the pillow out from under the man's head. His eyes opened, and he gave her a disarming smile. Gingin, who had been curled up at the foot of the bed, leapt to the floor with an indignant yowl.

"Hello, Louisa."

"What are you doing in my bed, Reggie Grant?"

He rubbed his eyes and sat up. "Waiting for you, darling. Where have you been at all hours of the night? You look lovely, by the way."

"Out. Since when do my nocturnal activities concern you? I haven't seen you since my Ellen went to Ireland and then disappeared to God knows where."

Reggie sighed. "Louisa, I had no idea the Foreign Office was going to enlist Ellen and send her back to the Germans."

She didn't believe him. Out of habit, Louisa took out the pins in her hair, then realized she didn't want to let her hair down in front of Reggie. She didn't want to give him any ideas. Too late. Her tresses tumbled down over her shoulders in thick waves. "Your superiors didn't give her much choice, did they? She had to save her brother from the firing squad."

"I suppose it *was* underhanded. If I could have done something…"

"Stop. I don't want to hear it." She turned to him and glared. "Why are you in my bed? You don't belong there anymore."

"I'm sorry. I was tired. What with this Bernstorff thing and now Room 40 has decoded a message from the Germans to Mexico."

She wondered what that old philanderer Count Bernstorff had to do with Reggie in her bedroom. "Room 40? Reggie, what are you talking about? I'm tired and would like to go to bed. Alone."

"It will be in all the papers tomorrow, which you would know if you still worked at a newspaper. Count Bernstorff will be expelled within days because of this little missive." He pulled a telegram from his pocket. "Would you like to hear what the Germans have to say? *'Germany will meet the illegal measures of her enemies by forcibly preventing after February 1, 1917, in a zone around Great Britain, France, Italy, and in the eastern Mediterranean all navigation, that of neutrals included, from and to England and from and to France, et cetera, et cetera. <u>All ships met within that zone will be sunk.</u>'*"

Louisa sank down in the chair before her vanity and leaned over to pet Gingin who was rubbing her head against her legs. "What does this mean for the United States? No, don't tell me. I know what it means. We can't remain neutral after this."

"As Germany continues to sink American ships, the public will demand war. And once they find out about the Zimmerman telegram to Mexico…"

"The what?"

As the British Naval Attaché, Reggie knew all the latest scuttlebutt. He rubbed his hand over his hair and stood up. "Naval Intelligence, or as we call it, Room 40, has decoded a bombshell. The Germans colluded with Mexico to invade the United States."

Their eyes met in the mirror. "You broke into my room to tell me this? What can I do about it? Is Ellen involved somehow?"

"Ellen is not involved, but I need a favor."

Louisa removed her earrings. "You always need a favor, don't you?"

He paced the floor as he had often done when cooking up some plan. "I would like you to visit Countess Bernstorff tomorrow and give her a letter in private. It contains a code she can use to get our attention. She's an American, and I don't think she'll be at all happy to return to Germany in the middle of war. Berlin is a hellish place these days if ever there was one."

Louisa took the tortoise-shell handle of her hairbrush and ran the brush through her thick mane of hair. "Thanks to the British blockade, I understand the German people are starving."

"War is not pretty," he said. "I'm sure the countess will want it to end, and she may be privy to information that could be useful to us." He paused and then continued, "She usually skates in the afternoon."

"You truly think Countess Bernstorff will spy for you?"

"Perhaps. She is an American, and she may be a patriot, for all I know."

"America is still neutral."

"Not for long."

Louisa took off her shoes. After all that dancing, her feet ached. "What should I tell the countess?"

"That we want to give her the option to help her country. If she uses the code, we will contact her."

She wiggled her stockinged toes. "And if she's not interested?"

"Give her the letter anyway. If she doesn't use it for this war, perhaps she will for the next one." He dropped the letter on her vanity table.

"The next one? Aren't you cynical? This is the war to end all wars."

He smiled indulgently. "Of course it is, dear. I hate to end our cozy tête-á-tête, but duty calls. Nice ring, by the way. Who's the lucky fellow?"

"His name is Francis Holland. He's an attorney. And we're very much in love."

For the briefest moment, Reggie lost his superficial gloss and said, "Then I'm happy for you, Louisa. You deserve that. By the way, his majesty will pay you for your service." He kissed the top of her head, before slipping out of the window onto the fire escape.

"Reggie," she called to him. He stopped and peered through the window at her. "Ellen's brother and mother want to know if she's safe."

"I honestly don't know. The last I heard she was in Germany." He climbed down the metal stairs and dropped to the alleyway below.

Louisa shut the window behind him and locked it. She wondered why he couldn't tell her that Ellen was safe. Perhaps the British weren't keeping good tabs on their double agent. What would she tell Martin next time she saw him? These thoughts plagued her as she tried to sleep. She should be happy. She was engaged to a fine young man. Instead, Europe's war sat on her heart like an incubus, draining her happiness while an infernal noise clamored in her head.

The next morning as Louisa was having her break-fast of Quaker Oats and reading the morning paper, a letter arrived for her. She opened the envelope and pulled out a sheet of paper.

"Who's it from?" her mother asked.

"It's a copy of a telegram," Louisa said. She read it quickly.

The Secretary of State to the Ambassador in Great Britain

Washington, February 5, 1917, 5 p.m.

Arrangements are being made for Count and Countess Bernstorff, their household servants, members of the Embassy staff, and all of the German consuls in the United States accompanied by their families, a party of about 200 in all, to leave on the Scandinavian Line steamship Frederik VIII which will sail from New York for Christiania in one week. It has been suggested that the examination of the ship by the British authorities might be made at Halifax and so avoid passage through the danger zone. Please take up the matter immediately with Foreign Office and request safe-conduct for Count Bernstorff and his party.

Reggie's meaning was clear. She had to deliver the message to the countess that day.

"Where did you get that ring?" her mother asked.

Louisa glanced at her hand. She'd meant to take it off until she and Francis made their announcement.

"Pretend you didn't see it, Mother," she said.

"See what?" Anna asked. "And where are you going?"

"Skating." Louisa gulped the last of her coffee, which had gotten cold, and went upstairs to get dressed.

Chapter 8

Ellen

The women in the bread line were a garrulous group in spite of the ungodly weather. They gossiped, complained, and occasionally guffawed. They were mothers, grandmothers, teenage girls, wives of soldiers and factory workers, and servants like herself. Children clung to the women's skirts or fought amongst each other. She had thought the women might be docile, defeated by hunger and cold. They were anything but defeated or docile. Rage simmered in their eyes.

As the days passed, Ellen recognized them and they her. She may have been a foreigner who slept under eiderdown at night, but she stood with them in the line for hours in the biting cold, and that made her one of them.

An old woman with sunken eyes and a black wart on her chin studied her. She reminded Ellen of her own gran, who swore she saw fairies and leprechauns and could tell the future by the flight of birds. The old Russian woman held up a gloved hand and with her other hand shook the empty pinkie finger slot.

"What happened?" Ellen asked.

"The pump took it off," she said.

"Pump?"

Another woman, younger, explained, "Old Sonya used to pump the water in the courtyard every morning. Her job. Everybody chipped in to give her a little something for doing it. Then. WHOMP. Her finger gone. Like that."

"Jesus, Mary, and Joseph!" Ellen exclaimed in English, causing the women to laugh.

Every day, Ellen picked up more tidbits about the plight of the poor in Petrograd. Women chained to their benches in the clothing factories to keep them working, sewing uniforms for soldiers. While other factory owners claimed they were out of materials as punishment for strikers so they'd have no work. Nursing mothers who had no milk for their babes. Simmering under all the grumbling was the memory of 1905, when the Tsar's Cossacks had slaughtered thousands of peaceful protesters. A bitter brew had stewed for a dozen years now. She knew the taste of that bitterness. She had drunk of it herself growing up in Ireland where the tyranny of the British loomed over the people like a bloated whale.

A teenage girl, who would have been in school had she been from a different sort of family, spoke up, "We will rise up like a fountain of fire. And from the ashes we will build anew!"

Ellen smiled. "Aren't you the poet?"

The girl bowed, her long braids swinging like ropes from the gallows.

The problem with Ellen's job was that she had no opportunity to speak to the man of the house, Lord

Greystone, and he was her only hope of getting a message to London about her whereabouts – and to ask after her family. She had been working for the Greystone family for more than a week and hadn't yet spotted the man aside from that first night, and then she'd only heard his voice.

She had just slipped into her flannel gown when someone knocked on her door. Opening it she found Jones, standing in the gaslit hall in her black dress, her face a mask of indifference.

"You are not to go to the bread line tomorrow. Instead, you will accompany Lady Greystone on her visit to the hospital for Russian soldiers."

"Why?" Ellen asked.

"She did not inform me. I am only delivering a message. She leaves at nine a.m. sharp. Make sure you are ready." With that, Jones marched off.

Considering Ellen had been getting up at five each morning to be in the bread line, her heart leapt in delight at the thought of sleeping in for an extra few hours. What a luxury.

Ellen lay in bed until the scullery maid got up, then managed to doze off, only to dream she was back in Dublin in the prison courtyard. This time she was too late and Martin's bullet-riddled body lay in a bath of blood. The despair in her soul at the sight of himself was as real as the bed in which she lay.

Jones' voice jerked her into consciousness. "Malloy, get up."

Ellen rubbed her fists over her eyes to rid them of the images of her dying brother. She looked out the window. Sleet pelted the glass. She desperately wished for a fur hat and vowed she would buy one or steal one if she had to. In the meantime, she tied a scarf over her head. At least she wouldn't have to stand in line today.

Lady Greystone wore her usual morose expression when Ellen met her in the foyer. Ellen had never seen anyone so dour. Draped in furs with food aplenty, and still she was dissatisfied with her lot in life.

"Top of the morning, Lady Greystone," Ellen said.

"Come along. The carriage is waiting."

They plowed outside into the punishing sleet and dashed to the waiting phaeton. Ellen thought it strange that the wealthy families in Russia still rode in horse-drawn carriages while even middle-class New Yorkers got around in motorcars. Everything in Russia was lodged in the previous century.

"How can I help you, your ladyship?" Ellen asked, once they were ensconced in the carriage, two dark horses trotting through the sleet and snow. Ellen pondered the cost of keeping those horses fat enough to withstand the weather.

A bearskin rug lay atop Lady Greystone as if the thing had died on top of her. Ellen found a wool blanket on the floor and covered her lap with it.

"How well do you speak Russian?" Lady Greystone asked.

"Adequately. I manage to get the bread and vegetables every day. Why d'you ask?"

Lady Greystone ran a finger along the edge of her fur collar. "I want you to spend today visiting with the patients in the hospital. Find out how the war is going."

An odd request, Ellen thought. "Can't you learn that from the newspapers?"

"I don't trust the papers. They all say Russia is winning, that's the official line. But if Russia is winning, why are the hospitals flooded with men? I believe it's a lie."

"Aren't there any English- or French-speaking soldiers? Officers?"

"The officers won't tell the truth. They are terrified. Of the Tsar. Of their own men. I need someone who can speak to the soldiers. They are the only ones I trust to tell the truth."

"And what makes you think they'll tell me anything?"

Lady Greystone hesitated, and then cleared her throat. "You have more in common with them than I do. Most of them were peasants or factory workers before the war."

"I see. Because I'm a servant, you assume I come from peasant stock."

The British woman's eyebrows rose. "Oh, did you come from wealth?"

"No, ma'am, I did not." Ellen failed to mention that briefly she'd been wealthier than Lady Greystone, thanks to her inheritance from Hester French. But she'd left her fortune in New York with the Murphys, who now had her child. Ellen was not ashamed of her origins and didn't miss the money. Hers were a people who had survived the Great Hunger along with centuries of oppression. "Tell me, your ladyship, why is this information so important to you?"

The woman twisted a handkerchief nervously.

"I'm frightened for my children and for myself. If Germany defeats Russia... If the Germans take over Petrograd..." She shuddered. "I simply must get my family out before that happens."

"But doesn't your husband work at the Embassy? Wouldn't he know these things?"

Lady Greystone shook her head in disgust. "He stupidly believes the Russian people will never defy the aristocracy, but when I look in those soldiers' eyes, I don't see obedience."

Ellen leaned forward. "What do you see?"

"Fire. Fire, death, and destruction. You can only stand on the throat of a people for so long. Why do you think Britain has a constitutional monarchy? In the last century, the British aristocracy saw what the abuse of power led to in France, and we were not willing to have our heads chopped off. Better to share power as Victoria did."

Ellen crossed her arms. "Except with those whose lands you have invaded."

Lady Greystone didn't have an answer for that.

"I've spoken much too freely," she said. "Will you do as I ask?"

Ellen nodded. Why shouldn't she? It was an opportunity for herself as well. The more she learned about the situation the better. If she were to eventually join with those plotting a revolution, she'd best learn what they were up against.

While Lady Greystone strode off to tend to the Russian officers, Ellen prowled through the crowded ward, where the infantrymen lay in cots jammed so close that sometimes only inches separated them. The stench of gangrene and misery hung in the air like a yellow miasma. Men had lost feet, hands, arms, and whole legs. Some were blind, others deaf, and some had only half a face left. These were the lucky ones, the ones who would not be sent back to the front unlike those with less catastrophic injuries or illnesses.

"Ledi," they called out to her as if she were one of the fine ladies devoted to charitable work. "Write a letter for me." "I'm thirsty." "I can't feel nothing below my waist." "Talk to me, please."

So, she stopped and listened to their complaints and fears or their memories of home. She fetched water from the barrel in the hallway. She adjusted a blanket, lay a comforting hand against a forehead, read a letter aloud.

One fellow wanted to know all about her, where she was from, if she had siblings. When he learned she was the daughter of a fisherman, he clapped his hands. "My family, too, plows the sea."

She sat on the end of his bed where his left leg would have been had he not lost it and shared stories of storms, schools of herring, and days when the nets came up bursting with the tiny silver fish like bright coins. The other men listened to them talk, thankful for any distraction. When she felt they were comfortable enough with her presence, she broached the topic of the war.

"We hear so much in the news of your great successes on the battlefield. The war should be over soon, shouldn't it? A great victory for Russia, they say."

A hush descended over the room. In the next bed, an older man with a patchy beard and one good eye barked a laugh. "You're a fool to believe it. It's worse than a slaughterhouse out there. The Tsar has destroyed us. Russia hasn't a prayer. Best learn to speak German. For the wolf will be at the door before you can fix your petticoats."

Ellen glanced around the room to see if any would disagree with his assessment, but none did. Tears rolled down the cheeks of several of the injured soldiers. One clutched a Bible. Another waved his stump of an arm and cried out, "Where is my hand? Brothers, where did my hand go?"

At the end of the grueling day, Ellen settled onto the leather seat of the carriage. Her employer stared at her, eyebrows raised in expectation.

"I'm afraid your fears are justified, your ladyship. The war is not going well on the front. The consensus among the men in the ward is that the Germans will defeat Russia in short order."

Lady Greystone gazed out the window as they passed the fine houses along the riverfront. "I thought as much. Thank you."

Then she shook her shoulders like a bird readying itself for flight.

Chapter 9

Louisa

The crowd of skaters at Van Cortland Park may not have known the identity of the attractive middle-aged woman in the sable jacket, who glided effortlessly around the lake, but Louisa spotted her right away. She waited until the woman skated around the bend in the lake and then aimed straight for her target, Countess Bernstorff, the former Miss Jeanne Luckemeyer. The countess was the daughter of an American importer, an upstart who turned Gilded Age society on its head 30 years ago with a dinner party featuring a table with a swan-filled lake in the middle. Louisa's parents had been guests at that famous display of conspicuous consumption.

"Hello, Countess," Louisa said, skating alongside her, keeping her hands warm in a fox fur muff.

The countess kept a strong pace, swaying from one foot to the other, skates hissing with each stride. She glanced over at Louisa.

"Louisa Delafield, what a surprise. My husband is quite annoyed with you, I'm afraid." That was no shock.

Two years earlier she had tricked the count into giving her information useful to the British. He hadn't known for certain that she was responsible for the subsequent release of certain documents to the press but he suspected as much.

"And you? Are you annoyed with me?"

"Of course not. I'm American like you. I understand why you didn't help him when he wanted you to write favorable stories about Germans."

"I did write a lovely review of *Die Fledermaus*."

"So you did. Besides, I'm not very happy with Johann myself right now." The countess rubbed her gloved hands together as they leaned into the curve. "I dread the idea of leaving New York."

"Then it's already happened? You've been expelled?" The countess was a fast skater, and Louisa strove to keep up with her.

"Apparently. What a nuisance. We'll have to take the whole household with us to dreary old Berlin."

They slowed down to pass a couple skating in tandem, the girl going backwards, the boy guiding her. Louisa thought of Reggie's prediction that America would enter the war soon and wondered if that boy would be one of those to go off and fight in the trenches.

"This war," she said.

"Yes, this war," Countess Bernstorff agreed. "And what do we women have to do with it? We didn't start it. We never do. It's always the men."

It had been the countess who had first approached Louisa two years earlier to become a part of the German propaganda machine in America, but much had changed in two years. She looked older, tired, still beautiful, of course, but faded. The count's philandering probably didn't help. They skated along the edge of the lake and passed a girl in pigtails practicing her spins.

The countess slowed her pace. "My legs are getting rather tired. I'm not as young as I once was. Shall we have a seat?"

They glided across the ice to a bench, their skates spraying white flecks of ice as they came to a stop.

"I do love New York," the countess said as they sat and watched a band of children playing chase. "It pulses with life while the rest of the world wallows in death."

Once upon a time, Louisa would have envied the former Jeanne Luckemeyer — a stylish heiress who married a count. But now Countess Bernstorff would be exiled from her home country — away from her friends, away from society. Dreadful. Far better to be marrying her young, handsome lawyer. He wasn't titled, and he wasn't yet wealthy, but that's what it meant to be an American. Birth did not determine your fate.

"Countess, I have a message for you from the British Naval Attaché, Reginald Grant."

"Of course you do. I asked you to write propaganda for my husband two years ago and now here you come with a return request." She brushed snowflakes from her dark velvet skirt.

"I wrote a very nice profile of your handsome Military Attaché, Franz von Papen, as you asked me to," Louisa said.

"And then I believe you were somehow responsible for his expulsion from the United States," the countess retorted.

"He was his own worst enemy," Louisa said.

"Was he? I suppose you're right. Terrible what he did to that girl. You took her in, didn't you?"

Louisa was surprised the countess knew that von Papen had sliced Carlotta's face. She wondered what else she knew.

"I did."

"Kind of you. Of course, it never would have happened if you hadn't enlisted her help to expose him, would it?" The countess was right about that. Louisa would always feel responsible for the scar that had ruined Carlotta's beauty. "Well then, what do you have for me?"

"A letter. With a code to use if you should ever want to contact British Intelligence."

"Why would I do that?"

"Because you're an American, as you yourself pointed out. And we're allies with Great Britain. We won't be neutral much longer."

"I'm also a wife."

"To a man who cheats on you. Publicly." A picture had been published in one of the newspapers the previous summer of Count Bernstorff at the beach with a couple of "bathing beauties."

The countess sighed and held out her hand. "Let's have it."

Louisa handed over the letter.

The countess tucked it in the pocket of her sable jacket. "You've delivered your message, Louisa." The countess stood. "Do give my regards to your mother."

"I will."

Countess Bernstorff gazed down her long aristocratic nose at Louisa. "By the way, your friend is in Russia."

Louisa stared at her in confusion. "What friend?" Why would she have a friend in Russia?

"The Irish woman, Ellen something-or-other. The two of you worked together on that magazine."

"What is Ellen doing in Russia?" Louisa was mystified.

"Spying for the Germans, of course." The countess skated away.

Louisa tried to absorb this new information. She knew the British had sent Ellen back to Germany to offer her services as a spy for their intelligence services. But Louisa imagined the Germans would have sent her back to America or to Ireland where she knew the lay of the land. Ellen had never even been to Russia. The countess had to be mistaken.

Louisa took off her skates, slipped into her boots, and headed to the train. Enough skullduggery. Soon she would marry Francis Holland, Esquire, and that would mean an end to any more favors for Reggie Grant. And yet a sense of dread followed her like a shadow.

Chapter 10

Ellen

Ellen shivered. She would never get used to Russia's arctic blasts. Most days the temperature hovered well below freezing, and this day was no exception. She stood in line for bread as was her job. A good two hours before the sun would peek over the horizon. The women were tired and angry, but for now they were still getting bread. Ellen wondered what would happen if that stopped.

Bands of soldiers roamed the streets, which confused her. "Why aren't the soldiers at the front fighting?" she asked one of the women.

"The Tsar has an army here in the capital to keep their boots on our necks should we dare to lift our heads. A bunch of louts with too much time on their hands."

At the servants' table, the maids and footmen chattered about the rumors floating in the air. "They say the Tsar is a fool." "Revolution is boiling." "A catastrophe is coming."

Let it come, she thought.

Ellen had dutifully sent a telegram to her cousin Olga in Berlin. "Would you send some tea? Cannot get it here. Hope Mother gets well soon, but she's very ill. Windy here." Captain Boehm would read the meaning. *People are hungry. Russia is ill. Change is in the wind.*

She had no fake cousin in London to whom to send a telegram, and if she sent one directly to the British Foreign Office, it would surely get back to the Germans. However, if the British didn't hear from her soon, she feared what might happen. Could they go back on their promise? Might they whisk Martin out of New York in the dead of night and send him to some farce of a trial in Dublin?

She had been working for the Greystone family for three weeks, getting up each morning except for Sunday to stand in line and wait six or seven hours to purchase a loaf of black bread or some moldy vegetables. The lines grew longer, the loaves smaller. On Sundays, she rode in a borrowed motorcar with the servant of another family out to the country to pick up eggs, butter, milk and even a couple of chickens. The cost was astronomical, but the rich foreigners would not have to go hungry. Not yet.

Lord Greystone had some sort of position in the British consul's office. His job, according to the other servants, was to repatriate British subjects stranded in Russia. One morning before heading to the bread line, she snuck into his study and snooped around while the house slept, but found nothing of interest.

The servants were always eager to blab. Lady Greystone's maid Jones, especially, was a veritable fountain of gossip. One night after returning from a trip to the country with Lord and Lady Greystone, Jones regaled the servants around the kitchen table after the master and mistress had gone to the ballet.

"You would think there isn't a war going on at all. We took the most sumptuous train imaginable, all brass and mahogany, and then everyone got in sleighs with fur rugs. It was like a fairytale with wolves howling in the distance, moonlight glistening on the snow." Jones leaned over the table. "The reception was in a glittering ballroom with gilded mirrors everywhere and what seemed like thousands of electric lights. Lady Greystone got to meet the Tsar and said she never met someone so uninterested in his duties. Thin and pale as a ghost."

"A ghost is what he will be if he doesn't find a way to feed his people," Mr. Myers said. "A monarch should care about his people. Yet he seems to think they should care about him. Not the other way around."

That was the problem, Ellen thought. An autocrat gets to decide for himself what he should or should not do. Perhaps he'll be a good ruler or perhaps not. His whims determine everything. Disgust at the arrogance of monarchs festered in her blood.

"What did they eat?" the cook asked.

"Sandwiches! And they drank copious amounts of sherry. Then we all came home. Lady Greystone says everyone has a terrible case of nerves. And the Tsar won't listen to reason."

"We are all sitting on a powder keg," Mr. Myers concluded.

Over the next few days, Ellen felt increasingly restless. What was she accomplishing? In spite of the cold, she preferred to be in the bread line, where she was surrounded by the tongue of Mother Russia rather than ensconced in the privilege of the British household.

Even when she didn't understand all the words the women around her spoke, she heard the music in the language. The poetry rolled off their tongues. Teenagers sometimes came by with pamphlets, which she studied in an effort to become more fluent. Her tutor had taught her the Cyrillic alphabet, and she had managed to acquire quite a bit of vocabulary. Studying the pamphlets taught her even more.

In the evenings she questioned Mr. Myers, the butler, about the politics of the country. He explained that there was something called the Kadet Party, moderate men and women who supported a constitutional monarchy. They made up the majority in the Duma, which was something like Britain's parliament but with no power. The Kadets were the liberals, he said, the "intelligentsia."

"The sooner they are running the country the better. I don't believe the Tsar and his minions have any friends anywhere," he said.

But the pamphlets she read made no mention of a constitutional monarchy, no mention of continuing the war with Germany, no mention of "allies." The pamphlets spoke of the people, of the need to take Russia out of the capitalist war and wrench the land out of the hands of the gentry. "Peace, land, and bread!" they demanded.

From Mr. Myers' information and what she read in the pamphlets, Ellen learned there were two groups in Russia opposing the Tsar and his ministers. One group wanted reform. The other group wanted revolution. The British favored the first group. The Germans, the latter. Each group then had factions within it, and all vied for the people's support. Meanwhile, the war was breaking the country's back.

Each night before bed, Ellen said her prayer for Hester. She locked her fears and concerns about her friends and family in little boxes in her mind, but the box where her brother resided rattled in her head. Was he safely in America with her mother and her other brother? Or had she sacrificed her entire life in New York for nothing?

The lord and lady had separate bedrooms, but according to Jones, the lady's maid, Lord Greystone was a randy fellow who visited his wife's bedroom most nights of the week. Ellen sat in a comfortable chair in his bedroom in the shadows, a woolen shawl wrapped around her shoulders, while a fire burned in the fireplace. Even with all the shortages, the British managed to keep their bedrooms warm — or at least not freezing.

The door to the room opened, and Lord Greystone entered, singing in a tenor voice, "By the Light of the Silvery Moon." He took off his robe and hung it on a hook against the wall. The singing turned to soft humming. Ellen stood up and cleared her throat.

"Good God!" he exclaimed. He wore silk pyjamas and sported the fat pink face and cold eyes common to English noblemen. Those faces beamed with a smug satisfaction at their lot in life. They were Englishmen, by God.

"Now, now, Lord Greystone, I've no ill intentions toward you." She stepped into the light of the gas lamp.

"Who the devil are you?"

"My name is Ellen Malloy. I'm a servant, hired by your wife to wait in the bread lines."

"What are you doing in my bedchamber, you strumpet? Get out." His face turned red, pale eyes bulging at her.

Ellen rubbed at a kink in her neck. "It's not sex I'm interested in." She thought but did not say, *If that were the case, I would be in your wife's room, not yours.*

"Then explain yourself and do it quickly before I have you thrown out."

"I need you to get a message to Sir Basil Thomson, head of Metropolitan Police in London. Tell him your wife recently hired a maid out of Ireland with the initials E.M. and tell him I said he needs to send assurance back that my family is safe."

The man's brow furrowed in disbelief. "You want me to do what?"

Was she talking to a petulant child, she wondered. "Lord Greystone, we're in the middle of a war."

"I know that. But what do *you* have to do with Basil Thomson?"

"I work for him." Thomson had been responsible for the arrest of her brother, and he'd been the one to authorize her mission to Germany.

"Are you some sort of spy? How do I know you're telling me the truth?"

"Ask Sir Basil."

His lordship frowned. "Rather nasty fellow, I believe. Ran prisons before the war."

"Now he works with the Foreign Office." In fact, Basil Thomson had been instrumental in the execution of several Irish rebels, and she despised the man, but it was on his orders that her brother was freed and living in New York. And he was her contact in London.

"All right, all right. Now, get out of my room. Of all the impudent..."

She interrupted him. "Thank you for your help, Lord Greystone."

She left his bedroom and padded quietly down the hall to the back stairwell leading to her quarters. When she reached the hallway to her room, she found Mr. Myers standing at her door.

"What are you doing out of your room at this time of night?" he asked.

"Couldn't sleep. What are you doing?"

He had no answer, so she went in the room and shut the door. The scullery maid's snoring sounded like a swarm of bees.

Chapter 11

Louisa

Standing in the courtroom with her hand on the Bible, Louisa wore a satin-lined, black-and-white-checked suit with large velvet lapels. The skirt was barrel-shaped, a style that was all the rage and quite to her liking for its roominess.

"I do," she said, promising to tell the whole truth and nothing but the truth. She mounted the witness stand and sat primly on the straight-back chair. The eyes of the old woman in the defendant's box glared at her. She'd heard the expression "shooting daggers," but these angry eyes were more like machine guns.

Louisa had never had to testify in court before. A deposition had always been enough. She felt both nervous and a bit self-important at the same time. The questions were clear and easy to answer. Had she been hired by Francis Holland, Esquire, to investigate the possibility of a theft at the Silk House? Had she been posing as a clerk at the Silk House when the defendant, Sassy Turner, entered and offered her an envelope –

which the prosecutor produced with a flourish – containing 500 dollars. Had the defendant brought in a nine-year-old boy with her and left him in the establishment?

Yes, yes, and yes, though she wasn't sure the exact age of the boy.

The defendant's attorney had only one question for her.

"Miss Delafield, how much were you paid to entrap my client?" he sneered.

The prosecutor objected and the attorney withdrew his question.

Louisa held her chin high and her back straight as she left the stand and walked through the swinging gate back into the gallery. The whole time, the old woman's eyes never left her. What harm could that old harpy do? She would be in Sing Sing soon enough. Louisa didn't stick around for the sentencing.

Francis met her outside in the hallway. "How'd it go?"

"Splendidly, I think," she said. "I told the whole truth and nothing but."

"Good work. I've got a civil case this afternoon, but I have time for a hot dog. How about it? I know this lovely little place."

"The stand outside the courthouse?" she asked.

"The very one." He took her elbow and led her down the hallway.

They had not yet reached the door when she heard a voice. "Hey! Miss!"

Louisa turned around to see who was calling. A clean-shaven man, about 30, wearing a gabardine suit with a rather garish red necktie approached them. He doffed his hat when he reached them. His dark hair was parted in the middle and he had thick, straight eyebrows, forming a ledge over deep-set eyes.

"Miss, I seen you in the court there. Did I hear tell you do investigations?" His jaw worked on a piece of fruity-smelling chewing gum as he waited for her answer.

Louisa hesitated. "I do. But mainly for Mr. Holland here." She had taken on a couple of assignments outside of Francis' practice, but they were for well-off ladies with a need for some "discreet" help.

"Oh, well, see, my wife is missing..." He looked down at his hands. He had soft, uncalloused fingers with clean, manicured nails.

"I'm so sorry, sir," Louisa said. "That sounds like a matter for the police."

The man shrugged. "I thought you being a woman and all, maybe you would have a better chance of finding her."

Louisa smiled at the man, hoping she appeared reassuring. "There are women police officers. I'm sure one of them can help you."

"You don't say. Maybe I'll give that a try. Good day to you." He replaced his homburg and walked off in the opposite direction.

"Poor fellow," Francis said. "His wife probably wandered off to a greener pasture."

"Well, I'd hate to think something bad happened to her," Louisa said.

They ate their hot dogs on a bench in the tiny park outside the courthouse.

When they were done, Francis looked one way, then the other, before pecking her quickly on the cheek. "See you tonight at your house."

She watched him walk back into the courthouse and took a deep breath. After the announcement tonight it would be too late to back out. Her mother would be absolutely apoplectic if Louisa got engaged again and then changed her mind. She looked at the sapphire on her finger. Maybe this time she wouldn't be a fool. If only she could be sure.

Francis arrived that evening with a bouquet of hothouse flowers. Suzie and Pansy showed up with a plate of Suzie's famous cornbread.

"Mr. Sweet is sorry he can't make it, but they're having a farewell party at the German Club," Suzie said. Mr. Sweet was a butler at the club, which was actually a brothel owned by a German opera singer.

"For Count Bernstorff, I assume," Louisa said, placing the pot roast on the dining table.

"How did you guess?" Suzie said.

"Reggie Grant sent me a copy of the telegram ordering his removal from the United States."

Carlotta brought out a pitcher of water. "Is the count bringing his wife to the farewell party?" she asked innocently. The German Club was the same brothel where Carlotta had worked when she had betrayed the German military attaché and subsequently gotten slashed in the face. Carlotta knew good and well the countess would not be invited to *that* party.

"I doubt it," Suzie muttered.

When all had taken their seats and the food was placed on the table, Suzie said grace. As they passed around the platters, Louisa gazed around the table at the odd assortment: a woman who had been born in slavery on a Southern plantation and her great-niece, whom she'd only met a few years earlier; a former prostitute who had been born into a Mafia family; an older woman who had been born into the highest echelons of old New York Society only to lose her husband and her fortune and wind up living in Harlem; and a young attorney with marriage on his mind. This, Louisa thought, is my family. If only Ellen and little Hester were here, the picture would be complete.

During dinner the women politely asked Francis questions, and he regaled them with stories about his years at Harvard and the pranks the "boys" would play. In turn he asked each of them about their lives, their pastimes. When Pansy said she was going to France to be a nurse, Louisa noticed a downward shift in his gaze. He's ashamed not to be fighting in the war, she thought, even though America was technically neutral.

"Do we have any word from Ellen?" Suzie asked.

"According to Countess Bernstorff, she's in Russia," Louisa said.

Anna's head jerked up. "Countess Bernstorff?"

"You knew her as Jeanne Luckemeyer," Louisa informed her.

"Oh yes, a delightful woman," Anna said. "New money, of course, but she always had such a droll sense of humor."

"Ellen is in Russia?" Carlotta asked.

"That's what the countess said," Louisa said. "I don't know if I believe her. What would Ellen be doing there?"

"Stirring up trouble," Anna said.

When dinner was finished, and after Carlotta brought out a plate of cheesecake she had made herself, Louisa tapped her wine glass and said, "We have an announcement."

The others looked on with expectant expressions. They all knew why they were there, but certain formalities must be honored.

Francis stood up. "We want you to know that I have asked Louisa to be my wife, and she has consented."

Pansy squealed, Suzie beamed, and Carlotta smiled. Anna, as usual, had a caustic comment. "I suppose we're lucky she found anyone, given her age."

"Anna," Suzie admonished. The two women had known each other since they were girls, and while Suzie had been the family housekeeper, she'd also been more like an older sister to Anna.

Louisa took a bite of cheesecake. Anna's sniping didn't faze her, and Francis might as well get used to it. "Francis is not just anyone, Mother. He's extremely bright. Speaks perfect French and several other languages as well. And he's a very good lawyer," she said.

"Is he rich?" Anna asked.

"Not yet," Francis said. "But I intend to be."

"See that you are," Anna said. "I would like a lady's maid, and we desperately need an actual cook." Naturally assuming she would be living with them.

"I will do my best," Francis said, a smile tugging at the corner of his mouth.

"I'll create a splendid wedding dress," Suzie said. "I have just the lace for the overlay, and of course I already have your measurements. I'm thinking a cream satin for the dress itself. As you know, the long trains are out of style thanks to the war. But you aren't the type for a long train anyway."

"No, I'm not," Louisa agreed. "They're much too pretentious."

It was Louisa's turn to wash the dishes after dinner and Carlotta's turn to dry. Carlotta seemed unusually subdued that evening. She sighed as Louisa handed her a dripping plate.

"Is something wrong?" Louisa asked, hesitant to intrude, but she did want to know what was on the young woman's mind.

Carlotta placed the dried dishes in the cupboard while Louisa put some chopped chicken into the cat's bowl.

"You could say so. I'm missing Ellen and the baby something fierce. There was so much to do when they were here, what with taking care of the baby and Ellen publishing her magazine. Right there in the parlor. I never knew women could do so much till I saw her put those magazines out. Then one day it was all over. The baby gone. Ellen gone. No more Mr. Thorn coming over to boss everybody around. Nothing for your mama to do."

"But haven't you enjoyed helping me with the investigations?" Louisa asked. She pulled the rubber plug from the sink and let the sudsy water drain.

"Yeah, but..."

"But?"

"You didn't need me on your last job, and now you're getting married. Do you even want to keep investigating?"

"I'm not sure." Louisa hung up her apron, realizing she hadn't even considered Carlotta's future.

"Louisa, I'm 19 years old. I'm not like you. I don't have no education. And no man's going to want to marry me. Not with this face."

Louisa looked at Carlotta. The scar along her cheek and her lip had faded probably as much as it was going to. Otherwise, she was beautiful. Lustrous black hair, large dark eyes framed in a forest of lashes, clear skin with an olive hue.

"I barely even see the scar anymore," Louisa said. "Once you get used to it, it almost disappears."

"I see it. Every time I look in a mirror." Carlotta's voice wasn't exactly bitter, but it contained a thread of sadness.

"I'm sorry," Louisa said, softly.

"I don't blame you. I'd do it again. You and me and Ellen got that German spy kicked out of the country. We did something good. And I don't miss the brothel. Not even for a minute. It's just I want to feel like I matter. To somebody. I don't want to be useless. And once you're married, you won't be needing me."

Louisa washed the last glass and handed it to her. "What would you like to do?"

Carlotta dried it and put it away. "That's the thing. I don't know."

Louisa had no idea what to tell her. When she was Carlotta's age, she was in college and already knew she would write a society column. At the time, she had thought she wanted to be in that world, the milieu to which she had been born. Then she discovered how vapid, how insipid, how meaningless the whirl of society could be. She also witnessed the depths of the corruption of certain powerful men and women. So she turned to her discreet investigations, something she did quite well. All her steps seemed guided by some inner voice.

"Give it time," Louisa said. "You'll find something. We no longer live in a world where a woman has to do what a man tells her to do. You don't have to marry. Or..."

"Or trade sex for money. I'm done with that."

Louisa shook her head. "You will never have to do that again. Not as long as I'm alive."

"You say that now. But you're getting married sooner rather than later. I can clean a little house like this but we both know, I'm no servant. You'll be wanting a real maid."

Louisa's family hadn't had actual servants since her father's death nearly 17 years earlier. Suzie had been more of a major domo than a maid, but Carlotta had a point. As Francis' career grew, as he became wealthy, they would need one or two servants and Carlotta didn't have the temperament. But how would a former prostitute make an honest living?

With the dishes put away, they had no reason to stay in the kitchen, but they lingered for a bit. Louisa reached over and took Carlotta's hand. She squeezed it to reassure the girl. "We'll figure it out."

Carlotta returned the squeeze, then took off her apron, hung it up, and said, "I may not be able to make you a dress, but my ma makes the best wedding cookies. One taste of an Italian wedding cookie and you'll know what heaven tastes like."

At the swinging kitchen door, Carlotta stopped, turned, and looked at Louisa. "Do you love him? Francis, I mean."

Louisa was taken aback. She looked down as she untied her apron. "Of course I do."

"I was just wondering." Carlotta left, the door swinging back and forth in her wake.

Chapter 12

Ellen

Ellen had heard nothing back from Lord Greystone. He might not have even delivered her message. Of course, she wasn't sure how often the diplomatic pouch went out. And she hadn't had time to go to the telegraph office to see if she'd gotten a message from "Olga" in Berlin. So once again she stood in line with the other women and their children, who had grown so accustomed to hunger they no longer cried.

"This is our reward for our loyalty to the Tsar," a woman in front of her remarked bitterly. "To be hungry and wretched. Cowed by the Cossack's whips."

The grumbles in the bread line were louder than usual, and after several hours of waiting she managed to acquire only a half loaf of black bread. The cook would not be happy.

Ellen entered the house of Lord and Lady Greystone through the kitchen entrance as always, but instead of the usual warmth, she was met with a distinct chill. She called out for the cook and then for Mr. Myers, but no one answered.

Still clutching the half loaf, she went into the main hallway and looked up to see Lord Greystone strolling down the wide staircase, his hand sliding along the mahogany banister.

"She's gone," he said. "They're all gone. Except for Myers. I sent him to the Embassy."

Ellen looked around the empty hall. So, Lady Greystone had fled and taken the English servants with her.

"That leaves you and me." He reached the bottom of the steps and crossed the marble floor to stand uncomfortably close. The stench of juniper berries from his gin wafted by.

Ellen's mind raced. Where would she go now? She had no idea how to find the Bolsheviks as Boehm had directed her to do. He'd given her a few names, but no clear idea where to find them. She had asked some of the teenagers handing out pamphlets where she might find the authors of the pamphlets, but they had only glared at her suspiciously before walking away.

"Shall I stay here, Lord Greystone?" she asked.

"Now that my wife is gone, I do have certain needs." He leaned close, sniffing her as if to determine whether she was safe to eat. "You're not much to look at, but with the lights off, it won't matter."

Almost two years earlier, the German spy master Nicolai had forced himself on her. She recalled the grunting, the sweat, the pain in her womb. She tossed the bread to the floor and pointed a finger in his lordship's face as if it were a pistol.

"Lord Greystone, I am in the employ of the Foreign Office. Do you really think they did not train me in the art of killing a man?"

His head jerked back. "With your bare hands?"

"If I must."

He took a deep breath. "You probably would. Well, get your things and get the bloody hell out. I'm moving into the Embassy."

"Perhaps you should follow your wife to England."

"Perhaps you should go to Hell." He stormed into his study.

Ellen strode down the hall toward the servants' staircase and up to the servants' quarters. She would not dash off in the dark just to satisfy him. In the small bedroom, the scullery maid, a dark-haired Romanian girl not more than 18 years old, sat on the bed, her face tear-stained. Ellen had a bad feeling the girl may have already been subjected to his lordship's unwanted attention.

"Are you all right?" Ellen asked her. The girl only closed her eyes and lay down with her face to the wall.

On Ellen's bed sat a fur hat and a note: "Do not stay too long." A gift from Lady Greystone? Ellen lifted it and gingerly placed it on her head. She picked up the hand mirror from the dresser and observed her reflection — the fading freckles, green eyes, thin lips and narrow chin. Lord Greystone was right. She was no looker. And she preferred it that way.

Chapter 13

Louisa

For Valentine's Day, Francis wanted to take Louisa dancing, but she explained to him on the phone that she had other plans for them.

"We are going to a birthday party," she said.

"A birthday party? Who has the audacity to be born on Valentine's Day?" he asked.

"My goddaughter, Hester Murphy. And by the way, Mother will be joining us."

"How utterly romantic," he said. "What about Carlotta? I understand she looked after the baby when Ellen still lived with you."

"She has something else to do. Please pick us up at 6:45 sharp."

At 6:45 that evening, Francis knocked on the door.

"It's about time," Anna grumbled.

"Mother, Francis is punctual as ever." Louisa opened the door and greeted him with a kiss on the cheek.

"Ready?" he asked.

They went outside into the frigid night, bundled in their fur coats. The day before, the high had been 24 degrees and the low was zero. Fortunately, the temperature had warmed, and it was near 32 degrees as they piled into Francis' Model T.

Anna started to get in the back seat, but Louisa told her, "Mother, Francis is not a chauffeur and we'll be warmer if we all pile in the front."

"In my day, we took a coach and four, and we were encased inside it. Not exposed to the elements," Anna complained after Francis had cranked the engine and gotten in the driver seat. There were motorcars, of course, that were fully enclosed, but Francis' Model T wasn't one of them. At least, it did have a sturdy roof.

Louisa directed Francis to the Murphys' Central Park pied-á-terre and soon they were entering the luxurious 10th-floor apartment, handing their coats to the butler.

"How delightful," her mother said. Louisa could tell the presence of a butler warmed the cockles of her mother's heart. She did so miss her former life of wealth and privilege.

Anna assumed her most gracious airs, the way any lady of her breeding would. She was no longer "old money." Now she was just old. Privately, she might find some minuscule fault in the way Katherine or John, whose father had been a street sweeper, folded their napkins or held their forks. But she would be quiet about it.

"I finally have the honor of meeting the charming birthday girl," Francis said as Hester shyly tucked her face against Katherine's shoulder, only to turn back to him with a wide smile and point at his silk top hat.

"I think she likes you," Louisa said.

"You two must be getting serious," Katherine said to Francis, "if Louisa is introducing you to her goddaughter."

"We haven't formally announced it yet," Louisa said, taking off her kid leather gloves and holding out her hand to show off the ring, "but Francis and I are engaged."

Katherine gasped. "How marvelous! John, John! Louisa is to be married! To this nice young man."

John Murphy entered the room. He was a big, lumbering man. The sort of self-made giant who prided himself on building a nation with railroads crisscrossing the continent. He took Francis' hand and offered him a hearty congratulations.

In the dining room, a portrait of Katherine's sister, Hester French, hung on the wall. She had not been a great beauty, but the artist had managed to capture the kindness of her spirit in the painting. It had been a terrible tragedy when she'd died in the sinking of the *Lusitania*, but it seemed that her namesake, little Hester Murphy, had filled the hole in Katherine's heart.

"Who is that?" Francis asked.

"Katherine's sister," Louisa said. Then she added in a quiet voice, "And the woman with whom Ellen was in love."

Francis looked thoughtful. He had never met Ellen but had heard much about her. A modern man, he was not one to judge the choices others made when it came to love. This was one of the things Louisa admired about him. She could never marry someone with a closed mind.

They sat down to a repast of ham with cloves, boiled potatoes, and roasted squash. Hester insisted on sitting on her father's lap and trying the food directly from his plate. Louisa saw Anna's eyebrows shift minutely. She wouldn't approve of such laxity in child rearing, but Louisa thought it wonderful. She hoped that Mr. Murphy would shower his adopted daughter with love and attention the way her own father had.

"I remember the day she was born," Anna said. "In the room right next to mine."

Katherine cleared her throat, perhaps not wanting the reminder that the child had not been born to her.

Anna took a sip of Bordeaux. "Oh, don't worry, Mrs. Murphy. I won't say a word in front of her when she gets older. Let her believe she has always been your baby."

"She has been." Katherine's tone held the tiniest bit of peevishness. "After all, even before Ellen left, I often took care of the child." Louisa wondered if the Murphys would really keep Hester's parentage a secret.

Anna smiled and immediately disarmed Katherine by saying, "And you are an exemplary mother, if I may say so."

Katherine looked at the baby on her husband's lap. "I do adore her."

Louisa couldn't help but wonder if there was the tiniest shred of memory of the woman who gave birth to her and nursed her for the first three months of her life lodged in little Hester's brain. It made her sad to think that the child would never know the brave and clever force of nature that went by the name Ellen Malloy. Then she saw the way the child nestled against her adoptive father and how he looked down at her, his heart conquered. She turned to observe Katherine, whose eyes shined as she gazed at the child. No one would ever be more important to either of them than little Hester.

After chocolate cake, which covered Hester's small hands and cheeks, much to everyone's amusement, they moved into the living room, overlooking Central Park. Carved panels lined the walls, and an enormous portrait of John and Katherine Murphy hung above a fireplace. While Anna entertained Katherine with stories of her days as a member of high society's vaunted "Four Hundred," Mr. Murphy and Francis mused about the likelihood of America entering the war. Francis griped about the heart murmur that kept him from joining the military. John said it was just as well.

"Men are needed here to support the war effort. Why, my company alone has sold 12,000 railroad cars to the Russians so far. We are currently in negotiations for more."

"That's impressive, but I'm not sure as an attorney I'm doing much that could qualify as worthwhile in the war effort."

Louisa wondered if John Murphy might send some legal business Francis' way. She would prefer Francis concentrate on his career than on what he might do for the idiotic war.

"I wouldn't worry about it, son. Not everyone gets to be a hero," Mr. Murphy said. "Ah, here's the princess."

The nursemaid returned with Hester, all cleaned up and wearing a dainty lace gown.

"May I hold her?" Louisa asked.

The nursemaid put the child in Louisa's arms, and the two gazed into each other's eyes. Louisa had been surprised by how enchanted she had been by Hester even as a tiny baby — even when it seemed that Ellen had such difficulty adjusting to motherhood. Now the baby was becoming a child before her eyes. She noticed Francis watching her and turned her head away. As much as she loved the idea of being married, she wasn't sure she wanted to be a mother. Of course, once she was married, she would not have much of a choice.

Birth control was such a nuisance to get and not always effective. She knew because she'd written articles all about the topic for *The Ladies' Lantern*. On the other hand, she might not even be able to have children. There had been a few times in her past when a moment of passion had precluded the use of birth control and she had not gotten pregnant.

After a few minutes, Hester struggled to get down, so Louisa set her on the Persian rug. Hester crawled across the floor. Then to her surprise, Hester reached a chair and, tucking one leg and then another under her, pulled herself up. Then she let go and stood on her two short legs, wobbling.

"Look at that! She's standing," Louisa cried. "All by herself."

And so she was. If only Ellen could see her, Louisa thought.

Chapter 14

Ellen

According to the Russian calendar it was February 16, the day after Valentine's Day, but in America they used the Gregorian calendar, and it was already March there. Hester would have turned one year old on the American Valentine's Day. Ellen wondered what the child looked like now. Had she said her first word yet? Was she crawling? Or even standing? She also wondered what Louisa and Carlotta, and even snobbish old Anna Delafield, were doing now that they no longer had *The Ladies' Lantern* to keep them occupied. It occurred to her that she'd left Louisa in a financial lurch. She should have left part of her fortune with Louisa, but when she went to Ireland to save her brother, she hadn't known she wouldn't be back.

Ellen got out of bed and saw that the scullery maid was gone. She decided to find Lord Greystone and ask if he'd heard anything from London. He'd been in his cups the night before, but surely he'd sobered up overnight. She put on her dark wool dress, boots and sweater and went to his bedroom. If he were going to kick her out of the house, then she'd have no compunction about waking him. She knocked loudly on the door. No answer. She peeked inside. The bed had not been slept in.

She went downstairs and looked in the parlor, the library, the dining room, and the study only to realize she was all alone in the big house. Back to her room then to don her fur hat, scarf, and coat. Her suitcases would be safer left at the house, as she had no idea how long it might take her to find a new situation. And she must not forget the treasury bonds, still safely tucked inside her mattress.

She wondered how she might find the Bolsheviks as Captain Boehm had instructed her to do. From the women in the bread line, she had learned that the factory workers were always going on strike, and the factories were located on the Vyborg side of the Neva River, the same area where she had spent that first miserable night. A university was also located on the Vyborg side, and it made sense that she might find the revolutionaries there amongst the factory workers and the students. Over the past few weeks, her Russian had gotten stronger. Her accent was not perfect, but she had a good ear, and the women in the bread lines seemed to enjoy sharing their stories with her.

She took a sleigh to the Liteiny Bridge and decided to walk from there. Above her, starlings zigzagged against the pale blue sky, and a breeze as sharp as a scythe slid over the ice-bound river. She turned onto Lesnoy Prospekt, a wide boulevard filled with carts, tram lines, and a few motor trucks. A horse-drawn cart slowly passed her. A woman lounged in the back in white boots, her skirt hiked above her knees, smoking a cigarette. A group of men with full beards argued violently. A bearded Cossack in a splendid uniform trotted by on horseback, his saber bouncing in its scabbard against his thigh. A harried woman pushed a baby carriage with a toddler and a baby inside. In front of the doors to a metalworks factory stood a long line of women. A stocky man with a cigar in his hand harangued them. "The owner has had enough of you! No work today."

A youngish woman with watery eyes, a fringed shawl wrapped around her shoulders, stopped in front of Ellen.

"Where did you get that hat?" she asked.

"It was a gift."

"From a man? You a prostitute?"

Ellen studied the woman. Something pugnacious in the angle of her chin.

"You guessed right. And see that man over there?" Ellen glanced across the street at a shifty-looking fella, hands in his pockets, shoulders all up around his ears. "That's my broker. If you lay a hand on me or my hat, he'll kill your children."

The woman stepped back, frowning. "No need for all that," she said. "I didn't mean nothing."

Ellen continued on her way. She wasn't sure where she was going or what she was looking for. She stopped to warm herself at a fire in one of the courtyards and remembered one of the names Captain Boehm had given her: Molotov. "He was the editor of *Pravda*, the mouthpiece for the Bolsheviks before the Tsar outlawed it. Our sources tell us he's back in Petrograd. All the other leaders associated with the newspaper are still in exile."

She hadn't seen any *Pravda* newspapers, so it must still be outlawed. That left her with the question: Where would she find one man in a city of a couple of million people? Eventually, she came up with a plan.

She would find one of the ubiquitous teenagers passing out pamphlets and follow him. She didn't have to go far to find one – a boy not more than 14 years old, a peasant's tunic under his coat and a leather cap on his head, standing on the corner, shoving tracts at passersby. She took one of the pamphlets from him and kept walking. Sure enough, it was full of Socialist slogans and quotations. She doubled back and lingered nearby. Waiting. Both the British and the German intelligence had taught her how to shadow a target. So she hung about, watching the thread-bare clouds drift across the sky.

By now she was used to standing in the cold, but she still hated it and thought of Lady Greystone, who was most likely already back in balmy England. She rolled her eyes, thinking of that gloomy little island as balmy. About half an hour passed before the kid had handed out all his tracts. Then he was easy to follow. He turned onto Baburina Street, walked several blocks, and hurried inside an apartment building. The granite building with its ornate decorations didn't feel like a hideout for revolutionaries. She entered behind him and heard footsteps in the stairwell. She hurried up the steps just in time to see him go through a door. She took a deep breath as she stood in front of the door. She knocked.

A woman yanked open the door and stared at her. A child clung to her skirt. "Who are you?" The woman was none too happy.

Ellen gave the woman a friendly smile. "Excuse me. I'm looking for Molotov?"

The door slammed in her face.

Ellen trudged down the steps and outside. This spy business is absolute bollocks, she thought as she walked past a bakery with yet another line of women, waiting for bread.

Frustrated, she leaned against the wall of a building and crossed her arms. What a waste of time. Here she was in a country where she knew no one, doing the bidding of the very same country that had casually killed the woman she loved along with more than a thousand other innocents. All because her brother had thought fit to overthrow the British. Oh, Martin, she thought. She still had no idea whether or not he was safe. She kicked her heel against the wall, which didn't make her feel the least bit better.

Then she heard someone singing in a pure and lovely voice. She looked around. A petite blonde woman who looked to be in her early twenties, wearing a red arm band and dark trousers walked along the line, singing the "Marseillaise" — the song of the French Revolution.

Allons enfant de la patrie
Le jour de gloire est arrivé
Contre nous de la tyrannie
L'étendard sanglant est levé
L'étendard sanglant est levé

Ellen knew the song. Every revolutionary, socialist, and anarchist in the world knew the song and what it meant, even if they did not know French: *The day of glory has come to rise against tyranny.*

Ellen ran after the singing woman. "Excuse me, Comrade."

The woman turned. "Yes?"

"I am looking to join the Bolsheviks."

The woman looked Ellen up and down. "Foreigner?"

Ellen nodded. "I used to live in New York but I'm from Ireland."

The woman tilted her head. "And how can you be of use to the Bolsheviks?"

"I have friends in New York who are eager for revolution. You've heard of Emma Goldman? She is my comrade. She told me to look up a man named Molotov." Ellen had known Emma, the "most dangerous woman in America,"; she had slept with Emma's editor, a blood-thirsty anarchist named Lulu; and she had smuggled out a letter to the public from Emma when she was in jail for speaking out in favor of birth control.

"Never heard of her."

Ellen scoffed. "You never heard of *Mother Earth*, a famous anarchist magazine? Emma Goldman fights for workers' rights, birth control, peace, and all manner of causes. She speaks to huge crowds all over America."

The blonde woman studied her and then asked, "So what? This is not America."

Ellen thought quickly. "I can be useful. I was in Ireland for the uprising last year. I'm no innocent. I can shoot. I can even build bombs."

The woman laughed. "Bombs? What is your name?"

"Ellen Malloy."

"My name is Irina Slamovna. Come with me."

She took Ellen by the arm and they marched along the street, dodging workers in their blue tunics and caps, singing:

Aux armes, citoyens,
Formez vos bataillons,
Marchons, marchons !
Yes, Ellen thought, *to arms, citizens, form your battalions, march on, march on!*

Irina stopped singing. "Why do you want to meet Molotov? He already has a girlfriend."

Ellen did not tell Irina the real reason she was not interested in being Molotov's girlfriend. "I asked for Molotov because I'm told he is the editor of *Pravda* and, in addition to bombs, I know a thing or two about newspapers."

"*Pravda* has been banned. All we do now is print flyers and pamphlets until the time we can resurrect the paper. I don't know how you can help us, but I will leave it to him to decide."

Irina took Ellen to a nondescript building not far away. They went inside, but instead of going up the stairwell, they went down to the basement. Ellen had to duck to enter through the low doorway. They walked through a room with a letterpress printer into another room. The second room was lit by kerosene lamps and one window high in the wall. The room was crammed with filing cabinets, a desk, and piles of paper. Posters plastered the walls and water leaked from a pipe into a bucket in a corner of the room. A samovar stood on a corner table. Around a table in the center of the room, three men in leather jackets sat, smoking cigarettes. The men stopped talking and stared at the two women.

"This is Ellen Malloy," Irina announced. "An anarchist from New York City. She's also Irish and took part in the uprising last year in Dublin. She wants to join us."

"How nice you have found a friend," one of the men said from beneath a cloud of smoke. "But what are we to do with her, Irina Samovich? She's not even pretty."

Ellen guessed this man was the elusive Molotov. She stepped forward. She'd cut her copper-colored hair short before leaving Berlin. She had a straight back and even under all the layers of clothing she exuded the strength of a woman who had hauled nets full of herring as a girl and learned to fistfight at her brothers' sides.

"Comrades," she said. "I believe you could use some help getting your messages out to the world. In New

York, I ran a magazine in support of workers' rights, women's rights, and against the capitalist system that sucks the very life out of the proletariat."

The man squinted through the cloud of cigarette smoke surrounding him. "What happened? Why are you here?"

"I went back to Ireland when I learned about the plans for an uprising against the British. My brother was a member of the Irish Brotherhood, and I went to help him."

The men shifted in their seats. "That doesn't explain why you are in Russia," one of them said.

"Once the British quashed the uprising, they started executing revolutionaries. I was on their list. I escaped and got out as fast as I could. Went to Berlin, where I met some fellow Socialists. They told me about a man named Vladimir Lenin."

Suddenly, she had the room's attention.

"What about Vladimir Ilyich?" one of the men asked.

"I know he believes in a worldwide revolution. I came to Russia because the greatest hope of that revolution begins here."

Irina put her hands on her hips and said, "She's right. The worldwide revolution begins right here with us."

Molotov scoffed. "How do we know you're not a spy for the police? Our group has been outlawed. Our newspaper banned."

Ellen couldn't tell the truth. That her German spymasters were eager to get Lenin back into Russia and that they were more than willing to help fund a Bolshevik revolution in order to end Russian participation in the war. Instead, she took a seat at the table and looked at each man in turn, finally resting her eyes on Molotov.

"You don't seem to have much faith in the people, Comrade," she said with a certain quiet conviction. "Everywhere I go in this city, I see hungry mothers, sick children, refugees and wounded soldiers from a war the Tsar keeps fighting even though he is losing. I feel the rumblings, the anger, the impatience in the bread lines. These people, the women especially, they will not wait forever. They will not watch their babies go hungry much longer. Once the revolution begins, I will get the word out to publications in America. The Socialists and Anarchists don't want this war any more than you do."

"Even Lenin does not think a revolution will happen before the war ends," one of the men muttered.

Molotov looked unmoved.

"Where are you living, Tovarisch? How do you get by?" Molotov might look unmoved, but he had just referred to her as "Tovarisch," meaning comrade.

She decided to be honest. The fewer lies the better. "I took a job as a servant in a British household while I figured out how and when to join up with you. That is, if you'll have me."

She paused and gazed around at the men once more. They traded glances.

She leaned back and folded her hands. "I've seen the prelude to a revolution before."

"In Ireland?" Molotov scoffed. "A failed revolution."

"True. They weren't as hungry as your people. No one is as hungry as your people. Or as cold. You are in it so deep you can't see what is happening right in front of you. Not like I can, as an outsider. An earthquake rumbles deep in the earth. It is coming to the surface. Trust me on this. There will be blood — aristocrats' blood, police blood, maybe even your blood — on these streets before long."

She settled back. She had no idea if her prophecy was true. She was relying on the servants' whispers about a coming catastrophe, but as she looked at their faces, she knew they had been swayed by her words. Ellen Malloy was nothing if not a storyteller.

Molotov nodded. "When we are able to publish again, we might use you to translate our pieces and send them to the west. But until then, what can you do?"

Ellen tapped her finger on the table. "I can work a printer, lay out a page, post flyers on walls. Comrades, in New York I was an anarchist. In Russia, I am a Bolshevik."

She could play this role because the more she saw of war, the more she saw of hunger, the more she believed in revolution. The uprising in Ireland may have failed, and 12 years ago, an attempt at revolution in Russia had been disastrously dealt with. That did not mean these revolutions would fail forever. Someday the poor and oppressed would turn the tables on their overlords. Those who had kept their boots on the necks of the laborers, of women, of the hungry would face a raging conflagration rising out of embers that had been burning for centuries.

"She can stay with me," Irina said. "I do not mind having another woman around. And I'll help her with the translations."

Ellen looked at her gratefully. The accommodations would probably not be as comfortable as Lady Greystone's, but the company was far more suitable.

Molotov threw up his hands. "Apparently, you are one of us now, Ellen Malloy."

"I have to get my clothes and my last wages," she told Irina as they left the building.

"My flat is in that building. Third floor." She pointed to a brick apartment building next door to the building with the Bolshevik headquarters. "Another girl shares the place, but she's never there. You can sleep in her bed."

"Where is she?"

"Usually in Comrade Molotov's bed," Irina said with a grin.

"I see. Well, I will return shortly." Ellen hurried away, eager to close out one chapter of her Russian adventure and start a new one. As a free woman, not a servant. A voice in her head mocked her and asked, *When is a spy ever free?*

Chapter 15

Louisa

Gingin was on the dining-room table again. Louisa picked her up and placed her on the floor. The little orange cat scampered off.

"Was that creature on the table again?" Anna said, her cane stomping the floor as she came in.

"No," Louisa lied and sat down. Carlotta had already put out coffee and biscuits and was nowhere to be seen.

Anna sat down and poured herself a cup of coffee. "I suppose I was merely having visions of cats on tables."

Louisa took the section of the paper with international news and gave her mother the local section as was their morning ritual. She wondered how different it might be after she was married. With a male presence at the table, would it be like her childhood? She remembered how her father used to talk to her about current events as if she were a small adult. She smiled thinking of his gentle nature. Unlike Francis, he would probably have welcomed a heart murmur if it kept him from having to kill people. For that matter, she couldn't imagine Francis in a battle – unless it was a legal battle.

"Oh, heavens, Louisa. You're in the paper. You do know that a woman's name should only appear in the newspaper three times in her life – when she's born and when she marries and..."

"And when she dies. Mother, have you forgotten that I was a society columnist? My name was in the paper at least three times a week. And not just one paper but papers all over the country."

Anna lowered the paper and peered at Louisa. "But not in the story itself!"

Louisa held out her hand for the offending article and Anna handed it over.

Louisa read the story. "Former society columnist Louisa Delafield helped police crack the case by posing as a clerk in the silk house. Miss Delafield's testimony helped convict long-time criminal maven Sassy Turner, who was tried separately from the three other thieves arrested in the operation. Delafield has helped police solve a number of crimes over the years, including a man trafficking in young girls. She also exposed German saboteurs, resulting in the expulsion of two German attachés."

Louisa's heart squeezed in apprehension. Her mother was right in this case. She was supposed to be a "discreet" investigator. She looked at the byline and her apprehension turned to anger. Billy Stephens? He should know better. In fact, it was Billy who initially helped her transition from writing about society to the world at large. She would have to speak to him.

"I suppose we should get ready for the graduation," Louisa said. "Do you still want to come with us?"

Anna set down her coffee cup. "Of course I do. I'm rather fond of young Martin."

Francis came to pick up Louisa, Anna, and Carlotta shortly after lunch. The four of them dashed through the snow and piled into a horse-drawn carriage.

"Keeps out the cold better than the Model T," Francis explained, but Louisa thought he was probably trying to please his future mother-in-law.

"I don't know why anyone would ride in anything else," Anna said, settling into the leather seat and pulling a blanket over her skirt.

"Where is the ceremony?" Francis asked.

"Police headquarters on Centre Street," Louisa said.

He slid a panel aside and gave directions to the driver, who pointed the carriage toward downtown. They were soon in front of a domed baroque building. Once inside, they were directed to a large auditorium on the fourth floor, where a crowd of family members and city officials had gathered to watch the graduation of the rookies. Paula Malloy had saved seats for them. She had her younger son on her lap, and Sean sat next to her in his suit like a little gentleman. Carlotta sat next to Sean and Louisa sat next to her with her mother next and Francis last in the row. She glanced over at Paula, who wore a proud smile on her face.

Up on the dais, Ellen's brother, Martin Malloy, sat with the other rookies in their crisp dark-blue uniforms. Louisa wished Ellen could see him. Of course, he wouldn't be up there if it hadn't been for Ellen. Instead, he'd be a cold corpse in an Irish graveyard.

"Gentlemen," Commissioner Wood said, "New York City is now worthy of the respect and support of the citizens. The day is no longer when criminals seek shelter from the law in our great city. Fingerprints sent here from all over the country and the world prove that the crooks are giving New York City a wide berth. Even our native crooks are taking up their abode elsewhere."

Louisa and Francis exchanged a glance. New York would never lack for criminals despite the commissioner's wishful thinking.

After the ceremony, Francis' uncle, Captain Tunney, came over and clapped Martin on the shoulder. "We're happy to have you on the force, son. We need all the men we can get. Once the country joins the war, I'm afraid we'll be losing a lot of good officers to the military."

Louisa glanced at Francis. His face showed no expression.

Martin cleared his throat. "Yes, sir. I plan to stay here to do my duty. I wouldn't leave Paula for anything in the world." He put an arm around his wife's waist.

Captain Tunney ran his fingers over his walrus mustache. "You're not a fan of the British Empire, are you? Heard you were involved in the Easter Rising."

"I was, sir, but I've turned over a new leaf."

Louisa assumed that Tunney, as an Irishman himself, didn't care one way or the other about Martin's involvement with the rebellion. The old hatred ran thick in the Irish blood.

Captain Tunney turned to Francis. "I believe congratulations are in order for you, as well."

Francis smiled and gazed at Louisa. "She's made me the happiest man on the planet." Louisa returned his gaze. She did not think he was the happiest man on Earth.

"Does this mean an end to your sleuthing, Miss Delafield?" Captain Tunney asked. He was the one who had introduced Louisa to his nephew the previous summer, when she was working on a case involving a blackmailer and a famous film star.

"We'll have to wait and see," Louisa answered.

After the ceremony, Francis found a motorcab to take them back to the brownstone while he walked back to his office.

Louisa turned to Carlotta. "You certainly have been quiet."

"I was raised to hate the police," Carlotta said. "They were the enemy." Anna's eyebrows lifted. After a long pause, Carlotta continued, "But they all seemed so proud. Like they were doing something important."

The driver turned the corner to go to the brownstone and slowed. A boy who looked to be in his late teens was hanging around the front of the house, gazing up at it.

"What do you suppose that scalawag wants?" Anna said.

Louisa leaned her head toward the window. As they slowed down, the boy spotted them and took off running.

"Looked like he was casing the place," Carlotta said.

Anna straightened her spine. "Indeed. Well, he's too late. I already sold all my jewels."

Louisa remembered her name in the newspaper that day. Her spine tingled, and voices chattered in the back of her mind.

Chapter 16

Ellen

Ellen took a droshky to the Greystone house on Furshtatskaya. It was eerily quiet inside. She was half-way up the staircase when the front door opened. She turned and saw the master of the house standing in the doorway.

"You there!" he called out, slamming the door and striding inside.

She leaned over the banister and said, "I'm only getting my things. I'll be out of what little hair you have left as soon as I'm packed."

"Not so fast," he said with a malicious grin. "The Scottish Chap wants a conversation with you."

"Who?"

"He's with the Foreign Office."

Finally, Ellen thought. Irina was expecting her, but she'd have to make time to see this man. She had to find out if her family was safe. "When? And where?"

"Tonight. At the ballet."

Her jaw dropped. "The ballet?"

"Yes, of course." He sneered at her. "By George, you have never been to the ballet, have you, you Irish bumpkin?"

It was true. She had never been to the ballet or the opera. When Hester French was alive, they mostly went to lectures by writers and activists. And even though Ellen was friends with Louisa Delafield, an avid fan of the theater, Louisa had never taken her to any sort of performance.

"What I don't understand is why in the midst of all this unrest, this suffering, you and your ilk still indulge in such frivolities," Ellen retorted.

"Maintaining some semblance of civilization is no frivolity, I'll have you know." He stomped up the stairs past her. "You better meet the man if you know what's good for you." Then he added, "Or your family."

He stood at the top of the stairs and looked down at her.

"I'm not exactly dressed for the ballet," she said.

"That is what we're going to rectify." He strode along the hallway as she hurried up to the stop of the staircase. He stopped at the doorway to one of the rooms. "Come on."

She hesitated, not trusting him in the least. And yet, she had no choice. "Why would I go into a bedroom with you?"

He scoffed and rolled his eyes. "I'm afraid I gave you the wrong idea yesterday. I'm not interested in your sort. We're merely going in here to get something for you to wear."

She held her ground. "Why can't this man meet me at the Embassy or even here?"

He shook his head and said slowly as if she were a five-year-old child, "You cannot be seen going into the Embassy. What about your cover? Oh, yes. They told me all about you. You're a double agent. Well, I certainly don't want the Scottish Chap in my house."

Ellen took the measure of him. Was he telling the truth? If he wasn't, she knew the proper placement of an elbow into the soft part of a throat. He disappeared into the room. She walked down the hall, stopped at the doorway, and peered inside.

It was indeed the bedroom of an upper-class British woman, complete with a painting of St. George slaying the dragon on the wall and a high bed with a gilt-trimmed, cushioned headboard. Sir Greystone stood in front of a huge walnut wardrobe, the doors wide open, pulling out dresses and tossing them onto the bed.

"She left her clothes?" Ellen asked.

"She took ten trunks with her. These were the dresses no longer in fashion or that no longer fit her. They'll fit you though if I'm any judge of a woman's body – and I am."

"Do you actually believe there won't be German spies at the ballet? What if they see me?" she asked. She'd been told by Captain Boehm that the Tsarina's court was full of German spies. She didn't know if any of them knew about her, however.

He shrugged. "German spies are everywhere, I assume, but they won't recognize you."

He walked over to the vanity and opened a drawer. From it he extracted a satin bag and tossed it to her. She looked inside.

"A wig?"

He shrugged a shoulder and said, "Sometimes I want to bed a blonde."

She brought out the wig and shook it out. It was finely made with real human hair.

"Be ready in 30 minutes," he said and walked out, shutting the door behind him.

Just to be safe, she locked the door before examining the dresses. They were all beaded and sequined and layered, with plunging necklines. Not the sort of thing she would be caught dead in. Not to mention, it was freezing outside. Then she spied something that might work. Velvet. Dark green. She held it up and looked in the mirror. It even had a reasonable neckline.

She stripped off her clothes, went into the washroom, and used a washcloth to take the day's sweat off her. No time for a proper bath. She dried off and found some lilac-scented talcum powder in the vanity along with some leftover rouge.

Thirty minutes later she stood in the hallway downstairs — a blonde wearing a necklace of rhinestones, a velvet gown, and a velvet cloche.

"What about a coat?" she asked.

He walked to a closet in the foyer and pulled out a full-length, dark wool coat with a sable collar and cuffs.

Ellen slipped on the coat. She had never worn anything so luxurious in her life even after she had inherited Hester's fortune. She knew what happened to the wealthy. They were seduced by luxury and easy living, and they would trample anyone who tried to take it from them. She understood the temptation and was happy to leave her unearned fortune in New York with the Murphys.

"What is the name of this Scottish fella I'm s'posed to meet?"

"We just call him the Scottish Chap."

He opened the door and waited for Ellen to exit, watching her with eyes as cold as the snow.

Chapter 17

Louisa

Louisa stood in Suzie's parlor and shook her head. "I would never have dreamed of a sight like this in a million years."

Anna sat on the sofa, spectacles on, carefully sewing beads onto a piece of green crepe de chine. "Why not? You think I'm a helpless old lady, don't you?"

"Not at all, Mother. It's simply that I have never seen you sew anything in your life."

Louisa exchanged a look with Suzie, who suppressed a smile.

"Old dogs can learn new tricks." Anna got up and stalked off to retrieve her coat and cane.

Louisa leaned close to Suzie. "Thank you for making her feel useful."

"She actually is useful. I don't enjoy beading, and she's good at it."

"Of course I am! Come on, Louisa. Let's go see what dreadful excuse for a meal that Italian girl has come up with for dinner."

They left Suzie's brownstone. Louisa raised her hand to hail a cab, but Anna clutched her arm and said, "Let's walk. We finally have a break in the miserable weather."

It was true. The sun showed its face for the first time in a week. People sat on their stoops or walked along the sidewalks just for a taste of it. Louisa was always glad when Anna wanted to walk. For years, her mother had pretended to be an invalid. Now, she still walked with a cane, but she relied on it less and less. Some people got feebler with age. Anna was just the opposite.

"Louisa, did you know that some of Suzie's friends are planning what they call a silent protest?"

"I did not. What is it about?"

"They are protesting these lynchings! Suzie's friends want a federal law against lynching because some states refuse to prosecute the perpetrators. Can you imagine? They are getting away with murder!"

Louisa gazed at Anna. "Mother, you astound me. I think Ellen Malloy must have rubbed off on you."

Anna raised an eyebrow. "You do remember that my mother was an abolitionist. That's how Suzie wound up living with us in the first place. Just a poor, orphaned girl, born into slavery. Suzie gave us so many years of her life. It's my turn to give something back to her. I might even join the protest."

Louisa did not point out that the marchers would be going a bit faster than she was used to, so she changed the subject. "Mother, I do hope you approve of Francis. He's no blueblood, but he's kind and a brilliant lawyer."

"I would approve of the milkman if it meant you were finally getting married."

"I don't know why you're such a fan of marriage," Louisa said.

Anna sighed. "Your father may not have loved me in the way that most men love women. But he did love me. And I loved him. He was my companion. I wish I had understood that was enough. Things would have turned out much differently."

Neither of them wished to revisit Anna's confession about what happened when she found her husband in a seedy hotel room with another man.

After a long pause, Anna said, "I do approve of your young man, dear. But you must admit there's something melancholy about him."

"Melancholy?" Louisa asked. "I don't think he's melancholy. He loves to laugh and dance."

Anna shrugged her shoulders. "I only know what I see."

Louisa scoffed. Her mother knew nothing about who Francis really was, but as they walked along the street past the stores and the shoeshine stand, she wondered if Anna might be right. Was Francis' disappointment in not serving in the military greater than she thought? Every woman must wish that the man in her life loved her beyond any sense of "duty" to his country, but some men had a need to fight for a noble cause. How else did they manage to have these pointless wars?

As they came around the corner of their street and headed home, Louisa scanned the street for strangers. To her relief, no one was about. Then Carlotta stepped out of the house, wearing her long camel coat and hat.

"Where do you suppose she's going?" Louisa asked.

Anna huffed. "She's been going somewhere every day. Says her sister is sick, but I don't believe her."

"Mother! Why would Carlotta lie?"

"How do I know? I only know there's something furtive about her these days."

As they climbed the steps of the brownstone, Louisa watched Carlotta turn the corner and disappear from view. Perhaps her sister *was* sick. Since reconciling with her family last year, Carlotta did spend more time with her sisters and mother.

As Louisa stood on the doorstep, a rushing sound like a waterfall filled her head followed by a clamoring as of women yelling in rage. She took a deep breath. Who were these angry women, she wondered.

Chapter 18
Ellen

Lord Greystone sat across from her in the carriage just as his wife had a few days earlier on their way to and from the hospital, the horse's hooves clopping along the street.

"How did you become a spy?" he asked. "It seems an unlikely occupation for an Irish woman whose main job qualification is that she can wait in lines."

"Comes natural," she said. She had no intention of sharing her personal history with him. The truth was that after Hester's death, Ellen had acquired the ability to shut off her feelings. A useful skill in her line of work.

He cleared his throat and crossed one leg over the other. "As a matter of fact, I did hear you were on the *Lusitania* when it sank. That must have been dreary."

Dreary? Hours stranded on a lifeboat in the Irish Sea, bloated bodies floating by, and then the bodies, like Hester's, never found. "It was no picnic."

"Tell me, are you spying for Britain out of love for the British Empire or for revenge on the Germans for shooting a torpedo into the *Lucy*?"

"I'm doing it because it was the only way to save my brother from the firing squad," she admitted. "What is the name of this ballet we are going to see?"

"How do I know? I just try my best not to fall asleep."

Was the ballet boring, she wondered.

The carriage took them over a bridge crossing one of the canals that cut through the city and parked in front of the Mariinsky Theatre, a massive lime-green building with white columns and arches. In spite of Russia's impoverished state, the building reflected the grandeur of Imperial Russia. It also signified the importance of the ballet to the Russian people.

The bust of the Empress Maria greeted them at the entrance. Apparently, the theater had been named after her. Must have been a better time for the autocrats, Ellen thought. The marble floors and the sparkling chandeliers showed not a drop of the peasant blood and sweat that funded such extravagance.

The theater itself astounded with its royal-blue curtain and golden eagles prominently perched above the auditorium. The place looked as if it had been drenched in gold. She gazed up at the tiers of boxes where the wealthy aristocrats, robust women and men with scented beards, ensconced themselves.

"Stop gawping," Lord Greystone said.

An usher in a gold-braided uniform showed them to their seats while an orchestra played national anthems from Russia, England and France in a tired effort to stir up enthusiasm for a war that was grinding the army down like cornmeal.

The ballet, called the "Trial of Damis Karsavina," was anything but boring. Ellen completely forgot her reason for being there as she sat, enraptured by the elaborate sets, the costumes of lacey frills, and the magnificent bodies of the dancers. How could they possibly soar through the air like that? She overheard a couple of women in the seats behind her raving about the beautiful Obukhov — a godlike dancer whose leaps made her wonder if he could actually fly. The ballerina who was his partner was a dark-haired, swan-like creature constantly twirling on one impossibly long leg. Ellen felt a pang and realized she desperately wished her beloved Hester French occupied the seat next to her. How she would love this.

Instead, she sat next to a rather nondescript man about 30 years old, she guessed. It wasn't until intermission when he spoke to her that she realized he was a Scotsman.

"It's nice to meet you, Miss Malloy," he said in a thick Scotch accent. "Basil Thomson sends his regards."

"I doubt it," she answered. "He's a pig."

"I suppose he was rather beastly to the Irish. But he has his talents. Recruiting you, for one thing."

She snorted. "I haven't done much so far."

"We're curious. Why did the Germans send you to Russia? We thought they'd send you back to Ireland to foment rebellion."

"Obviously, rebellion in Russia is more important," she said. "They want me to join the Bolsheviks. In fact, I have already met their leader and am going to live with one of the women."

"Why the Bolsheviks?" he asked.

She clasped her hands and gazed around the room as she spoke. "They are the most likely to end the war, freeing up the Eastern Front, as I'm sure you know."

"I see. Well, it's obvious to anyone in Russia that revolution is weeks, perhaps days, away. Next time you communicate with the Germans, you might tell them that the British expedition was a resounding success."

Now she was confused. "What expedition?"

"Och, an embarrassing affair when various dignitaries came to convince Russia of the advantages of staying in the war."

Ellen remembered Lady Greystone's maid talking about some fairytale trip they made to the country where they met with the Tsar. "I heard about that."

"Tell the Germans we have thoroughly persuaded Russia to stay in the war and we do not expect any sort of revolution until the war has been won."

"They won't believe it. I was told the reason the German spies are openly friendly with the Tsarina is to instill hatred for the royal family, making revolution inevitable."

The Scottish Chap smiled as if they were merely trading pleasantries about whatever trivial things ballet aficionados discussed during intermissions.

"I agree. The Tsar and his ruthless policies don't help. He's an unreasonable man. I hate to say it, but he deserves whatever is coming to him. Are the Germans doing anything to foment this rebellion?"

"Money."

"Money? Through you?"

"Indeed."

"Well, don't give it to them, for God's sake. Look, even if there is a revolution, and I'm sure there will be, the Bolsheviks won't win. The moderate Kadet Party has the full support of the Allies."

"Then what does it matter if I give the money to the Bolsheviks?"

"Miss Malloy, you must *not* do it."

With that, the lights dimmed and the performance resumed.

She understood that dancers were supposed to be thin, but even so, the lot of them looked like they hadn't eaten a decent meal in months, and she suspected that like most everyone except the elite they couldn't get their hands on enough food.

Her conversation with the Scottish Chap had yielded nothing. He had not even told her if her family was all right. As soon as the curtain fell after the final ballet, he got up to leave. She also stood. Greystone grabbed her arm but she pulled free and followed the Scottish Chap out of the auditorium while the audience clapped and roared its approval.

"Oi," she called to him once they were in the lobby. He stopped and she caught up with him. "What about my family? Are they all right?"

"As far as I know, they're fine."

She didn't trust his bland expression. "I want proof."

He shrugged. "I'll see that you get it. In the meantime, do not give any money to the Bolsheviks. Do you understand? We won't like it if you do."

She understood the look in those pale blue eyes. She nodded her assent, and he walked out of the building and disappeared into the swirling white snow.

She shrank against the wall to wait for Sir Greystone as the giddy audience poured out of the auditorium. Ellen watched them curiously – the bejeweled women, the portly men with their monocles and their noses in the air, forcing "carefree" laughter. Perhaps it was not so easy to ignore the poverty on all sides now that shortages encroached on their own lives. Still, they must console themselves that at least they still had caviar and warm beds and servants to do their bidding.

Not everyone dripped in jewels. The poorer people streamed down from the balcony and Ellen understood how a couple of hours in the dark watching lithe bodies in feathers and tulle leap across the stage provided a small respite from the struggles of poverty and the banality of wealth.

Her scanning eyes doubled back to a column of blue – a woman with auburn hair in an elegant sheath with a lace border crisscrossing the bodice, accentuating her slender figure. A single strand of pearls glowed against her pale skin. Was it Ellen's imagination, or did their eyes meet for the briefest of seconds? In the next moment the woman had passed by, and Lord Greystone huffed up to her.

"There you are. I had half a mind to leave you."

Ellen made no retort as she followed him to the line of carriages, destiny's breath on the back of her neck.

Chapter 19

Louisa

The orange-peel scent of the steaming tea wafted over the table in the Greenwich Village teahouse while the chatter and laughter of women filled the air.

"You can have your choice, Louisa," the *Evening World* journalist Nixola Greeley Smith told her. "The ejected ambassador's wife or the opera singer. I can't be in two places at once."

Louisa blew on her tea before sipping.

"I'm not the interviewer that you are, Nixola," she said.

Nixola waved the comment away. "Oh, my dear, you are a fine interviewer, and you're a fine reporter. I don't need a full-blown interview of either one, just a description of the event, which you do extremely well. I still remember your vivid description of the Grand Central opening."

Louisa considered the options. "All right, then, I'll take Ambassador Gerard's wife. To think the Americans traded Count and Countess Bernstorff for the beleaguered ambassador and his wife."

"Do you know Mrs. Gerard?" Nixola nibbled a cookie.

"I met her when I had my society column. She was pleasant enough, if a bit dull."

Nixola chuckled. "Aren't they all? Take Francis with you. Make a date of it. How are things going with him, by the way? Shall I be receiving an embossed wedding invitation soon?"

Louisa smiled and held out her hand with the sapphire ring. "We haven't set a date yet. We haven't even made a public announcement."

Nixola tilted her head as she examined the ring. "Lovely setting. What's holding you up? Is it the prospect of war? He's not thinking of joining up, is he?"

Louisa stirred her tea. "He wants to serve his country, but he's already been rejected from the military because of a heart murmur. It's nothing serious, but they won't let him fight."

"A heart murmur? Let his heart murmur for you then. This damnable war."

"At least it gives you plenty to write about." Louisa admired Nixola tremendously. The granddaughter of the great newspaper man Horace Greeley, Nixola consistently churned out incisive articles, never forgetting the plight of women in peacetime and in war.

"That it does."

Mrs. Gerard's train was two hours and 40 minutes late, during which time Louisa and Francis played a game of gin rummy in the lobby of the Ritz Carlton with Billy Stephens, her old pal from *The Ledger,* who had recently taken a job at *The Times.*

"I've been meaning to speak to you about something, Billy." Louisa laid a card on the table. "Did you have to mention me in your article on the silk thieves?

That wasn't helpful for my reputation as a discreet investigator. Also, I saw someone skulking outside my house right after that story came out."

Billy took a sip of his Gibson. "Sorry. It was my last article for the police beat. I needed it to be good. But here I am in politics now. You know, the Krauts wouldn't release Ambassador Gerard and his family until that swine Bernstorff was safely returned to the bosom of the fatherland."

"That's a distasteful manner in which to refer to the German people," Francis said. He turned to Louisa. "You know the count, do you not, dear?"

Louisa's eyes met Billy's. They'd known each other too long for her to take offense at anything he said.

"I'm afraid my colleague is correct when it comes to Count Bernstorff." She laid down three jacks. "He's absolutely up to no good. Funding saboteurs and spreading propaganda to try to keep America out of the war."

"So you aren't a 'peacette,' Louisa?" Billy asked. "I thought you'd turned into a communist when you were writing for *The Ladies' Lantern*."

Louisa exhaled. "Gin. Of course I'm not a 'peacette' or a communist. I do think humanity would be better off, however, if we didn't decide to wipe out half the young men every generation or so." She glanced at Francis, ever thankful for his murmuring heart.

At a few minutes after 8 o'clock, Mrs. Gerard arrived at the hotel accompanied by family members, a policeman for security, and a couple of friends.

"Here she is," Billy said. "Let's get our quotes, kiddo."

A space was found in the lobby of the grand hotel for a press conference. Louisa took out her notebook, but Mrs. Gerard had little to say about the fact that her husband, the U.S. ambassador to Germany, had been unceremoniously booted out of the country — an obvious provocation on the part of the Germans.

"Home! Home! I'm very, very happy to be here. Say that for me. But I'm so tired after the long trip, really too tired to talk. Anyway, what talking there is to be, must be done by Mr. Gerard."

Louisa took note of Mrs. Gerard's appearance, including the dark circles under her eyes. and wrote, "Mrs. Gerard wore a dark traveling suit under a long seal coat with a sable collar. A jaunty black sailor hat trimmed with medallioned brocade topped her blonde hair, and she carried a bouquet of small red roses."

"Mrs. Gerard," she asked, "what were conditions like in Berlin before you left?"

Mrs. Gerard's eyes widened in recognition. "Oh, hello, Miss Delafield. The conditions were horrid. People are hungry. Young women widowed with children. Wounded soldiers begging in the streets." She shuddered. "Why, oh why, do they keep fighting?"

No one had an answer for that question, so the tired woman dismissed the reporters and went upstairs to the apartment reserved for her and her husband, who was still in Washington being debriefed by officials.

Louisa gazed at her fiancé. Francis itched to be in the war, and the image of him as a wounded soldier, perhaps missing a leg or two, popped vividly into her brain.

"I hope Nixola wasn't expecting much," Louisa said as the elevator doors closed on Mrs. Gerard and her family.

"Perhaps you could make something up," Francis suggested. "'Mrs. Gerard demands invasion of Germany to retrieve her Pomeranian puppy.' Something like that."

"Oh, yes, that will work. My debut as a fiction writer. Shall we get something to eat while we're here?"

They were seated at a secluded table in the rooftop lounge, finishing off a bottle of red wine and a couple of sirloins. It wasn't as if Francis could afford these expensive dinners every night, but something about a world at war made practical considerations less urgent.

"You and Billy Stephens must have been rather chummy at some point," Francis said.

Louisa chuckled. "I don't have brothers but I imagine if I did, they would be like Billy. Annoying nuisances, but on one's side in a pinch."

"Good-looking fellow. Is he married?"

Oh, Louisa thought, so this is about jealousy. Billy *was* handsome in a devil-may-care way. More handsome than Francis, whose thin face and prominent nose gave him the look of a man who often had his head in books. And yet that smile and the cleft in his chin...

"No, he is not married. He wouldn't want to give up the dance-hall girls. I, personally, have never found him remotely attractive." She ran a finger over Francis' palm and gazed up at him with a flutter of eyelashes. "Unlike a certain young attorney."

He laughed. Jealousy quelled. "You know you looked awfully sweet with your little god-daughter Hester the other night."

A shadow fell over the table.

"Louisa?"

She looked up and there stood Forrest Calloway, the man she had once loved. She was so surprised to see him she had no idea how to react.

"Forrest...it's been ages," she said. Her heart beat off-rhythm, as if it were listening to some Chicago-style "jass" music no one else could hear.

"I don't believe I've seen you since the wedding." His mahogany eyes were warm and, as always, seemed to see her and only her.

"Has it been that long?" She felt like a fool. Poor Francis must be utterly flummoxed. "Forrest Calloway, allow me to introduce Francis Holland. Francis, Mr. Calloway was my publisher when I worked at *The Ledger*. Until he went and sold it out from under us all." For heaven's sake, why did she say that? She sounded petty, perhaps even bitter. And why didn't she mention that Francis was her fiancé?

"Pleased to meet you, Mr. Holland. Louisa, we're here celebrating Sadie's birthday. Do drop by the table before you leave. Sadie would love to see you."

No, she wouldn't, Louisa thought. Louisa and Sadie had shared a look shortly before the wedding, and in that look Louisa's true feelings for Forrest had stood naked. Sadie had reacted with kindness and grace because she was a kind and gracious woman, but Louisa doubted she would be thrilled to see the younger woman who was once in love with her husband.

"Of course I will. I have been meaning to catch up with her," Louisa said. It sounded like the lie it was.

Forrest headed back to his table, and Francis looked at her curiously.

"You seem rather flustered." Francis knew she'd once had a lover, but he didn't realize he had just met the man. She found it ironic he had just been jealous of Billy, but it wouldn't occur to him that the man she had been in love with had been her publisher. This wasn't information she ever planned to divulge to him.

"It's just that I have a difficult time forgiving him for selling *The Ledger*. I was a syndicated columnist and when I lost my home paper, I lost the column. Of course, when Ellen started *The Ladies' Lantern*, I thought that would provide me with enough work. Then she went off to Ireland and didn't come back." Louisa was horrified to realize she was crying. "Oh, take me home, Francis. I'm a wreck."

"Darling, have another glass of wine. You'll be fine."

"I don't want any more. I just want to go home."

"All right," he said in his infinite patience. He truly was perfection, and yet her heart ached. She was no longer in love with Forrest, she reminded herself. She was going to marry Francis.

"Let's put our engagement announcement in the paper soon," she said as he helped her with her jacket.

As she sat on the passenger side of the Ford, Louisa gazed down at her engagement ring. Was she doing the right thing, she wondered. Was it fair to marry Francis when she was still unsure of the depth of her feelings for him? A dark mood settled on her. Her mind catapulted back sixteen years ago, standing beside her father's grave, feeling as if she no longer had a heart, as if her chest were an empty shell. She had sworn not to marry until she knew the truth about his untimely death. She had finally discovered the truth and she was free of that oath. And yet he would not be there to walk her down the aisle. What a dismal...

"Whoa," Francis said in an alarmed voice. He was staring at the rectangular mirror on the outside of the motorcar. He sped up and Louisa turned around to see what was happening. The bright headlights of a truck were inches away from the rear of the motorcar.

"Some fellow is driving like a maniac," Francis said.

"Pull over," Louisa said. "Let him pass."

His eyes darted from one side of the street to the other. "There's no room." Finally he whipped the car down a side street, the Ford careening on two wheels.

"My God!" Louisa said. She turned and saw the truck continue on its way, but she could have sworn she saw the driver grinning at them.

Francis stopped the car and took her in his arms.

"It's all right, darling."

She had the feeling nothing was all right.

Chapter 20

Ellen

Ellen waited till the next morning to pack her two suitcases and make her way back to the Vyborg district. She took the wig and velvet dress as well as her maid's outfit. She might need the disguises. She wanted to keep the sable-trimmed coat for its warmth, but it wouldn't do to call attention to herself with such an obvious sign of wealth. The fur hat was chancy enough.

Fortunately, she only had to clamber up two flights of steps to get to Irina's flat. With two beds, a table, two chairs, and a coal stove, it was luxurious compared with the apartment where she'd slept that first night.

"I thought you were coming back yesterday," Irina said as she lit the stove.

"So did I," Ellen said, "but my employer wouldn't give me my wages till this morning."

"The bed here isn't free, you know."

Ellen handed Irina a bit more than half the rent. The slight extra amount pleased her new roommate. Even the most die-hard socialist liked an extra bit of coin.

"Have some tea," Irina said.

Ellen's next telegram to Olga in Berlin said: *Met new friends. Wore a pretty red dress to a party. Will write soon.* She had learned to write in actual cyphers, but an obvious code would raise flags at the telegraph office, so she and Captain Boehm had created a code of their own. To him this message would mean she had joined the Bolsheviks and had assumed the role of a reporter.

She also sent a telegram overseas to a woman activist she knew at *The New York Call,* one of the only English-language Socialist newspapers in New York. *Dear Rose. Interested in news from Petrograd? Ellen Malloy, former publisher of* The Ladies' Lantern.

Ellen and Irina got along famously. Irina loved to talk, and Ellen's job was to listen. Irina never talked about her childhood. Instead, she carried on about Vladimir Ilyich Lenin and his treatise, "What Is to Be Done," which she had read cover to cover. When she wasn't talking about the Socialists or the futility of war or quoting Comrade Lenin, she talked about the men she'd slept with. Her descriptions of male anatomy – mushroom top, toy soldier, little fatso – made Ellen laugh so hard she cried. "You're what we call a 'trollop' back home."

Irina accepted the designation with pride. Then she asked Ellen questions about New York and the anarchists there. Ellen told her about the protests at Rutgers Square, the day the Army of the Unemployed occupied a church only to be reported to the police by the priest, the Ludlow massacre of mine workers' families, and the winter night when she had stayed at a facility for homeless men, women and children and truly understood the depths of misery engendered by capitalism run amok.

During the day they created pamphlets and broadsheets while drinking tea and smoking cigarettes of *makhorka*, a black Russian tobacco from the Caucasus. Ellen had never been a smoker except for once shortly after Hester's death, but now it became a part of her transformation. She made herself useful, loading broadsheets onto the old printer, selecting type from the cases, inking up the cylinder and hand-cranking the machine to roll out the pages. She liked the way a plain sheet transformed into print before her eyes. Back in New York, she'd been awestruck by the thundering presses at *The Ledger* newspaper where she had worked before starting her own magazine — the incredible noise and the thrill of the thousands of sheets of paper coming off the rollers. But she also found it gratifying to make these broadsheets by hand — each one a missive to the world.

"Everything we're doing is illegal," Molotov had warned her. "If caught, you could be shot by the Tsar's police."

Ellen understood the risks.

One evening Ellen asked Irina what the name Molotov meant. It didn't sound like a traditional Russian name.

"It means sledgehammer," Irina said, tossing her blonde hair behind her shoulder. Many of the Bolshevik women had cut their hair short, but Irina was vain about her golden locks.

Molotov didn't look like a sledgehammer. He had a pleasant face with dark hair, a high forehead and a neatly trimmed mustache. He told Ellen he'd been involved with the publication of *Pravda* from the beginning, though for the past three years the Bolshevik newspaper was outlawed. While the leaders of the Bolsheviks were off in exile somewhere, Molotov had come back and evaded the authorities.

It seemed as if the promised revolution was in a perpetual half-conscious state, but then in late February the Tsar dissolved the Duma.

"What does this mean?" Ellen asked.

"That's how the Tsar solves every problem. Take away the toy of the people," Irina said. "It's as if the King of England told Parliament to go home. But in England he can't do that. Only in backward Russia."

"Perhaps this time the toy will get up on its hind legs and refuse to be cowed," Ellen said.

"We shall see."

Two days later Ellen woke up and noticed the air was somehow different. Her muscles felt looser on her bones like they weren't clinging on for dear life.

"Today is International Women's Day," Irina announced.

"So?"

"Get dressed, you lazy slug. We're meeting Molotov and the others at a café in the Military Hotel."

Bundled up in her fur hat, wool coat and knit scarf, Ellen trundled after Irina down the streets of the Vyborg district. This day *was* different from the other days. For one thing it felt warmer. The stranglehold of winter had begun to ease. And on this day, hundreds of women poured out of the factories, crying, "Down with the war! Down with hunger! Bread for the workers!"

Throngs of women filled the lanes. When they passed the Havana Cigar factory, the women outside called through the windows, "Come out, workers! March with us!"

Irina threw a snowball in a window. Other women picked up on the idea, tossing snowballs into all the factory windows they passed. Within minutes workers streamed out. They were seized by the marchers and kissed on their cheeks as they set off down the Bolshoi Sampsionevsky Prospekt.

"To Nevsky! Down with the war!" the marchers shouted at they approached the Kalinkin Bridge. The excitement was infectious.

Ellen's breath caught in her throat when she saw on the bridge a blockade of police on horseback, holding their whips high. The stymied marchers halted. Then they grabbed ice chunks and threw them at the police.

"Across the ice!" Irina yelled to the crowd. In front of people, Irina exuded a magnetic power Ellen had not seen before.

The crowd cheered, "Hurrah!" and soon they were crossing the ice-coated Neva to the Petrograd side.

"To Nevsky!" the marchers shouted and proceeded toward Nevsky Prospekt.

Ellen had seen demonstrations in New York, but nothing like this. Tens of thousands of people filled the streets. An ocean of women, and she was just one drop.

Once they were in the city, Irina pulled Ellen out of the crowd of demonstrators, and they hurried along a side street to the Military Hotel.

Ellen gazed at the elegant building and said, "How is this a military hotel?"

"It used to be the Hotel Astoria but it was owned by Germans, so the Russian government confiscated it when the war began."

They shook the snow off their boots before going inside. No one else had arrived except for Molotov and his girlfriend, Maryuska, a willowy creature who never had much to say, but occasionally rolled her eyes at some pronouncement Molotov uttered.

Lowering the newspaper he was reading, Molotov pushed his spectacles onto the bridge of his nose and graced them with a rare smile. "Good morning, Comrades. Have some coffee. I paid for a whole pot."

"Molotov, why are you sitting here on your duff? Huge protests! Right now on Nevsky Prospekt." Irina's voice thrummed with excitement.

"I know, I know. Have some coffee. They will be marching all day," he said.

They sat down and each poured themselves a cup of coffee.

"I'd kill for a lump of sugar," Irina said.

Molotov pulled from his pocket a wrapped lump of sugar, which Irina happily snatched from his hand. The café still had bread, a stale black loaf that tasted like sawdust. Ellen took a piece from the basket on the table. She wondered if she'd ever get used to the constant hunger. She didn't miss the servant's life with Lady Greystone, but her clothes were getting looser. Decent food was hard to come by at any price.

"What's the plan?" Ellen asked.

"International Women's Day is vital to the Socialist cause," Molotov said, giving them each a handful of flyers.

Irina studied the flyers. "Where did you get these? We didn't print them."

"From the Interdistrict Committee. We must present a united front against the war," he said. "Deliver these to the marchers."

Irina read the pamphlet out loud: *"Because of this war, factory owners turn workers into serfs. We cannot afford to live. Hunger knocks at everyone's door. From the villages, they steal the cattle and the last morsels of bread — all to feed the war machine. For hours, women stand in line for food. Children work at dangerous machines until late at night. Suffering surrounds us. Not only in Russia, but in all countries."*

While Irina read the contents of the pamphlet, Ellen heard another voice behind her, speaking in English. "That was some dead brilliant whiskey in the pouch, lad." Then a man's laughter. Ever so slowly she turned her head. The Scottish Chap stood by a table with another fellow. He didn't see her. Wouldn't have recognized her anyway without her wig and velvet dress. A point in her favor. Two points actually. Now, she knew where he was staying.

Irina continued reading aloud, gesticulating: *"Comrades, who wins when war is waged? Need we kill Austrian and German workers and peasants? German workers do not want to fight either. War is waged for the sake of the capitalists, the war profiteers who fish in troubled waters. They become rich in wartime. After the war, they will not pay military taxes. Workers and peasants are the only ones who pay the costs."*

Irina's voice attained a mesmerizing quality when she spoke, and Ellen found the message stirred something in her breast. Ellen and Molotov's girlfriend clapped when Irina finished.

One of Molotov's cronies burst in with a triumphant gleam in his eyes. "Comrades, the factories are empty. Already a crowd of more than a hundred thousand is swelling in the streets."

"This is it!" Irina said, as if she were witnessing the Second Coming. "This could be the Revolution."

Molotov turned to Ellen. "You spoke of rumblings in the earth. Go see the quake."

Irina grabbed her arm and out they went, clutching the pamphlets.

Ellen's sighting of the Scottish Chap reminded her that she still had no idea about the safety of her family, but finally she sensed her sacrifice was worth something, for she was helping to usher in the future. Her whole being felt light as a soap bubble.

Chapter 21

Louisa

Carlotta tapped her fingers on the table while Louisa tried to read the *Evening World*. On the front page was a story about the Zimmerman telegram that Reggie had talked about. It was all out in the open now. In fact, the German foreign minister admitted he had written the telegram inviting Mexico to attack the United States. The editorials were screaming in rage.

Carlotta cleared her throat. "We haven't had a client since your job at the silk house. And we need money, Louisa. Food costs keep rising. Onions are sky-high. We're supposed to boycott onions, but how am I supposed to cook without onions? Ay, me."

Louisa hadn't wanted to think about the lack of work, but she knew she would have to come up with some way to pay bills and soon. When she decided to hang out her shingle as a discreet investigator after solving a sticky problem for the film actress Theda Bara, it had seemed so easy. She'd had several clients in a row, but with the prospect of war at America's doorstep, all other concerns had faded into the woodwork, and women no longer required her help or at least they weren't willing to pay for it. Reggie had given her a payment for delivering his message to Countess Bernstorff, but that wouldn't last much longer. She couldn't go to him with hat in hand like some beggar. She also did not want Francis to know their situation. He might think she was marrying him just to get out of a financial jam. She had been supporting herself and her mother through her writing for years. She'd just have to drum up some more assignments.

"Did you know it's 40 cents for a pound of onions?" Carlotta held up one of the offending vegetables. "Last year it was six cents! Bread was 12 cents. Now, it's 37 cents. Even potatoes are a luxury. We're dining on fine china, but we're going to run out of food to put on that fine china. You want I should take it to the pawn shop?"

Louisa shook her head. She hadn't had to worry about money for several years, and now poverty had reared its ugly head again.

"I'll visit Nixola today. She can always throw some stringer work my way."

"I have something to do today as well. Your mama will be fine?"

"Of course," Louisa said. "But where are you going?"

Carlotta shrugged. "To see my sister."

When Louisa went upstairs to change, she felt a weird ache along the inside of her skull. She heard those angry voices again. Then they faded and all she heard was a bird outside, longing for spring.

"Louisa dear, impeccable timing." Nixola looked up from her typewriter. "Would you be interested in covering these food riots?"

"Riots?" Louisa asked. She preferred not to cover any sort of riot.

"I thought that was the sort of thing you wrote about for *The Ladies' Lantern*. This is a women's cause. Apparently, poor mothers are absolutely up in arms."

"Why aren't you covering it? You're known for your feminist outlook."

"I have an interview with Mr. H.L. Mencken, who is more of a feminist than you or I."

"How so?"

"For one thing, he claims that women are more intelligent than men."

"My goodness, that's quite radical for a..." Louisa looked over Nixola's shoulder and read, "*a shining member of the all-star sex.*" "I agree with him, of course, but what's his evidence?"

"He says it's obvious. For one thing, women choose a mate based not on looks or social graces, but on his capabilities, whereas men look for a wife who is merely pretty."

"He has a point," Louisa said. Francis was good-looking enough but he was no movie star, and he certainly wasn't a member of high society, but he was brilliant and he enjoyed a good laugh. And he was hard-working. She had chosen well, she told herself. "All right. I'll cover this women's food riot. Carlotta has been complaining about this very problem."

"Marie Ganz is speaking at Madison Square this afternoon."

"Isn't she the one the reporters call 'Sweet Marie'?"

"The very one," Nixola said with a laugh, "because from my understanding she's a bit of a hellcat and swears like a sailor."

Louisa grinned at Nixola as if they were old chums. "Perhaps she'll teach me some new vocabulary."

On the subway, Louisa read the articles Nixola had tossed at her about the lead-up to today's protest. Apparently just a few days ago, women had rampaged through the poultry market, enraged at the prices. One woman had turned over a pushcart when she found she couldn't afford her purchases. The riots lasted for more than two hours. Louisa wondered how she'd missed this news. Had she been so ensconced in pondering marriage to Francis, she'd lost touch with reality?

Louisa exited the subway station and emerged onto Rutgers Park. Already a few hundred women were gathering, many of them bare-headed with only a shawl to stave off the cold. They held babies in their arms, and their faces were gaunt with hunger. The crowd milled around before they took up a chant. "We want bread! We want bread!"

A woman, most likely the infamous Sweet Marie, stood on the edge of the fountain and shouted, "Follow me to City Hall!"

Louisa took out her notebook and quickly jotted down her observations as she hurried along with the crowd. They marched down East Broadway through the Bowery, all the while shouting, "Feed us now!" in both English and Yiddish.

"Excuse me," Louisa said to a young woman with a toddler on her hip. "I'm a reporter. Can you help me explain to the public the concerns of the mothers?"

"Concerns? You bet your keister we got concerns. The butchers no longer cut the fat off the meat, and then charge us higher prices, ya know. The chicken sellers are all in cahoots. And I had to pawn everything my bubka left me – her wedding ring, her silver spoons – just to put food on my children's plates, ya know. As for me, I don't eat nothing for lunch or dinner – just a half a potato for breakfast."

Louisa scribbled as fast as she could as the marchers continued on their way. They made it to City Hall Park, and a few hundred women dashed up the steps of the building only to have police hurriedly close the iron gate in front of the door.

A furious roar rose up from the crowd. "Feed our children!"

A few minutes later, one of the mayor's representatives appeared at the window. Louisa could not hear what he said, but one of the women yelled to the crowd, "The mayor says he will meet with us later today, but you must disperse quietly."

The women around her grumbled, but it was cold out, and Louisa had no doubt they would all rather be home. Not to mention policemen on horseback were riding through the crowd with their bludgeons held high. As the crowd turned to leave, Louisa edged toward the steps in the hopes of getting a quote from one of the leaders when the woman known as Sweet Marie stood on the steps and yelled, "Don't leave! Where is the mayor? Off to a nice lunch that's where! Whilst you cannot feed your children, he and his cronies dine on steak and apple pie!"

A police officer shouted from the back of his big white horse: "Mayor Mitchel has promised to meet with three of your representatives, but only if you will kindly disperse. He has heard your concerns. But you must disperse now."

The women grumbled. Would they disperse? Or would they stay and listen to Sweet Marie?

A middle-aged woman clutched the hand of a little boy. "Let's go home. It's too cold out here," she grumbled.

Others nodded, resigned. The excitement quickly faded.

"Hell no!" Marie yelled to the crowd. "We canna trust what this big shot says. It's a bunch of baloney!"

The women in the crowd hesitated.

Louisa noticed a black-haired young woman now stood beside Sweet Marie, fists on her hips, like a sentinel. Recognizing the tough-looking young woman, Louisa felt the ground wobble beneath her. What was Carlotta doing there?

Chapter 22

Ellen

As Ellen and Irina hurried toward the gathering, thousands upon thousands of women, housewives, students, women workers, and even society women poured into the streets, striding forth like Roman soldiers. They carried banners and shouted, "Bread and peace!"

At the front of a line, a woman in a black turban caught Ellen's eye. She was holding onto one end of a banner. She seemed encapsulated in a bubble of joy. The Socialists and the Bolsheviks all scowled. This woman smiled. Something about her seemed familiar.

"Do you know that woman?" Ellen asked Irina. "The one in the turban."

A dark expression came across Irina's face. "Oh, yes, I know her. That is Countess Sofia Panina."

"A countess is marching with students and workers?"

"They call her the Red Countess because she feeds the poor, but does she give up her mansion here in Petrograd or her estates in the country? No. Women like her are happy to help the poor as long as they can continue to live in luxury."

Ah, Ellen thought. Similar to the society women in New York who spend their days involved in various charities and hold outlandish parties at night. Except for Hester French, who spent her days delivering food and medicine to the tenements and her nights in Ellen's arms.

They separated to pass out flyers to the strikers and the marchers. As the women marched, more striking workers flowed over the icy river to join them. An enormous release swelled with the shouting voices. Someone began singing the "Marseillaise" and soon the din of thousands of voices rang in her ears. Ellen had never felt anything quite this intoxicating.

Suddenly shouts erupted.

"They are rioting. The women are rioting!" a boy shouted. "They're throwing rocks and breaking windows of the shops! They're demanding bread!"

The peaceful protest was no longer peaceful. Ellen watched dumbfounded as women took up stones and threw them through the window of a popular bakery. The cries grew angrier: "Death to the Tsar!"

Police on horseback came riding through the marchers, swinging their clubs. Ellen threaded her way through the hordes of women and striking workers toward the Liteiny Bridge and found Irina at the foot of it, holding a red banner.

"This is savage!" she yelled to Irina, gleefully.

"You are witnessing the birth of the new Russia." Irina waved the banner. "Viva la revolution!"

That evening they joined the Bolsheviks in Molotov's flat, drinking vodka and laughing about the grand day's events. Molotov played the violin. Although his sympathies were with the factory workers and the peasants, he had grown up in a wealthy family. He had turned his back on the bourgeois family he'd been born to, so that he could champion the rights of those who had been denied their rights for so long. Tonight he played a cheerful peasant tune, and the men danced. These people she barely knew had become like kinfolk.

They were all living through an actual revolution. Nothing would ever be the same. What would her old comrades in New York would think when they heard the news? Wouldn't Emma Goldman and Lulu, Ellen's one-time lover, wish they could be here to witness it? Soon a red wave would circle the globe, and workers would rise up. No more Rockefellers. No more robber barons like Frick, Carnegie and their ilk, men who brought in soldiers to maim and kill striking workers.

When Molotov was done playing, he lifted his glass and said, "To *Pravda!*"

"To Truth," Ellen said in English.

"Truth," they all said and drank.

"We will resurrect the only newspaper in Russia that does not lie!" Irina said.

Molotov leaned close to Ellen. "We will have much work for you, Tovarisch. Because this is a worldwide revolution of workers. That is the most important goal of all."

When she and Irina returned to their own flat, Ellen felt happier than she had in ages. In New York when she had joined up with the anarchists, she was never really one of them, even if she did believe in their various causes. She'd been trying to find out who among them had wanted to kill Louisa. Besides, her darling Hester French did not approve of anarchists. Too radical for her tastes. But here and now, Ellen had no restraints. The Germans were happy to have her imbedded with the Bolsheviks. And the British asked only that she not give money to them. She could do what she wanted in Russia. She could follow her heart. And her heart was a Bolshevik. She was so tired she fell asleep without saying her prayer for little Hester.

Ellen awoke the next morning with misgivings. She'd been so confident in the revolution the day before, but now she wondered how long it would last or if any permanent changes would result. She thought of Ireland and how swiftly the British had crushed the uprising last Easter. Were the bread riots merely another temporary outburst?

"Will any of this matter?" Ellen asked Irina, as they huddled next to the coal stove, drinking their tea."Won't the Tsar send in his Cossacks to quash the troubles? Like in the uprising in 1905?"

Irina rubbed her hands together. "There's a difference now. The country has been ground down by this war with the Germans. The people have nothing left to give. The ruling class has sucked them dry, as you say." Irina paused in order to get a gander at Ellen. "Nice jacket."

Ellen had bought the leather jacket from a hungry student the day after joining the Bolsheviks, but it had only just gotten warm enough to wear it.

"Seems to be the uniform of the Bolsheviks," she said.

Irina poured more tea from the samovar into Ellen's cup.

"Who's in charge of the country now?" Ellen asked, warming her hands on the hot cup. Outside the sun had crept up the sky like a guest who's not sure if he's invited.

Irina sipped her tea, dipping her tongue in first, an odd little habit that reminded Ellen of Louisa's little orange cat, Gingin. "The members of the Duma, for now. They will form a Provisional Government."

"That's a good thing, isn't it?" Ellen asked.

"Ha! They are bourgeois puppets. When Comrade Lenin returns, we will rip the land out of the greedy hands of the gentry. The Soviets will control the factories. The army will revolt. And we will have a dictatorship of the proletariat."

If the Germans had their way, Lenin would already be on the way back to Russia, Ellen knew.

Irina finished her tea and stood, eyes bright with the prospect of mayhem. "Let's go to Molotov's. He'll surely be resurrecting *Pravda*, and you must let your American friends know about the new Russian freedom."

Fifteen minutes later Irina and Ellen were in Molotov's flat, smoking cigarettes with the mysterious Maryuska. Irina was jealous of the way the men all eyed Maryuska, but she pretended she didn't care. Two young fellas sat on the couch, cleaning guns.

Molotov entered, shirtless, scratching his head. "Go out and cover the protests. Witness everything you can. We will print an issue of the new *Pravda* as soon as we are set up."

"Set up where?" Ellen asked.

"We will have a press shortly," Molotov said and looked over at the two men on the couch. "Won't we, Comrades?"

The two men exchanged a look. One of them smiled broadly. His teeth were yellow.

"By noon tomorrow."

What could they possibly be planning, Ellen wondered.

Molotov said, "Irina, go to the workers' soviet and insist they continue the strike while we have the momentum." He turned to Ellen. "Tovarisch, once we are up and running, you will write articles for the New York papers. In the meantime, go and see how the revolution progresses."

Ellen grinned. She would help spread the word — revolution was possible. If revolution was possible, peace was possible. First, the old world must burn.

Ellen left the flat and crossed the bridge from the Vyborg district into a city of chaos. The revolution was in full swing. A dozen policemen on horseback stood sentry near the Nicholai Station. In front of the station, Ellen came to a circle about twice the diameter of Columbus Circle in New York with an enormous statue of a man on horseback — the emperor Alexander. Suddenly shots rang out. She ducked behind the statue and peeked over its base. Policemen fired into the crowd of people at the station. Would this be another massacre? Like the one in 1905? The crowd scattered, hiding behind any barricade they could find, leaving the bloodied bodies of two women and a child on the ground. Ellen's legs trembled as she slid down to the ground and assessed what she'd seen. She couldn't make sense of it. The women were hungry. They wanted to feed their families, and for that, the police had shot them.

A pounding of horses' hooves on the street. Again, Ellen peeked over the base of the statue. Cossacks. She held her breath. The Tsar relied on the Cossacks to do his bidding, and they themselves had crushed the revolution in 1905. Would they do it now? She trembled as one of the Cossacks on a huge black horse pulled out a revolver. An old woman fell to the ground in terror.

To Ellen's shock, the Cossack shot the police captain. The Cossack then shot two more police before the rest of them turned and fled.

The people emerged from their hiding spots, shouting, "Hurrah! Hurrah!"

They surrounded the Cossacks, cheering them. Ellen sat on the ground and jotted down the events as fast as she could. She rose and walked toward the crowd. The Cossacks were joking around with the workers, their wives and children. She'd heard so many tales of how the Cossacks terrorized the poor people of Russia in the last revolution, beating them to the ground and running roughshod over them. But everything was topsy-turvy in 1917 Petrograd.

Later over beer and cigarettes, the Bolsheviks parsed the day's events.

"The Cossacks shot the police," Ellen told the others. "I thought the Cossacks were on the side of the Tsar."

"They have seen the light," Molotov said, gleefully. "Why should they kill the wives and mothers of soldiers? Some soldiers are even rising up against the officers."

"The tide is turning," Irina observed, "when soldiers refuse their orders."

"But why are the police still on the side of the monarchy?" Ellen asked, trying to keep track of these strange shifting loyalties.

Irina explained that the police were the most hated officials in the land. They had too much power. These men could have been, should have been, at the front fighting the Germans instead of on the streets of the city, slaughtering the wives and children of soldiers for trying to get bread.

That evening Ellen and Irina stood on the bank of the Neva, looking across the ice-bound river at the city. A huge fire blazed.

"What is that?" Ellen asked.

"The hall of records," Irina said. "Every criminal, every political prisoner – all their records, their mug shots going up in smoke."

She slipped her arm in Ellen's and together they watched the past burn. As they stood there Ellen felt a ghost at her shoulder. 'Twas her da. Laughing in delight.

Chapter 23

Louisa

Louisa sat in the parlor looking at an article in *McCall's* about how war had affected wedding dress styles, but it may as well have been written in Greek. She was too immersed in mulling over the events of the day to concentrate on the words on the page.

At the protest, someone had shoved Carlotta off the steps and into the crowd of women, and two policemen had taken Sweet Marie by the arms. The demonstrators stood stunned into silence as the police dragged the screaming, cursing woman to the paddy wagon. Carlotta ran back up the steps and turned to face the crowd. "Stay calm! Stay calm! The leaders will meet with the mayor tomorrow and see what he has to say. If they don't fix the problem, then we'll show them what for. Now you can take your children home and get some rest."

She had a power in front of the crowd that Louisa had never witnessed. The women, hungry and cold as they were, assented, and the crowd slowly dispersed. Louisa pushed her way through the bodies to Carlotta to confront her. "So, this is what you've been doing?" she asked. "I thought you had a sick sister."

"She is sick. Sick of being hungry and having nothing to feed her kids."

As they headed back to Harlem on the 9th Avenue El, Carlotta explained that she'd been going to meetings of the Mothers' Anti-High Price League. "America hasn't even declared war, and we already have food shortages, not to mention the price gouging of those so-called merchants."

"What do you think the mayor can do?" Louisa asked.

"They can sell food at a fair price. They can give free lunches to schoolkids. If they don't there will be more marches. And more destruction. We already burned down a poultry market."

"Oh, Carlotta, please be careful. You could wind up in a jail cell next to Sweet Marie."

As Louisa sat with Anna sat in the parlor, remembering this exchange, Anna asked,

"You aren't going out to dinner with your fiancé?"

"He can't afford to take me out every night of the week," Louisa answered and turned the page of the magazine she wasn't reading.

Carlotta popped her head in the doorway and said, "I'm going out."

Louisa looked up, alarmed. "Not another meeting of those mothers, is it? The mayor did acquiesce to their demands."

Carlotta shook her head. "Not one of those meetings. A different kind. I won't be late."

Louisa rose and followed Carlotta to the hall credenza where her coat hung.

"What sort of a meeting?" she asked in a low voice.

Carlotta shrugged. "It's...political."

Political? Carlotta had never shown an interest in politics, and now here she was getting involved in all sorts of causes.

"What is the meaning of this?" Louisa asked. "Since when do you care about politics?"

Carlotta shrugged on her coat and stuck her hands in her pockets as she gazed at Louisa. "You don't know what it was like, Louisa. To be a ...a toy for men to play with. To be helpless as they did whatever they wanted to my body. Rich men. Powerful men. I was nothing..."

Louisa's chest constricted. She hated to imagine Carlotta's life in the brothel. "I'm so sorry that happened to..."

Carlotta didn't let her finish. "From the Mother's League, I find out there are people who want to take power away from those men. To give it to people who are" – she searched for the word – "oppressed. Like me."

"But you aren't still oppressed, are you?" Louisa asked. "Haven't I given you a nice home?"

"We all are oppressed. Even you, Louisa," Carlotta said. "My family turned to crime to gain power. But I won't do that. There's another way."

Louisa realized that when Ellen was publishing her magazine about labor unions and birth-control activists, Carlotta had been paying attention.

"They call themselves socialists," Carlotta said. "The meeting is close by. The Lenox Casino on West 116th Street."

"Oh, Carlotta. It's too dangerous for you to go there by yourself," Louisa said, unsure how to dissuade the young woman.

"Then why don't you come with me?" Carlotta threw the question at her like a challenge to a duel.

Louisa took a minute to contemplate the idea. What could it hurt? "Mother, will you be all right alone tonight?" she called out.

"Of course I will. Stop treating me like an invalid."

"All right then. Carlotta and I are going to a meeting of socialists at the Lenox Casino."

"What is a socialist?" Anna asked.

"Someone you would not like," Louisa answered.

Louisa knew several socialists among the Bohemians in Greenwich Village, and they seemed to be fine people, if somewhat overwrought. But while she fully understood the pacifist point of view, the world had chosen war, not peace. And all their anti-war speeches were so many daisies between railroad ties. The train of war would run right over them.

Louisa grabbed her wool coat. She would not wear fur to a meeting of socialists. She and Carlotta left the apartment and strode side by side through Harlem to the casino, on 116th Street. Despite its name, it was not a gambling establishment but a dance hall with various vaudeville shows and concerts. Only lately, the socialists had been renting it for their meetings.

The pungent smell of working men and women laced the dance hall. One fiery fellow got up on the stage and gave a speech about how the capitalists want to drag America into the war for profit. Another stood up and demanded that all workers unite – not just the cigar makers or the truck drivers but all workers. Louisa looked around at the crowd. So different from the types of people she had once covered as a society writer. She heard Yiddish and Russian tongues. But a sense of futility surrounded them as if they were crying for help from a cold, dark pit.

Louisa noticed Carlotta smiling up at a well-dressed, dark-haired man with a gaunt face and a thick black mustache. He looked to be around 40 years old. Louisa had never seen Carlotta show any interest in a man, but the two of them were deep in conversation when she felt someone at her back. Someone's warm breath brushed against her neck. She smelled a fruity scent. She turned around, but couldn't tell in the crowd who had been behind her. Then she noticed a teenage boy watching her. When she approached him, he darted into the crowd and disappeared.

Then she heard a voice, close by. "Where's your boy-friend?"

Again she wheeled around. All she saw was the back of a man in a fedora as he hurried off.

"Let's get out of here," she said to Carlotta.

"So soon?" the man with Carlotta asked. "Will you come again?"

"You betcha, Abe. It was nice talking to you," Car-lotta said. Then she took Louisa's arm and they walked out of the casino.

"Let's take a cab," Louisa said.

"But it's not far."

Louisa already had her arm up, and a taxicab pulled to the curb. They got inside and Louisa looked around. A man stood on the sidewalk, watching as they drove away.

Chapter 24

Ellen

Molotov's men had forcibly taken over another newspaper in a large stone building on the Moika River. Excitement filled Ellen as she heard the familiar rumble of the huge printers in the depths of the building. But there was little time to enjoy it.

"Out!" Molotov demanded. "Out into the streets."

Petrograd seethed with revolutionary fervor. Every hour the crowds grew larger. Not only students and factory workers, but tram drivers, waitresses, postal workers joined in. Red banners and flags sprang up everywhere. People ripped imperial emblems off walls. They toppled statues. The rallying cry was no longer "We want bread!" Instead, they proclaimed, "Give us land!" and "Down with the Tsar!"

The mounted police tried to manage the crowds by rounding them up like cattle, beating them with their loaded whips, lined with steel shot to inflict the most damage, but they may as well have tried to herd cats. The people, wearing metal plates under their hats and padded clothing, no longer feared the police, and the

Cossacks had lost all interest in doing the Tsar's dirty work. The soldiers as well had transferred their loyalties. Ellen interviewed a member of the Petrograd Garrison who told her, "Why should we kill our brothers and sisters, our brides? They have done nothing wrong."

Ellen and Irina prowled the streets, gathering information to share with readers. On Nevsky Prospekt some soldiers beckoned them inside their armored car.

"Get in!" a soldier yelled to them. "The police have machine guns on the roofs."

They jumped into the car, and indeed as they rode down the streets, the sound of ricocheting bullets surrounded them, and showers of snow erupted where the bullets slammed into walkways. Instead of hiding, citizens and soldiers in armored cars, armed with one-pounders, shot the daylights out of the police. Centuries of oppression crumbled around them, and giddiness infected the citizenry.

After the shooting died down, Ellen and Irina leapt from the car and hurried along the Bolshoi Kenushava, a side street, when a group of mounted lancers with nine-foot weapons resembling harpoons charged down the street. When they tried to escape into a nearby restaurant, the doorman shut the door, but Ellen managed to get her snow shoe in the opening, and Irina grabbed a brick from the street.

"I'll break every window you have!" she yelled at him.

He relented, and they pushed their way in. A policeman followed, screaming curses at the doorman, but Ellen and Irina didn't stay around long enough to see what happened next. They dashed through the kitchen and out the back door to an alley.

"Why are the police still on the side of the royalists if the Cossacks have switched sides?" Ellen asked Molotov later.

"In any street problem, the policeman has been both judge and jury. His pay is so small he has gotten used to living off graft. His greed gets the upper hand, and so he is not popular. It may simply be too late for him to change his spots."

The next day the shooting started about 11:30 in the morning. Irina suggested they help out at one of the makeshift infirmaries in the lobby of one of the cheaper hotels.

"We'll see the real effects of the revolution but out of the way of the bullets." She grinned. She was having the time of her life.

At the infirmary, automobiles dropped off bloodied men and boys. Ellen bandaged gunshot wounds and applied splints to broken bones. One poor fellow died while she was tying a tourniquet around his arm. She placed a hand on his chest and whispered a prayer before moving on to the next victim. There was no time for fear or sorrow. As soon as one body was taken to the pile in the back, another injured person needed help.

One delirious man with a stab wound in his side ranted in German.

"A spy," one of the soldiers said.

"How do you know?" Ellen asked, trying unsuccessfully to stanch the bleeding.

"Listen to him."

Ellen shook her head. The average Russian soldier had no idea that the German high command fully supported the revolution. The Russian soldiers didn't want to fight, and Germans didn't want them to fight. Russians feared that German soldiers would swarm their countryside, but in reality, they'd be pulled back to fight the French and the British if Russia would sign a peace agreement.

Outside, volleys fired back and forth as horses galloped to and fro. The shooting and the rising body count continued all afternoon. The trams had stopped by the evening, and the electric streetlights were out. But a searchlight on top of the Admiralty Building with its golden spire kept the street bright enough to stroll around. Venturesome souls were out and about. Their lack of fear amazed Ellen. The fighting seemed to have that effect on many people. Either you'd get killed or you wouldn't.

"Look, Ellen," Irina said, pointing to a proclamation posted on a pole.

"What does it say? Something about workers?" The writing on the sign was barely legible.

"'All workers who are not back at their jobs by Monday morning will be immediately drafted.' Stupid Royalists!" Irina ripped the sign down.

A throng passed by. "To the armory!"

Ellen and Irina glanced at each other. The armory?

"Let's go," Irina said. Ellen didn't have to be told twice.

Walking down the street with the Nagant revolvers they had managed to liberate from the armory, Ellen noticed a preternatural calm in the air. The gleam in the eyes of the people told of the storm on the horizon. This revolution was nowhere near done.

They took a droshky back to the Vyborg side, and the old *izvozchik* told them, "The police are all in hiding. The people will have the upper hand soon. They will not stand for shooting down the wives and children of the soldiers at the front when they ask for bread."

"What about you?" Ellen asked. "What will you be doing tomorrow? Isn't everyone going on strike?"

"I will be killing policemen," he said with a nonchalant shrug.

Peals of Irina's laughter echoed in the gloaming.

When they reached their room and got into bed, Ellen could not fall asleep. She thought of the failure of the Easter Rising in Ireland, how the British overlords kept their boot on the necks of the Irish, how they had executed the poor foolish heroes. The Russian workers and peasants had been defeated when they tried to rise in 1905. It took time to kill the beast of oppression. Time and blood. Someday Ireland would throw off her own yoke. Ellen hoped to be around to see it.

Her mind wandered across the ocean to New York. She wondered how her brothers and mother were faring. It had been ten days since she met with the Scottish Chap. He'd promised proof of Martin's safety, but how would he get it to her? It occurred to her that as the revolution progressed, foreigners would be leaving in droves. The Scottish Chap would have no reason to stay. She looked over at the sleeping Irina. She didn't want to leave her bed for the cold outside, but she pushed the blanket off and quietly got dressed.

Chapter 25

Louisa

Louisa was dreaming of Francis. The two of them were in a rowboat. He was in the front with his back to her. She kept calling his name but he wouldn't turn and face her. He couldn't hear her over the sound of the women shrieking in rage. Then she heard her own name.

"Louisa. Louisa."

As she swam into consciousness, she felt a weight on her bed, too heavy to be Gingin. She opened her eyes.

Carlotta sat on the end of the bed. "Wake up. I've got something to show you."

"For heaven's sake." Louisa rubbed her eyes. "Let me wake up first." Outside rain pounded against the window.

She sat up, and Carlotta pointed to the bedside table where a cup of coffee sat. Louisa hooked a finger in the gold-plate handle and sipped. Plenty of cream, just the way she liked it though ideally it would be a touch warmer. After the caffeine started percolating in her brain, she asked, "All right. What's so urgent?"

Carlotta handed her a newspaper.

"The *New York Call*? The Socialist paper? Why would I read this?"

"First of all, the Russians have had a revolution."

"They're always having revolutions, and the Tsar is always crushing them. Quite violently if I remember my history correctly."

Carlotta leaned forward. "Turn the page."

Louisa did so, her eyes scanning the newsprint and then she gasped. It was a short article directly from Russia.

The headline read "A Comrade in Russia." Louisa read the story: *"On the 18th of February, women took to the streets to demand bread. Four days later, more than half a million people were demanding peace, bread and land. A spontaneous protest by workers, by the hungry and those who have been yearning for freedom. Now the proletariat dream is coming true. All the old symbols of Imperial Russia have been ripped from the walls. No more censorship. The doors to the prisons have been flung open. A new Russia is born. Wake up, American workers. The time has come."* And it was signed, Ellen Malloy.

"My God," Louisa said. "I can't believe it."

"We have to go back to the Lenox Casino," Carlotta said.

"Why?"

"Trotsky will be there tonight to talk about the revolution."

"Trotsky? Who is that?"

"A Russian. Abe told me that Trotsky came here in January with his family after they were expelled from Spain. He has been imprisoned many times by the Tsar for standing up for the people. A hero to the Russians here in New York. He knows all the leaders of the revolution."

"Wait. Who is Abe?"

"You know. The poet I met at the casino."

"He's a poet?"

"Yep. He's been in New York raising money for the revolution for the past five years. A very important man."

"How do you know all this?"

"He told me. We meet at Rutgers Square and go on walks."

Louisa stared at Carlotta in surprise. Then she sighed. "All right. I suppose I better find out exactly what Ellen's gotten herself mixed up in."

She threw back the covers. Her bare feet landed on the cold floor. So, Ellen was in Russia as the countess had said. Had she become a communist? She certainly sounded like one. Why would the Germans send her to Petrograd?

As Louisa donned the charcoal-gray skirt that Suzie had altered to land just above the ankles in keeping with the style, her white silk blouse, and gray jacket, she thought of the last time she had been so worried about Ellen. The sinking of the *Lusitania*. Then she had also been recently engaged, and she immediately called it off. She grimaced at her reflection as she tied the bow at the neckline of her blouse. She would not make that mistake again. Of course, this time Ellen was not in danger of drowning, but to be in the middle of a violent revolution surely had risks of its own.

"Where are you off to?" Anna asked as Louisa came through the parlor.

"*The Evening World*. I want to make sure my engagement announcement gets in the paper," Louisa said. "And I have to pick up my payment for the food riot story."

"But you haven't even set a date yet."

"I'll leave it out."

Louisa strode toward the el platform, wishing she had the money to take a cab. She must find a steadier source of income, especially if she planned to have any sort of wedding. Unless she got another client for her discreet investigations, she would need to drum up more writing assignments.

"Have you got any other stories you need covered?" Louisa asked Nixola after she had dropped off the engagement announcement at the society desk.

"Nothing at the moment, but I'll let you know," Nixola said.

"What about this revolution in Russia?"

Nixola looked at her with an expression of mild confusion. "What about it?"

"It's a big deal," Louisa said. "What if I wrote about it from a New York angle?"

Nixola shrugged. "If you can find a New York angle, be my guest."

"You've got it." If she was going to have to listen to some Russian communist at the Lenox Casino, she might as well get paid for it. Now to stop by Francis' office and cancel their dinner date.

Chapter 26

Ellen

On Monday a raging snowstorm shut down Petrograd, and Ellen slept in. The night before she had donned her blonde wig and gone to the Hotel Astoria. After skulking in the lobby, ignoring the advances of drunk military officers for what felt like hours but was only about 45 minutes, she saw the Scottish Chap stumble in, dressed as if he'd been to a party. A party! The oblivious rich were still having parties.

"Do you have my proof?" she asked.

He peered at her. "Oh, it's you. The Irish spy."

She glanced around to see if anyone had heard the fool, but no one was paying attention to what looked like a transaction between a prostitute and a potential client.

"My family? Are they still in New York? Are they all right?" she asked.

He shrugged. "I'll let you know when I find out something." He gazed across the lobby at a group of boisterous officers. "The revolutionaries will get here soon enough, and those bloody bastards over there will be rounded up and shot. Soldiers are already killing the officers at the front. Who can blame them? They didn't start this war. I'm only surprised it doesn't happen in every war."

She looked into his eyes. Even drunk he possessed a cold and calculating glare. She turned and left, empty-handed.

The next day the shops reopened. The droshky drivers started working again, trams were running, and the city felt remarkably normal. But a closer look showed that nothing was really normal. The revolution was going full steam ahead. Practically every automobile in the city had been confiscated by soldiers. If it was already occupied, the soldiers demanded that drivers, at the point of a bayonet, take them around to arrest royalists.

That afternoon Ellen and Irina took to the streets again. Ellen managed to get into one of the automobiles where a soldier offered her a French pastry.

She took a bite and moaned in pleasure. "Where did you get this?"

"We took over the kitchen at the Military Hotel," he said with eyes twinkling, his rifle pointed out the window. More proof that some places got flour while the masses starved.

The Scottish Chap had said the revolutionaries would get there soon enough. She wondered if the officers were all dead. She didn't ask. Soon they were chasing down a squad of about two dozen mounted police. The police scattered, but not before the soldiers managed to shoot three of them off the backs of their stampeding horses. Ellen gasped as the bodies tumbled onto the street only to be trampled by the horses of their fellow officers. She felt a sharp stab of horror at the blood-shed but then swept it away. When the whole world was on fire, you had to expect some embers.

She got out at the next corner and took a tram to the *Pravda* office. She quickly typed the English version of what she had witnessed, and was rereading the story when Irina came in crowing, "The royalists in the Admiralty have surrendered because the two regiments guarding it have come over to our side."

"Where are the Cossacks?" Ellen asked.

"Patrolling the outskirts of the city to prevent any attacks from troops that may still be loyal to the old regime."

Irina noticed the full typed page in Ellen's hand. "That's too much for a telegram."

"Sure, but the postal service never fails. It might take a month or two but it'll get there. My friend at *The New York Call* will make sure it gets to print."

"And who is this friend?" Irina asked. "Was he a lover?" She was always curious about Ellen's nonexistent love life.

"Not at all. Her name is Rose, and she's married to a millionaire – both of them socialists."

"Millionaire socialists," Irina scoffed. "You can't trust them. Just like our Countess Panina. You wait. She'll betray the revolution. The French knew what to do with them." She made a chopping motion with her hand and laughed.

Irina was the very definition of a true believer. Even the anarchists back in New York would be no match for her.

Ten days after the revolution began, *Pravda* came out of the gates with a four-page Sunday newspaper.

"We're back!" Molotov said, opening a bottle of champagne that had been confiscated from some palace or another. This was one of the problems the revolutionaries faced – soldiers and factory workers discovering caches of wine bottles in the houses they looted. Molotov explained to Ellen that Lenin's idea of the paper's mission was to be "not only a collective propagandist and a collective agitator but also a collective organizer." Drunken revolutionaries were not easy to organize.

Then three days later the miraculous happened. Tsar Nicholas II abdicated. The centuries-old monarchy was over. Just like that. Ecstasy exploded in the streets like confetti. As she walked through the city, Ellen saw men and women kissing out in the open, on park benches, in doorways. It shocked her and reminded her how empty her own love life was. She'd been so busy with the revolution she hadn't felt it, but now, with a lull in the action, an ache yawned inside her. She'd felt that way before she left Ireland for America, knowing she was somehow different from other girls, having no interest in a husband or children. She had not known there were other women like her until she found a teahouse in Greenwich Village where women gathered to meet each other not just for friendship but for something else, for the possibility of love, the possibility of sex. Then she'd met Hester French, and the world opened its arms to her.

She wished she had someone to share *this* moment with. Unbidden came an image of Lulu, the anarchist with whom Ellen had once had a brief but torrid affair. Lulu was in New York, however, and Ellen might never see her again. Then another image snuck into her head — the woman in the turban, the Red Countess. Surely not, Ellen thought.

Chapter 27

Louisa

When Louisa and Carlotta returned to the Lenox Casino for Trotsky's talk, the atmosphere was radically different from their first visit. The huge room was filled with Russian immigrants waving red flags and singing Russian songs. Abe, Carlotta's Jewish friend, found them, and Carlotta's eyes lit up. Louisa shouldn't have been surprised. Of course, Carlotta would find a man someday, but a socialist poet? And he was probably twice Carlotta's age. In spite of his fancy cravat, he didn't seem like much of a prospect to Louisa.

"Wait here," Abe said to them before ascending the dais and leading the entire auditorium in a Russian song. The thronging voices lifted and rang in the air, and joy swirled all around. Louisa felt as if she were a stone in the midst of a rushing river. Finally, Abe quieted the crowd and told them, "My friends, the day of freedom has come. Welcome our comrade from Russia, Leon Trotsky!"

Clapping. Whistling. Shouting. A handsome man in his 30s with black hair, a smooth black mustache that flared out above his mouth in the European style and a small goatee stood on the dais, his eyes like two pieces of burning coal. He spoke in Russian, and though she couldn't understand the words, she felt the cadence in her bones, and she could tell by the reactions around her that this man had untold power. Funny, she'd never even heard his name until that morning.

When Abe returned to them, Louisa said, "I'm a stringer for the *Evening World.* Could I talk to Mr. Trotsky?"

He nodded. "That can be arranged. There is someone here from the *Times,* too.

"Does he speak English?" she asked.

"He does."

The poet took her to the back room after the speech. Billy Stephens from the *Times* was there. That was good luck. He could vouch for her as being with the press. As it happened, this Trotsky fellow didn't care about credentials. He leaned back in his chair, puffing furiously on a cigarette, and signaled for the two reporters to sit.

"Tell us about the People's Revolution," Billy said.

The man's fierce eyes moved from Louisa to Billy and back as he spoke. "The people are war-weary," he said. "All their resources have been depleted. Our aim is not simply to end war in Russia but in all of Europe. You cannot understand what it's like. To have no coal in the winter, to have no food, day after day, week after week. You are so well fed here in America. Even if your president and your Congress decide to enter the war, you will not know even a fraction of the suffering that Russians endure."

Louisa felt the truth of his words penetrate to the marrow of her bones. He was a magnetic force on the stage, and up close he was positively mesmerizing. "Will you return to Russia now that the Tsar is gone?" she asked.

"Oh, yes." He smiled. His teeth were yellow and the imperfection made him even more disarming. "I must go and guide the revolution. The mothers of Russia started the revolution with their food riots. You see the importance of women in our new Soviet republic, Miss Delafield? You Americans pride yourselves on free speech and yet a woman can go to jail if she advocates for birth control? Men can go to jail for selling a glass of beer on Sunday? What sort of freedom do you really have in this country?"

"What's next, Leo?" Billy asked. "Where does the revolution go from here? Will Russia have a democracy?"

Trotsky scoffed. "The bourgeoisie of Europe and America say the revolution has been won and is complete. They know nothing about mass movements. This is only the beginning. The Provisional Government will not last. Believe me, the Bolsheviks will make sure of it."

Louisa was perplexed by this pronouncement, but at that moment an attractive woman came in with two young boys. Trotsky rose and kissed her cheek and chucked the chins of the two boys. The interview was over. Louisa was astounded at what a nice ordinary family they appeared to be. In a matter of seconds, the great man had become a simple husband and father.

Outside she found Carlotta. Fortunately, there had been no unpleasant encounters with strange men or watchful teenage boys this time. The man who had bothered her last time had probably been a masher just looking for a woman by herself. And she had allowed herself to get spooked.

The next day when she read the short piece in the *Times*, she noted that Billy had referred to the man as "Leo Trotsky." She was quite sure it was Leon. Then again that was probably a made-up name. She wrote up her own article and dropped it off at Nixola's desk at the *Evening World*.

"Who is this Trotsky?" Nixola asked. "I never heard of him."

"You might not have heard of him, but half a million Russian Jews living in New York know who he is."

Nixola shook her head. "I'm not sure our readers will care."

Louisa worried her story might wind up in the bin. "*The Times* was also there. They ran a piece this morning."

Nixola shrugged. "All right. I'll fill the hole on page 19."

As Louisa left the building, she remembered the wild joy that had filled the Lenox Casino. The waving flags, the songs. Something momentous had happened, and yet the American citizens of New York barely heard a whisper. She wondered what role Ellen played in all this, and she thought of the clamoring voices she'd been hearing off and on for weeks. Would they die down now that those Russian women had had their revolution? And what about the American women who might soon be sending off their husbands and brothers. And fiancé.

Chapter 28

Ellen

In just a few weeks' time, Petrograd had transformed from a cauldron of repression, fear, and hopelessness into an oasis of freedom. Newspapers of every stripe could be had for a song. Men gloated in the streets over broadsides showing cartoon images of the former empress indulging in orgies with Rasputin. On every public building were empty spots where once the double-headed eagle of the empire had perched. Soldiers wore their caps backwards and women wore trousers. Every hall and street corner was occupied with someone making speeches or some group holding meetings. The Russians loved the sound of their own voices almost as much as the Irish, Ellen thought.

Ellen and Irina also donned trousers. They were more comfortable and easier for running should they need to make a hasty exit. Ellen felt a freedom wearing them. There was something equalizing about wearing the same legwear as soldiers.

But Ellen could make neither heads nor tails of the new government — or governments. Some beleaguered prince was in charge of the Provisional Government with a cabinet of "Kadets" and conservatives while various soviets, or committees, claimed as much power.

When Ellen arrived at the *Pravda* office one morning in March, she found men hoisting the printing press into the back of a truck.

"Where are you going with the printer?" she asked.

"We're taking over a concubine's palace!" The men laughed gleefully.

She went inside and found Irina gathering stacks of papers.

"A concubine?" Ellen asked.

"Mathilda Kschessinska, a ballerina," Irina said and twirled. "The slut was a mistress of the Tsar as well as the Grand Duke. Nicki made sure she was the top ballerina in the country. With all her acquired riches, she built a mansion. And now it is ours."

Ellen picked up a stack of papers and followed Irina out to a commandeered armored car. She wondered what had happened to the ballerina. Had they shot her? "But why her place?"

"Because her love nest is located on Kronverksky Prospekt, just across the river from the Winter Palace where the Provisional Government meets, and also close to Peter and Paul." The Peter and Paul fortress was the old prison where the Tsar had sent political prisoners. It squatted across the river, glowering at the citizens — a constant reminder of their fate should they incur the imperial wrath.

The Kschessinska mansion, a two-storey granite building with a balcony, a domed turret, and decorative metal work, stole Ellen's breath.

"She must have been quite a ballerina," Ellen said as they approached the entrance.

"Mathilde Kschessinska did some dancing all right," Irina said and made a lewd move with her hips. "Wait till you see the inside. It stinks of sin."

Ellen gasped as they walked through the elaborate double doors into a hallway of marbled tiles and faced a white staircase under a glittering chandelier. Even the stone balustrades were carved. She followed Irina through one enormous room after another, each filled with statues, white and gold molding lining the painted ceilings. A pig wandered around, grunting in confusion.

"That was her pet," Irina said with a laugh. "He'll be on the table soon enough."

Ellen enjoyed rashers with breakfast but she felt bad for the poor little pig. She'd had to stab a pig in the heart when she was training with the British. They wanted to make sure she understood how it felt to pierce flesh with a blade. Not an experience she relished.

"What happened to the ballerina?"

"She fled somewhere. Here's our new office." Irina strode into what was once a small boudoir. A mattress had been propped against the wall and the bed taken apart to make room for the mahogany writing tables brought in from other rooms. Gold curtains framed the tall windows, and the parquet floor gleamed.

They dropped their papers onto the tables.

"It's about time the gluttons got their due." Irina pursed her lips, fists on her hips, as she gazed around the room.

Ellen agreed. The ostentation of the Russian elite in a world of so much hunger and despair was utterly disgusting. The pig wandered into the room and grunted.

The Bolsheviks, the organization favored by the Germans, were small in number with only Molotov and one other fellow in charge. But within weeks of the revolution, whispers floated about a new leader — one who had returned from exile in Siberia.

"He's egotistical and violent. A criminal, but a charming one," Irina said. "Just the sort of man we need."

"What's his name?" Ellen asked.

"Joseph Stalin, but we call him Soso."

By the gleam in Irina's eyes, Ellen sensed that Irina's admiration came from her loins as much as from her head. And for the first time since the Tsar had abdicated, she wondered if the revolution was doomed to create a system not so different from the old one. She shook the idea out of her head. She had to believe they were creating something brilliant and bold. Otherwise, why had she sacrificed everything?

Chapter 29

Louisa

"Nobody's heard of Trotsky *yet*," Louisa told Francis as they walked along Central Park West. "But I have a feeling the public will know his name before long."

"Does he think Russia will make peace with Germany now that the Tsar is gone?"

"He said no, but he also said that the three things the revolutionaries want is bread, peace, and land, so I think we'll have to wait and see."

They strolled along the street, coats open. The sun shone, melting the snow, shrugging off winter's harsh edge. Spring was officially knocking on the door. They turned down West 67th Street toward the Cafe des Artistes.

"You'll love this place," Francis said, holding open the door for her. "I hear it's where Marcel Duchamp comes when he's in town."

She ordered the Dover sole with asparagus and hollandaise while Francis, practicing his French with the waiter, ordered the pot-au-feu — a hunk of beef, striated with fat, mixed in a broth with carrots and potatoes, and horseradish sauce on the side.

"How did you learn to speak French so well?" Louisa asked.

"I lived in Northern France for several summers. My father's nana was Bourbon."

"The drink?" she teased.

"The place, silly."

Over lunch Francis admitted his feelings of frustration. "I want to join the army desperately. I feel perfectly healthy. I don't understand why they won't accept me simply because of a heart murmur. We all know we'll be going to war soon. Perhaps I should join the French Legion."

"Don't you dare. There's plenty to do right here. Besides," she admitted, looking down at the sparkling blue stone on her finger, "I couldn't bear to lose you."

He looked thoughtful. "I suppose I'm fated to live a long life."

"I do hope so." Louisa thought it wise to change the subject. "I'm looking forward to meeting your friends Friday night."

Francis wiped his mouth with the linen napkin. "And they want to meet you. I plan to ask Paul to be my best man."

"And what is his wife like?"

"Nice girl. She seems to be with child every time I see her."

Louisa grimaced. "That sounds dreadful."

Francis' fork hung in the air. "Dreadful? You don't want children?"

"Not really. One at the most," she said. "Is that a problem?"

He set the fork down and shook his head. "One would be fine."

If she could even have one, she thought. Poor Francis. Did she not love him enough to give him a home full of children?

The clock in the hallway chimed. Francis would arrive any minute for their dinner date to meet his friends. Louisa grabbed her beaded purse. As she descended the stairs, her silk skirt swishing against her ankles, the phone rang. She hoped it wasn't Francis ringing to say he'd been delayed.

"Delafield residence," Carlotta said. "Just a moment."

"Who is it?" Louisa asked.

"I don't know. They asked for your mama."

"Me?" Anna stood in the doorway of the parlor. As she took the phone receiver, she whispered to Carlotta, "I'm her mother, not her 'mama.'"

Carlotta shrugged.

Louisa took her old mink jacket off its hook and slipped it on, wondering who could be calling her mother.

"You look swell, Louisa," Carlotta said.

"Thank you. Francis is taking me to Delmonico's. We're meeting an old college friend and his wife. I think it's important for me to meet the best man and his wife before the wedding."

"Have you set a date yet?"

Carlotta's eyes flicked up at her. Louisa remembered their conversation in the kitchen.

"No, dear. Please don't worry. It won't be for a while."

The brass door knocker thudded. Louisa would have to talk to Carlotta later, to reassure her somehow that they wouldn't simply abandon her.

She opened the door. Francis stood on the stoop and smiled. "Hello, beautiful."

She turned to say good-bye to her mother, who was now off the phone.

Anna held up her hand. "Oh no you don't. Louisa, you must go to the St. Regis right away."

"But, Mother, Francis and I have a dinner date. Why would I...?"

"Edith needs to see you. She said it's very important."

"Edith? Edith who?" Louisa asked in exasperation.

"How many Ediths do we know? Edith Wharton, of course. She's staying at the St. Regis. You must go there right away."

Louisa had only met Edith Wharton a few times, and last she'd heard the novelist was living in Paris, helping the French in the war effort.

Francis touched her shoulder. "Louisa, if your mother says it's important, then we'll go straight there. Our dinner reservation can wait."

Louisa looked at him. The perfect gentleman. Of course he would accede to her mother's wishes.

"But your friends, Paul and Rosalind?"

"I'll call Delmonico's and explain. We can meet them some other time."

"Very well. We'll go see what is so important," Louisa said. She raised her eyebrows at her mother. Satisfied? Anna nodded and then headed back to her chair in the parlor and the side table where her glass of sherry waited. Francis called Delmonico's and asked them to deliver a message to his friends.

"Have a good evening," Carlotta said as they headed down the stairs to Francis' Model T. Louisa waved without turning around, heard the door shut, and got in the car.

After Francis cranked the engine and got in the driver's side, she leaned toward him. "We don't have to go right now."

"I'm happy to oblige your mother." He let out the clutch. "After all, I hope to be seeing a lot of her in the future."

"I suppose you're right. But I hate to disappoint your friends."

"They'll survive. Who is Edith Wharton, by the way?" Francis asked.

"She's old Old New York," Louisa said, shivering even in her fur coat. Winter had returned for one more swipe at the city before leaving. "I'm surprised you never heard of her. She wrote *The House of Mirth*, *Ethan Frome* and other books."

"Oh, that Edith Wharton. Haven't read her work, but I know who you mean. A friend of your mother's?"

"From back when Mother was one of New York's elite. Edith was quite kind when the whole scandal happened with my father, and many people weren't."

Louisa had told him the whole story. Well, not the whole story. Not the part about her mother murdering her father. She told no one that. But the rest of it. The beloved father who managed to lose the family fortune in a swindle and then was murdered in a hotel room in Greenwich Village. How they had scraped by for years on what was left of a small life insurance policy. How she'd become a society writer since she knew the world of society. How, even, she had fallen for a wealthy man, but that it hadn't worked out.

Francis parked near the imposing brick hotel, and they hurried to the huge glass doors, which the doorman opened for them. The St. Regis was one of the most exclusive New York hotels. Of course Edith Wharton would stay in a hotel built by John Jacob Astor, husband to her late cousin, Caroline Astor.

They took the elevator up to the tenth floor and knocked on the door to her suite. The maid answered and invited them in. They found an imposing woman, looking out the window.

"Madame, your guests have arrived."

"Guests?" Edith turned to face them. "I was only expecting one person."

Louisa was taken aback at the sight of the great writer. She had perfect posture, the cool gaze of an empress, and the glow of a woman decades younger, but her eyes were those of someone who had witnessed the horrors of war.

"I'm sorry, Mrs. Wharton," Louisa said. "Mr. Holland and I were about to go to dinner when my mother received your phone call."

"I'm happy to wait downstairs if you prefer to speak in private," Francis said.

Mrs. Wharton appraised him quickly.

"You aren't a journalist, are you? No one is to even know I'm here."

"No, ma'am, I'm an attorney."

"An attorney? Good. Let me hire you and then everything I say in this room will be held in strict confidence. How much do you charge for a retainer?"

"How about one dollar?" he said. "That will legally bind us."

Mrs. Wharton smiled and asked the maid to get a dollar from her purse.

"Would you care for a drink? I believe the specialty here is the Bloody Mary."

"I'll have the blood without the Mary," Louisa said. "It sounds as though we might want to keep our wits about us."

"Good plan. Doris, would you bring three glasses of tomato juice?"

The dollar having been paid, the glasses of juice brought forth along with crackers and cheese, Louisa and Francis sat on the sofa while Mrs. Wharton settled into the armchair.

"What is the situation like in France?" Louisa asked.

"Unimaginable, my dear. The troops are struggling to hold on. Disease is rampant. I don't think France stands a chance if America doesn't join the war effort."

"Is that why you're here?" Francis asked. "To persuade Wilson to declare war?"

"I wouldn't dare interfere at such a high level. It is an awesome responsibility to ask young men to sacrifice their lives for the sake of another country."

"Then, if I may ask, why are you here? And why did you want to see me?" Louisa asked.

"Because if... no, *when* America does join the war, she will need a network of intelligence officers. And as of now, there is no coordinated effort to gather intelligence and perform counterintelligence."

"Counterintelligence? What does that mean?"

"It means exactly what you were doing, my dear, when you spied on Count Bernstorff and helped expose the Germans' sabotage network here in New York. Yes, I know all about that. I'm friends with members of the Foreign Office and British Naval Intelligence. Now, I have been asked to present a case to the high command in the U.S. as to why an American intelligence agency is so desperately needed."

Louisa and Francis exchanged a glance.

"I don't mean any disrespect, but why you, Mrs. Wharton?" Louisa asked.

"Please call me Edith. I met your mother when she was 12 years old, and we went to cotillion together, not to mention all those tedious debutante events. I adored your father. He and I shared a love of poetry. I was devastated by the news of his death."

To her chagrin, sudden unwanted tears surfaced in Louisa's eyes. She batted her eyelashes to tamp them back down.

"Thank you, Edith."

Francis leaned forward. "Do you mean to say that America has no intelligence agency? No map makers or code breakers? And here we are on the brink of entering the war?"

"That's exactly right," she said. "But I'm expecting another guest, and he can explain the situation better than I. More tomato juice?"

"No thank you," Louisa said. "I still don't understand how you became involved."

There was a knock on the door.

"There he is now. I'll let him answer your question."

Doris ushered in a distinguished looking man of military bearing with a long, narrow face and pale eyes. He was wearing a dark suit at the moment, but there was no mistaking him for a banker. Something about the set of his shoulders and the spine straight as a plumb line.

"Come in, Major. I'd like to introduce you to Louisa Delafield and her fiancé, Mr. Francis Holland," Edith said. "This is Major Ralph Van Deman. He famously established the only effective American intelligence system in the Philippines."

Louisa had read something about his work. He had created a network of spies, but she couldn't remember the details.

Francis stood and shook the man's hand.

"I apologize in advance. I'm not good at small talk, and frankly I don't have the time for it," Major Van Deman said, sitting down in a wingback chair. "Doris, could I have a bourbon on the rocks, please?"

Doris brought his drink and he took a sip.

"I have been trying fruitlessly for three years to get the War College to take the establishment of a strong military intelligence agency seriously, but so far, all my concerns have been falling on deaf ears," he said.

Edith interjected, "The War College has something called a military intelligence committee, but I don't believe they have the slightest idea what they're doing."

Reggie Grant had mentioned the committee to Louisa once with a tone of disgust and said the Americans were an ineffectual gang of ostriches with their heads stuck in the sand and their "thumbs in their arses." She had said she didn't think ostriches had thumbs.

The major set down his drink and leaned forward. "To call a chair a table does not make it a table. It still remains a chair. And to call the personnel of the War College Division a Military Information Committee does not make it one. They seem to believe we can rely on the British and the French for information, and that those agencies will happily hand over anything we desire."

Edith raised her glass of tomato juice and waggled it in her hand. "That is why the major has enlisted my help. You see, I met Major Van Deman when he escorted me on a tour of military installations, requested by the secretary of war, who happens to be my friend."

The major gazed at their hostess as if she were royalty. "Mrs. Wharton is greatly admired in military circles for championing the Volunteer Ambulance Corps in France and working with the hospitals there. I've enlisted her help to convince the Secretary of War we need more than this hodge-podge system of attachés that we have now. We must have a strong American intelligence unit in the military."

"Why will he listen to her and not you?" Louisa asked.

The major sighed in exasperation. "I have been specifically forbidden by the chief of staff from approaching the secretary of war about this issue. But Mrs. Wharton can speak to her good friend about the topic. And he'll listen."

Now Francis leaned forward. "Assuming the secretary of war is convinced, how will you go about creating an agency in such a short time? Wilson may declare war any day."

"The first thing would be to recruit well-educated, highly intelligent men who speak French and possibly German to become counterintelligence officers."

Louisa gazed down at her silk skirt, contemplating this information.

"Louisa," Edith said, "what I would like from you is an honest assessment of the threat here on our shore. If I am going to convince the general of a need for a sophisticated division of intelligence, I must have the facts at my command. I believe you worked with British Naval Intelligence in 1915, did you not?"

Louisa took a deep breath. She had never told Francis about her liaison with Reginald Grant, British naval attaché and spy.

"You are correct. At the behest of the British Naval Attaché, I formed a friendship with Count Bernstorff.

My assistant, Ellen, allowed herself to be recruited by Germany's intelligence unit, the *Abteilung III b*, while in Berlin. Then she returned to America and worked in the office of the Hamburg-American Shipping Line. The two of us helped to uncover a plot to blow up American ships at sea."

Edith rubbed her chin. "I see. Do you think the threat is over?"

"Not at all. The Black Tom explosion last summer is evidence of that. There are hundreds of thousands of German Americans in the city. Most are loyal to the United States but there are those who are loyal only to the Fatherland. Reggie, that is, Mr. Grant, expressed frustration to me quite often at the lack of an intelligence organization here in the U.S. The greatest asset was and still is the New York Police Department."

"And do you think from your experience there are enough civilians to fill the positions if we had a military intelligence division?" the major asked.

Louisa clasped her hands together as she considered the question. "I do. In fact, Francis' uncle is Captain Tom Tunney of the New York Police Department. The police detectives, especially those in the bomb unit, have been the most involved in uncovering the sabotage plots. And the captain would be willing to release some of his men for the war effort. Of that, I am sure."

Louisa detailed all the things she had learned during her undercover work. An hour after they arrived, Louisa and Francis left the hotel room and were on their way to Delmonico's for a late dinner.

Francis tapped his fingers on the steering wheel while he drove. "Did you hear what they're looking for, Louisa? Men who are well-educated and fluent in French. I can actually read German quite well. Maybe I can serve after all."

Dread filled Louisa. The idea hadn't even occurred to her, but now it was obvious. If Francis could find a way to be useful, he would not hesitate, and all her "happily ever after" plans would evaporate. This damnable war, she thought. The fact that Francis' heart murmur wouldn't miraculously go away was her only solace.

"They might not even care that I have a heart murmur." He grinned.

She hadn't thought of that. "Francis, you are not going anywhere. I forbid it."

Chapter 30

Ellen

As Ellen hurried through yet another snow shower to the ballerina's mansion, she bumped into Molotov.

"I've been thrown out." He raised his hands in dismay.

"By whom?" Ellen asked.

"By Stalin."

Ah, the exile. "Irina told me he's one of the leaders of the Bolsheviks, but could he truly walk in and be firing you like that, Comrade?" Ellen asked.

"He's older. He has more authority than I." He shrugged and trudged off, heading back to the Vyborg district, she assumed.

Ellen entered the building, past the soldiers, lolling about uselessly, smoking their cigarettes and dropping their trash in the hallways. The staff of *Pravda* had turned the upstairs bedrooms into their offices. She walked into the editorial office, which had once been the ballerina's boudoir, and found Irina and the rest of the *Pravda* staff standing around a short, thin man who exuded an immediate, almost overwhelming presence. He wore a clean black suit with a blue shirt and a striped scarf. His cheeks were hollow but his dark eyes smiled in amusement as he looked around at his new lackeys, swarming around him, offering congratulations. He smiled broadly under his thick mustache.

"Man of steel!" one of the Bolsheviks said, clapping the man they called Stalin or sometimes Soso on the back.

Ellen wasn't sure how she should act in the situation. Obviously, this was a man who expected people to fall under his sway. She saw his effect on the others, but she was impervious to his magnetism. His eyes assessed her quickly and then moved on. He must have decided she wasn't worth seducing.

He leaned against a desk. "The chariot of the Russian Revolution is advancing with lightning speed, but look around and you will see the sinister work of dark forces going on incessantly," he said. The Bolsheviks were forever going on about the "dark forces."

"What about the war?" Irina asked.

"We are not for or against the war," Stalin answered. "That is our official stance. For now, we will work with the Provisional Government."

"Vladimir Ilyich won't be happy," one of the men said. Their familiar name for Lenin.

"Lenin isn't here, is he, Comrade? I'm in charge, and I will determine who and what *Pravda* supports. For now, we make no waves." He spread his hands out to indicate a smooth surface.

The man who had spoken looked down at the floor. One could argue with Molotov, but she sensed Stalin wouldn't hear of dissent.

After the impromptu speech, Ellen found Irina downstairs in the room where they kept the printer.

The smell of ink and oil wafted in the air as she folded pamphlets for distribution.

"What do you think of our new boss?" Ellen asked.

"I think Comrade Soso is the sexiest man I've ever known," Irina said with a grin.

Stalin appointed himself editor of *Pravda* and as such he wanted to meet with everyone and learn their duties. When Ellen was summoned to his office the next day, he greeted her with warmth in the French language. She answered him in Russian, and he switched over with an approving nod.

"Tell me about yourself, Tovarisch." He lit a cigarette and indicated a chair for her to sit. "How did you come to be in Petrograd? Why are you working with *Pravda*?"

She sat in the chair but kept a straight back as she spoke. This was no time to relax. "I am here because I am a believer in the Bolshevik cause. In New York, I worked with the anarchists Emma Goldman and Sasha Berkman at *Mother Earth* magazine. Then I started my own magazine in New York to educate women about oppression. I know the power of the press both for good and ill."

He sucked on the cigarette and blew smoke through his nostrils like a bull. "Why did you leave New York?" He seemed genuinely curious.

"I went home to Ireland to partake in the Easter uprising. After that failed, I was on the run from the British and wound up in Berlin. The Socialists there told me about the fight for freedom and peace in Russia. I wanted to be part of history. And now I am. I feel it is my duty to spread the gospel to the West."

He seemed pleased with her religious reference. Did he fancy himself as the messiah? "But why would you leave Ireland in the first place? Why were the British after you?"

She cleared her throat and looked around the room as she thought about how to present her story. Her eyes rested on a Chinese vase filled with dead roses no one had bothered to throw away. "My brother was instrumental in getting funding from Americans, and so I knew all about the plans for the uprising. When he went to Dublin, I followed to try to protect him. The British captured me and threatened me with prison or worse if I did not tell them where the leaders were hiding."

Stalin stroked his mustache. "What did you do?"

"I pretended to seduce a guard. Then I took his gun and shot him. In the head. Now, the British want to put me in front of a firing squad."

She figured he would believe this and perhaps admire her. Irina had told her stories about the people Stalin had killed in his various adventures.

"I see. But you understand that England is Russia's ally, don't you? Why shouldn't we turn you over to them?"

"Why would you? You will not always be allies," she said. That is what Captain Boehm had told her. *If the Bolsheviks take over, Russia will turn its back on the Allies and the war.*

Stalin chuckled as he studied her. An element of malice lurked just beneath his surface. "I like you," he said. "You can continue to work here, spread our message to English speakers around the world and help us unite the workers of the world." Then he looked down at the papers on his desk. The interview was over.

As she left his office, a tremor ran through her body. This was not a man to be crossed. Why had she lied about killing a British guard? What an eejit. Already, she missed Molotov.

A few days later, the editors and writers for *Pravda* sat in the chairs or leaned against the walls of the ballerina's bedroom. Molotov, who had been let back into the fold, stood at Stalin's side.

Stalin smoothed back his black hair. "Comrades, the Petrograd Soviet has declared that we must honor those who have died for the revolution. But there will be no funeral rites. No churches. No so-called 'men of God.' You will all attend. Even you, Tovarisch." He pointed at Ellen. He paused, his eyes gleaming, and she couldn't help but think of a snake as he drew back. "Unless you are concerned someone at the British Embassy might spot you? After all, you are a wanted woman, aren't you? And the embassy is across the street from the Field of Mars."

Ellen shook her head and another lie popped out of her mouth. "They believe I'm dead."

Stalin said nothing, merely crossed his arms and gazed at her. She cursed herself for weaving this tangled web.

Chapter 31

Louisa

Louisa donned her favorite outfit. She'd purchased it a year earlier before everything got so ridiculously expensive. It had a jacket with a bow at the neckline and brass buttons over a blue overskirt with a peplum to create an hourglass shape. The good thing about the war was that no one cared if you wore last year's style. Carlotta wore one of the dresses that Ellen had left behind. And Anna had gotten Suzie to update one of her old dresses by taking the hem up a few inches.

They were gathered together in the hallway to wait for Francis when the phone rang.

Carlotta answered, "Delafield residence." Then she handed the phone to Louisa.

"Hello?"

"Louisa? Nixola here. I have an assignment for you."

"That's great, but we're just about to leave for the Malloys' citizenship ceremony."

"I know. I'll have a photographer there waiting for you."

"The citizenship ceremony is the assignment?" Louisa asked.

"Yes, you can handle it, can't you?"

"Of course…But how did you know…?"

"Wonderful. It only needs to be about ten inches, but do make sure to include a quote or two from the new citizens. The photographer will have more information if you need it."

With that Nixola hung up. Louisa turned to Carlotta and Anna.

"I just got a freelance assignment from Nixola," she said.

"Good," Carlotta said. "We need the money."

"Must you always go on about money? It's distasteful," Anna said, slipping on her kid leather gloves.

"You know what's more distasteful, eating dirt because we got no food," Carlotta replied.

The door knocker banged.

"That must be Francis," Louisa said and opened the door to find Francis standing on the stoop with a bouquet of red and yellow flowers. "Darling, how sweet."

Francis looked puzzled. "They aren't from me. I found them in front of the door."

Louisa inhaled sharply. Suddenly things began to make sense.

"Does it say who they're from?" Anna asked.

Francis shook his head and glanced at Louisa. Louisa shrugged, and Carlotta stepped up.

"They're probably from my new beau," she said and took the flowers. She left them on the hallway credenza. "I'll put 'em in water when we get back."

Louisa shared a quick glance with Carlotta. Carlotta knew as well as she did that the flowers were a signal from Reggie Grant. And, Louisa now realized, the reason Nixola knew that Louisa was going to the citizenship ceremony was that Reggie had told her. The question now was why. Why did Reggie want a news story of a citizenship ceremony?

The ceremony took place at the Bureau of Naturalization. Martin Malloy, his mother and his younger brother were all there dressed in their Sunday best. But the preponderance of prospective citizens were Germans. One after another, they stood up and renounced the Kaiser and pledged their loyalty to the United States. Generally the process of naturalization took at least a couple of years, but the bureau had put some foreigners on the fast track since they anticipated a need for men to join the military in the near future. Perhaps Reggie had played a role in getting the Malloys put in with that group.

Ah, she thought. That was why this ceremony had become a newspaper assignment. Reggie must need something to show to Ellen that her family was safe. Once they were American citizens, the British would have no more claim on them. And if Ellen was in Russia on some sort of spy business, how would she know?

When it was the Malloy family's turn, they renounced allegiance to the British Empire which was easy for them to do as they despised the British.

"Excuse me, Martin," Louisa said when the ceremony was done, "may I get a quote from you about your family's new status?"

"A quote?" he asked in surprise.

"For a newspaper article." She gave him a pointed look. "It will be seen the world over."

His eyebrows lifted as he understood Louisa's meaning. "Well, then. You can say that I am honored along with my mother and brother to now be a citizen of the greatest country in the world, and that as an officer with the New York City Police Department, I pledge to protect my fellow citizens of this great city."

Louisa scribbled the words down and then smiled. "You'll make a fine politician someday, Martin."

The photographer took a picture of the smiling family with the American flag in the background.

"Miss Delafield," Ellen's mother said, "do you have any notion where Ellen is at? We've heard nothing, and I'm worried to a thread."

Louisa hesitated, unsure what she should say.

"Mrs. Malloy, I don't know exactly where Ellen is, but I do know she's alive and well. And this article will let her know that you're alive and well, too."

"Really? Will she read it?"

"Yes, I promise you that," Louisa said. She had to trust Reggie to make it true.

She looked around the room for Francis and saw him deep in conversation with two of the new citizens. She walked over and put her arm through his and smiled at the gentlemen conversing with him. She couldn't understand a word they were saying.

"Practicing your German?" she asked Francis with a smile.

"I have gotten a little rusty." He turned to the two men and bowed. "Danke, Meine Herren."

She didn't ask why he wanted to practice his German. She knew why.

When Louisa turned in the story that afternoon, Nixola asked if she might attend the Knights of Columbus ball at Madison Square Garden. "I just need a couple of graphs. The thing starts at 8:30. It'll be fun."

Louisa wasn't at the point she could turn down work, so once again she decided to make it a date with Francis.

On the way to the ball, Francis asked if she'd heard anything yet from Edith Wharton.

"Why do you ask?" Louisa replied.

"You know why. If they start a military intelligence division. I intend to apply."

"But, dear, your heart murmur."

"I don't think it will matter," he said.

Louisa hoped he was wrong.

He parked the car on Madison Avenue, and they approached the arena along with droves of guests. A palpable excitement turned them into one giant mob. An enormous tower with a statue of Diana the huntress greeted them.

Inside they found their seats and settled in to observe a series of military exhibitions by the Squadron A Cavalry of New York, as well as several cadet corps, and even a women's battalion. The Squadron A band – trumpets, trombones, tubas and baritones and two huge kettle drums – created a patriotic fervor. Rousing stuff indeed.

It was a thrilling exhibition with men marching in formation, their leader calling out orders – "March!" "Double time!" "Halt!" – and older boys from the cadet corps demonstrating signals. This was how they drummed up the spirit for war, Louisa thought, but she was in no way immune to it. She turned to look at Francis and noticed his face was stiff and his eyes watery. If she was affected by it all, how much more so for him. Oh, how he wanted to be in the thick of it. She reached over and patted his knee. He looked down, frowning. Her heart nearly broke, he looked so ashamed.

After the exhibition, a parade of city officials marched around the arena. Then came the dancing. Francis had no interest in dancing, and Louisa had more than enough information to write her article.

"The man at the box office said there were at least 5,000 people in attendance," Louisa said as they left.

"It certainly was crowded." Francis smiled, but she could tell it was a forced smile. They reached the car which he had parked several blocks away and he opened the door for her. She sank into the passenger seat and waited for him to crank the engine and get in. An odd sensation crept up her spine and along the back of her neck. She wondered if she was getting a headache.

Francis got in the driver's seat, and off they went up Broadway toward Harlem. He was distracted and unhappy. She wished she could convince him he wasn't less of a man for not being able to join the war.

"Mother's already pestering me about my china pattern," Louisa said, hoping to distract him.

"Your what?" he asked.

"China. You know. Dinner plates, salad plates, cups, saucers, bowls of all sizes, and dessert plates. Every woman has to have a china pattern. I did see a pretty blue flowered Limoges pattern that I liked."

"That's nice," he said. She could tell he hadn't heard a word she said. And who could blame him? Men didn't care about things like china. She didn't care all that much either, but it was expec...

Something hard nudged the back of her head and a man's voice said, "Keep going or I'll shoot the dame."

Louisa's mouth dropped open. Her breath shot out of her lungs.

Francis looked over his shoulder, eyes wide. "Who the hell are you?"

"Don't worry about it," the man said. The smell of fruit chewing gum wafted past her face. Louisa couldn't see him, but she knew who it was.

"He's the man who came up to me at the courthouse, Francis. I don't think he wanted to hire me. I don't think he has a missing wife."

"Aren't you the clever one?" The man's voice was soft and oily.

"What do you want?" Francis asked.

"Just drive. Keep going north."

"Let me drop off the lady," Francis said. "You can keep me. I'll give you money."

The man chuckled. "Keep your money. The lady ain't going nowhere."

"Francis?" Louisa's hand trembled as she clutched the door.

Francis reached over to pat her knee. "We'll be fine, Louisa. We'll take this gentleman where he wants to go and then he'll let us go."

She didn't think that's what the man had in mind. "You *are* the man who came up to me after the trial of the silk thieves, aren't you? And you followed me at the Lenox Casino. A boy works with you. What is your connection to the silk thieves?"

He leaned forward, his breath hot against the side of her face. "That lady you put in Sing Sing for ten years, that's my ma."

Louisa exhaled. This man wasn't planning on robbing them. He had revenge on his mind.

"Were you part of the gang?" Louisa asked. "I thought all of them were caught."

"I wasn't with them that night," he said. "Hurt my back right before we was to go in and get the goods. If I'da been there, they wouldn't'ta taken any of us alive."

Louisa tried to think of other things to say to the man, but it was hard to keep from trembling with the hard barrel of a gun lodged against the base of her skull. The man directed Francis to turn on 145th Street toward the bridge. Louisa's knees shook uncontrollably. She thought of all the things she would never get to do if this man killed her. What would happen to her mother? Had she been a fool to think her life would smoothly unfold before her when the entire world seethed with violence?

They crossed the river and, after a mile or so, he told Francis to turn down a narrow road and drive down toward the river. "Go that way."

"Look, I'm an attorney. I'll represent your mother. I'm sure I can get her sentence reduced," Francis said.

"Ya think I'm some kinda dunce? Pull over."

Francis did as he was ordered. He turned in to a vacant lot between two warehouses. Moonlight rippled on the river's surface.

"Now turn off the motor." The engine went quiet. "Get out, come around the car, and let your lady friend out. Nice and slow. Any funny business, and I blow her brains all over your windscreen there."

Francis got out and walked around toward the front of the car. He kept his eyes on hers as he walked. When he reached the front of the car, he tripped and fell, but immediately he was up. He continued around to her side of the car. Louisa held her breath as she watched him, wondering how Sassy Turner's son planned to finish this. To think she had thought that Francis' heart murmur would save him from an early death. Now he'd die at the hand of some thug in an empty lot by the Harlem River.

Francis opened her door. Their eyes met. He held something close to his body with his left hand. He glanced quickly at the ground and then back up. She wasn't sure exactly what he meant to do. She put her hand in his free hand and stepped out. At the same time, the man with the gun opened the back door, all the while keeping the gun pointed at her.

Francis shouted, "Now!" and flung her away from the car. She flew past him, stumbled and fell hard on the gravel. The palms of her hands stung. A shot fired and at the same time the man howled in pain. Terrified, she rolled over and saw Francis with a crooked piece of metal in his hand – the hand crank for the car! – as he brought it down on the man's arm over and over again. He dropped the gun on the pavement. Louisa scurried over the gravel on her hands and knees and snatched it. The man knelt on the ground, groaning and cradling his broken arm.

Gasping for breath, Louisa managed to stand up and point the gun at the would-be murderer. "What should we do with him?"

"Tie him up and take him to the police," Francis said, calmly. "He can join his mother at Sing Sing."

While their misadventure had a good result, Louisa's heart felt as if it were made of granite as she lay in bed that night. She had never been able to imagine Francis as a soldier or as a spy, but that night he had shown he could think on his feet. He had proved he had cunning and courage. With his other skills, he would be quite an asset to a military intelligence division. Now she could only hope that Edith would be unsuccessful. She realized how selfish this hope was. If America was to succeed in the war, it would need spies. It would need men and women who could crack codes and read maps and unearth information.

As she thought about Captain Van Deman and his urgent plea, a memory surfaced in her mind. She shot out of the bed.

"What is it?" Carlotta asked when Louisa flicked on the light in her bedroom.

"I need to see the second issue of *The Ladies' Lantern*."

Carlotta pushed her covers aside and got out of bed. She knelt down, pulled a box out from under her bed and handed Louisa what she had requested. The cover featured a drawing of two women drinking tea, protest signs at their sides. Louisa sat on the bed and quickly thumbed through the magazine to the "Letters" section.

"There it is," Louisa said. "I knew I'd read about him somewhere."

"Him? Who?" Carlotta looked over her shoulder.

"The man who wants to ruin my life."

Chapter 32
Ellen

The day of the ceremony to honor the victims of the revolution was bright and sunny. Stalin gathered the staff, and they left the ballerina's mansion to march down to the Troitsky Most, a long bridge crossing the Neva. Below them pieces of ice floated as the river broke free of its confines.

Irina had worn lipstick and rouged her cheeks. Such a lovesick puppy. She would follow her "Soso" anywhere. The man did have a certain savoir faire and a disarming smile. Ellen was glad to be immune to his charms, but not many women were. Molotov's girlfriend had already succumbed. Even so, Molotov stood at Stalin's side. Apparently, a girlfriend was a fair price to pay to be allowed back into the inner circle.

"Why is it called the Field of Mars?" Ellen asked Irina.

"Because Mars is the god of war, and this is where our war heroes are honored," Irina explained.

All the various factions of the revolutionaries arrived. They were joined by a long procession of people tromping down Millionnaya Street. A band played Chopin's "Funeral March." Prayers for the dead were chanted – even though God was not supposed to be involved in the proceedings.

"Look at this," Stalin said, waving his arms at the red banners surrounding them. "A forest of banners."

As the day progressed, hundreds of thousands of people poured into the field. The ceremony began as they almost always did in Russia with a doffing of head coverings and then speeches, lots and lots of speeches. As each coffin was lowered into the trench, a cannon boomed from the Peter and Paul Fortress. Ellen shivered in spite of the sun. She thought of the mass funeral for the dead of the *Lusitania* and remembered the numbness inside her chest. She gazed around. The Russian people had a collective grief. They had lost so many loved ones to the Tsar's brutality, to the idiotic war, and now to the revolution.

Finally, the speeches ended and people milled about. Ellen wanted to leave. An oppressive feeling had settled into her shoulders, as if it wanted to pull her to the ground. A stray fragrance wafted past her. She lifted her head. Lavender — Hester's scent. She gazed around and saw a woman in a fur hat and a long, camel coat approach Stalin. Ellen was close enough to hear the woman's velvet voice.

"Comrade Stalin," she said.

Ellen inhaled sharply. She recognized her as the same woman in the turban at the International Women's March, the one she'd asked Irina about. The Red Countess. Ellen had only seen her at a distance, but up close she could see that the countess was in her mid-forties with milk-smooth skin and rosy cheeks. Stalin tilted his head and smiled. It was obvious he did not know who she was. Molotov jumped in.

"This is the Red Countess, Sofia Panina, a great friend to the people, Soso. Her stepfather founded the Kadet Party." Molotov said this last part with a dollop of disdain. He was strongly against any cooperation with the "bourgeois" Kadets, who thought the revolution heralded a democracy rather than a dictatorship of the proletariat. But so far, Stalin favored cooperation, so he smiled broadly at the countess, turning on his famous charm.

"So pleased to meet you," he said in his rough French.

The countess was out of Stalin's league. Although she smiled, her eyes showed nothing but mild amusement. It took a minute or so for him to realize his charm offensive had no impact on the woman. His own smile faded.

"The Provisional Government looks forward to working with the Bolsheviks," she said. "Together we will do great things."

At that moment a cannon boomed from the fortress. Ellen flinched. Another coffin was lowered into the ground. When her gaze returned to Stalin, the countess was walking away. A breeze touched the back of Ellen's neck.

The next morning Ellen stared out the window of the office she and Irina shared. The river gleamed in the spring sunlight. The revolutionary fervor was a palpable thing, like a bird's heart beating.

Ellen turned back to the story she was currently writing. She had the only typewriter with an English alphabet, procured from the house of the American ambassador.

"Soso wants to see you," Irina said.

Ellen had expected this. Stalin liked to know what everyone was doing. She walked down the hallway to the ballerina's boudoir. Stalin was bent over his desk, writing furiously.

"I have a job for you, Tovarisch," he said. "You will write a story for the American and English women about the gains of Russian women since the February Revolution."

"Other than getting to wear trousers, I haven't seen much in the way of progress for women," she said.

"You obviously don't know about our Red Countess, Sofia Panina. She has been given a role as a deputy in the city government. Unheard of for a woman."

Ellen sat down and crossed her legs. "I heard you talking to her at the Field of Mars. Are you trying to appease the Provisional Government?" Was Stalin, the wolf, trying on sheep's clothing?

He shrugged.

Ellen maintained a neutral mask, but she thought she understood Stalin's ulterior motive. His masculine pride had been injured because the countess did not fawn over him at the Field of Mars ceremony. She was beautiful, and he wanted to either own her or destroy her.

"Is she at the Winter Palace with the government? How do I get in to see her?" Ellen asked.

"I will make sure you have papers from the Petrograd Soviet. When you see her, explain that you are writing an article to show the great strides women are making in the new Russia."

"But what do you really want to know, Comrade?"

"She's a very wealthy woman. Where does her money go?" He leaned forward. A fleck of tobacco clung to his bottom lip. "More to the point, can she be persuaded to leave the Kadet Party and join the Bolsheviks?"

Ellen considered the request and then realized this was an order, not a request.

"What can you tell me about her?"

"Go ask Irina. Irina's mother was a servant on one of the countess's estates. As a matter of fact, she sent Irina to university here in Petrograd."

Ellen tried not to look surprised. She thought Irina was an open book, but she had kept secrets, hadn't she?

Ellen found her friend leaning in the doorway of the White Hall, smoking and telling jokes with the soldiers. Although Ellen had learned to speak Russian well enough, she found humor difficult to translate. She could laugh at their jokes but never attempted to say anything funny herself. Irina didn't mind. She liked being the funny one.

"Let's go into the garden," Ellen suggested.

Irina tossed her cigarette butt into a rose bed and followed Ellen along a garden path to a stone bench.

"Soso wants me to write a story on the Red Countess. He said your mother worked for her," Ellen told her.

Irina struck a match on the bottom of her shoe and lit another cigarette. She blew a stream of smoke at the ground. "The Panina family had estates all over Russia. My mother was the housekeeper at one of them."

"So that's where you grew up?"

"No, my mother couldn't keep me and still hold her position. I lived with my grandparents. Peasants. My grandfather was ... never mind, I don't want to talk about that. When I was old enough to work, my mother brought me to the estate. But the damage was done."

"Damage?"

Irina looked away. "I said I don't want to talk about it."

Ellen nodded. "How did you wind up in Petrograd?"

Irina studied the cigarette in her hand. "The countess paid for me to go to the university."

"That seems generous."

"Yes, it *seems* generous. She robbed me of my childhood but sent me to the university where I learned the truth about our imperialist society. It's like having a thief take everything you own and then throw you some crumbs. Tell me, Ellen, how does one family accumulate so much? They owned my grandparents. Owned them, do you understand? No wonder my grandfather was such a vicious bastard who drank himself to death."

"I do understand, Comrade," Ellen said. "My mother lost her ma and da and all her brothers in the Great Hunger. It was a different kind of oppression, but it leaves a bitterness that cannot be sweetened at any price."

Irina looked up at the clouds in the sky.

"When you go see the countess, slap the bitch in the face for me."

Ellen laughed. "I don't think that's what your dear Soso has in mind."

Ellen walked through the Summer Garden to the Palace Square. Along the walkways flowers of every hue bloomed. It's like a fairy tale, Ellen thought. When she arrived at Palace Square, she stared across at the enormous green building with its statues and vases decorating the parapet and wings spread like some colossal bird. Why was everything in Petrograd so massive, she wondered. Were they glorifying or challenging God?

As she strode across the square, she remembered that the revolution of 1905 had ended in the massacre of unarmed men, women and children on Bloody Sunday here on these very stones. Were their ghosts rejoicing now that the old order had been overturned?

Ellen entered the palace and stopped. She lifted her eyes and tried to take it all in — the soaring gold pillars, the statues of soldiers in the niches, the gleaming chandelier, and glistening marble floors. She had been impressed by the ballerina's mansion, but this was a thousand-fold more majestic. Awe mixed with anger. For centuries the people of Russia had toiled so these heartless despots could build obscene monuments to their greed and folly. At least they'd had the sense to turn part of it into a hospital at the start of the war.

She asked a soldier how to get to the office of the City Government. He dropped his lit cigarette on the polished floor and smashed it with his dirty boot. Then he pointed to his right with his bayonet.

Ellen had not been in many government buildings in her life, and she wasn't sure how it all worked, but she got the distinct sense that the new Provisional Government hadn't quite figured it out. Men in suits wandered about. They gathered in groups to gesticulate and yell.

She found her way to the city office and asked a clerk to be admitted to see Sofia Panina. She gave him a card with her name in Russian and English. One of the beauties of having a printer accessible.

After nearly half an hour of waiting, Ellen was shown into a high-ceilinged office with a chandelier hanging overhead. The woman seated behind the desk wore the sort of unadorned dark dress an English governess might wear. She looked up at Ellen with startling blue eyes. Her auburn hair was piled on top of her head. Curls framed her forehead. She was the sort of woman who took one's breath away and then immediately gave it back with the warmth of her smile. Ellen remembered what Irina had said and told herself not to trust that smile. The countess stood and held out her hand – something an aristocratic woman did not normally do when encountering an "inferior."

"How may I help you?" the countess asked in English as she sat down and indicated an ornate chair for Ellen.

Ellen accepted the seat. "Countess Panina, I would like to interview you for the American press."

"Interview me? Why?"

"I write for a socialist paper in America. Women there are thrilled to see the changes happening here. They still cannot vote in America, and here you are with a position as a deputy in the city government."

The countess looked surprised. "You don't sound American."

"Born in Ireland, but I also claim American citizenship. I lived in New York for several years."

The countess leaned forward eagerly. "What do you think of their form of government? I've always been intrigued."

"It's got flaws. The wealthy still have an obscene amount of power. Poor people still go hungry. I partook in several demonstrations with the Army of the Unemployed in 1914 and saw men brutalized by police and ignored by the clergy. Women have no legal access to birth control. In fact, women who try to provide information about birth control wind up in jail."

"And yet...?" The countess rested her chin on her hands.

Ellen sighed. "And yet...I suppose there is a sense it's in flux. In Ireland we were stuck. There was no moving forward, but my life in America changed radically. I went from being a servant to running a magazine. Change is possible in America, but it isn't fast or easy."

"Sounds like it was fast for you."

"A matter of luck, that's all." She didn't mention it had been bad luck that had caused her to inherit a fortune, a fortune she never wanted.

"I hope democracy will be possible here as well, but we have so much work to do. Speaking of work, I must get back to it." She straightened some papers on her desk. "In addition to my duties on the City Council, I have been given the task of making sure the soldiers' families get food to eat, building a playground for children, and creating a new soup kitchen."

Ellen hadn't expected to be dismissed so quickly. "I would still like to interview you. Perhaps somewhere else? At a more convenient time?"

The woman looked down at her desk. Something in her demeanor and the tilting of her long neck made Ellen's breath catch. Countess Sofia Panina reminded her for a split second of Hester French. Then she felt ashamed of herself. She should not be falling for this "liberal" aristocrat. They were the people Molotov and Irina despised. Ellen must not give in to sentimentality.

The countess looked up at her with ocean-blue eyes and said, "Come to my house tomorrow evening."

That was more than Ellen expected. "Certainly."

Ellen left the Winter Palace with the countess's home address in hand. She felt guilty for the strange elation she felt. She should not be so intrigued by this woman. She gazed up at the blue sky and a memory flashed in her mind – a woman in a blue sheath, smiling, her eyes scanning and then, for a fraction of a second, catching on Ellen's before moving past her. The countess was the woman in the blue sheath she had seen at the ballet.

Chapter 33

Louisa

The knock on the door came at the ungodly hour of 8 a.m.

"Louisa, your young man is here," her mother called up the stairs.

Did she have to refer to Francis as her "young man," Louisa wondered. He was only three years younger than she. And what was her mother doing up so early anyway?

"I'll be right down," she said.

She threw on a linen day dress, donned a pair of slippers, pulled her hair back, tied a ribbon around it, then hurried downstairs.

She found Francis, her mother, and Carlotta all waiting for her in the parlor.

"I brought the paper," Francis said.

"It's happened!" Carlotta said. "We're at war."

"Well, let's hear it." Louisa sat down next to Francis on the sofa. Carlotta sat on the other side, looking over his shoulder.

Francis cleared his throat and read from the front page: "At 8:35 o'clock last night, President Wilson appeared before a joint session of the Senate and House and invited it to consider the fact that Germany had been making war upon us and to take action in recognition of that fact in accordance with his recommendations, which include universal military service, the raising of an army of 500,000 men, and co-operation with the Allies in all ways that will help most effectively to defeat Germany."

"Well, it's about time. He should have declared war after they sank the *Lusitania* two years ago," Anna grumbled.

"Mother, please," Louisa said.

Francis continued, "American ships have been sunk, American lives taken, in ways which it has stirred us very deeply to learn of…. The challenge is to all mankind. …Our motive will not be revenge or the victorious assertion of the physical might of the nation, but only the vindication of right, of human right, of which we are only a single champion…."

Francis paused before reading the next sentence. "'The world,' Wilson said, 'must be made safe for democracy.'"

Louisa leaned back to absorb the import of this declaration. They had all known since February that a declaration of war against the Central Powers was likely. More than likely. But when it actually came, it felt like a blow. How many young men would lose their lives? How many families would be left bereft?

Francis continued skimming the article.

"He also mentions 'the wonderful and heartening events that have been happening in the last few weeks in Russia.'"

Carlotta clapped her hands. "He's talking about the people's revolution. The Russians know what to do with aristocrats."

Louisa wondered what the revolution meant for the war. Would Russia abandon the fight just when America joined in? "Well, what do we do now? We're a country at war, and this is no ordinary war. It is a world war."

Francis put down the paper. "I'm going to find Captain Van Deman and ask if he'll be accepting applications any time soon."

Louisa's heart sank.

After lunch, Carlotta also left. Louisa put a cello sonata on the phonograph while Anna looked out the window. Gingin had slipped onto the older woman's lap, and Anna gently stroked the cat, forgetting that she disliked animals.

"Where did Carlotta say she was going?" she asked.

"She didn't. But I imagine she's out with her socialist friends, bemoaning America's entrance into the war."

"Shameful," Anna said. "We must support our country now."

Louisa closed her eyes. Her mother was right, of course. But why? Why must they support death and destruction? When they ought to be planning a wedding? She was so angry she could scream.

That evening Louisa took the elevator up to Edith Wharton's hotel room, where the maid let her in and hung up her jacket. Louisa sat down and removed her kid gloves. Edith entered in a satin dressing gown.

"Louisa, I'm so glad you could stop by before I head back to France."

"I wanted to find out whether your meetings were successful," Louisa said.

"Splendidly. The secretary of war has authorized a new military intelligence division, which will be called rather unimaginatively MID. Captain Van Deman will be in charge."

"That's wonderful." Louisa didn't mention how unwelcome the news really was.

"Your information helped me convince the secretary of war," Edith sat down across from her. "Did Doris offer you tea or coffee?"

"I'm fine, thank you. May I ask you for a favor now?" Louisa hoped to emerge with at least one piece of good news.

"Of course, dear."

Louisa left the hotel feeling at once elated and despondent. Elated because Edith had been more than willing to grant her favor and despondent because Francis Holland was exactly the sort of man that Ralph Van Deman was looking for. The men must be "of good character, courage and unquestioned honesty." That description fit Francis Holland more than any man she had ever known.

Chapter 34

Ellen

That night Ellen took a droshky to the address Sofia Panina had given her. The countess's mansion stood across from the Fontanka River. When Ellen stepped down from the cart, her gaze floated up the facade of the yellow stucco building, three stories high and stretching out for seven windows on either side of the door.

Like the ballerina's mansion, the conspicuous display of wealth must have driven the starving Russians mad, and yet the new government had installed this woman on the City Council. Molotov was right. They were not forming a government of the people. Instead they were creating another handle for the aristocrats to hold onto power.

Ellen strode across the cobblestone street and knocked on the massive door. A butler answered and showed her inside. She gazed around the entrance hall with its huge marble columns and shiny marble floor. Statues occupied the corners. It was just as ornate as the ballerina's palace but the air felt dusty, as if there were not enough servants to keep it up. Dimly lit with gas lamps, the hallway was cold. The countess might still have her wealth, but the lack of fuel affected all.

"She'll see you in the study," he said in French. They passed an ornate drawing room, with paintings and antique furnishings. The butler indicated a room at the end of the hallway, and Ellen entered. A fire glowed in the fireplace and warmed the smaller room. Portraits of sneering men and haughty women hung on the walls. A tray of cheese, rolls, and herring sat on the table. Sofia Panina rose from the settee to greet her.

"Please sit and have something to eat, Miss Malloy," Sofia said in perfect English. "Food is so dear these days, but we still manage."

Ellen couldn't help herself. She sat and gobbled down the food, delighting in the soft white rolls, a rarity in Petrograd. The countess watched her with the same amused look Ellen had seen when she spoke to Stalin.

"What would you like to talk about?" the countess asked.

Ellen wiped the crumbs from the corners of her mouth and made sure to swallow before speaking. Her Bolshevik friends were always talking with their mouths full of food, spewing masticated bits into the air. Her own manners had gotten rusty around them. She took out her pad and pencil.

Countess Panina lifted a porcelain cup and sipped her tea. A voice inside Ellen's head told her she was being seduced by the woman's perfect manners, the velvet voice, and the food. She felt a surge of annoyance with herself.

"How did you become involved with the Kadet Party?" Ellen asked, pen in hand.

The countess leaned back in her comfortable chair and looked up at a portrait of a silver-haired man with a fleshy face, a gray goatee, and spectacles. "My stepfather, Ivan, and my mother founded the Kadet Party. I grew up listening to their debates about how to reform the government. Believe it or not, some members of the aristocracy have long known that Russia has to change. But the Tsar always stood in the way of progress. He had so many opportunities to save his legacy and he chose not to do so. He was a weak man. Good riddance, as you say in America."

"You did not care for him?"

She scoffed. "Not at all. He was an obstinate man with more loyalty to the autocracy than to the people. When he kissed the crown at his coronation, he signed away his soul." The countess frowned. "Now, the opportunity for reform may be lost."

"What do you mean?"

"I mean, the Bolsheviks. From what I can tell, they are in no mood for compromise. If they gain control, the country is doomed. Instead of a liberal democracy, we'll have a group of ruthless thugs in charge."

Ellen's anger returned full force. This high and mighty woman was calling the very people who had sacrificed so much, who suffered imprisonment and exile for the sake of the people, as "thugs." She gazed around the comfortable room with its velvet drapes and thought of the miserable little flat she shared with Irina.

"At least the Bolsheviks demand peace while this new government, these 'liberals 'support the continuation of the war with Germany. And how does that help the starving workers?" Ellen jabbed her finger in the air. "Poor people are the ones punished by war. They're the ones sending their sons, their husbands and brothers to fight." Ellen thought of her own brothers, one dead and the other two exiled. "They go hungry while sending grain to feed the horses and the soldiers. The wealthy manage not to suffer no matter what."

"That's not entirely true."

Ellen held up the piece of white bread. "Where do you get flour?"

"I have an estate in the country. We grow wheat."

"How nice."

The countess sat up a little straighter, lifted her chin and said, "I do know that I have an easier life than most. That is why I fight so hard to change our society, to uplift all that I can. Russia is in the throes of momentous change right now."

Ellen leaned forward, wishing she could rip the blinders off this woman's lovely eyes. "Yes, and you are a part of it. But does your government really intend to change anything? There is still no bread for the workers, no peace for the soldiers, and no land for the peasants."

"I thought you wanted to write about me, about what I do," Sofia Panina said, her voice containing a blade of sharpness it did not have before.

Ellen collected herself. She should keep her outrage in check. She wasn't even sure why she was here. If she still published a magazine for American progressive women, then the

countess would be perfect for a profile. But, she reminded herself, she was not a publisher anymore. She was a propagandist for the Bolsheviks. Molotov and Irina said that the Kadet government was nothing but craven cowards. They were right.

On the other hand, Stalin wanted her to conduct this interview and he wasn't a man to be ignored. She softened her voice. "I apologize. Tell me, what is your role in the new government?"

The countess sighed. "The imperial family supported schools and orphanages and many charities. Now that they are gone, we must determine the fate of those places. For example, the Smolny Institute was a school for girls. The military is already moving in, and now where will those girls go?"

"Daughters of the aristocracy, aren't they?" Ellen asked. Once again, disdain crept into her voice. "Did you go to school there?"

Now it was the countess's turn to lean forward. "I know what you think. You see all this wealth and ask what I have done to deserve any of it. The answer is I did nothing to deserve it except to be born. It was my ancestors who served the Tsars faithfully and were stewards of their estates, allowing them to accumulated the wealth."

Ellen gave up any semblance of objectivity. "How many people did your family *own* before the emancipation of the serfs?"

The countess looked down at her hands. "Thousands."

"How many thousands?" Ellen pressed. She didn't know why she was being so aggressive. This woman was sure to throw her out any minute.

"My grandfather owned more than 15,000 serfs, but he also drafted the legislation that freed them. My grandfather did his duty and freed them all. That is what my family does. We do our duty. And I do mine by devoting my life to uplifting the Russian people. You are a stranger to our land, Miss Malloy. You have no right to judge me."

Ellen let her eyes drift around the room, taking note of the priceless vases and figurines on the shelves. "Now that Russia has undergone a revolution, what are you doing with your immense wealth?"

The countess's eyes flashed. "Do you really want to know what I do with my wealth? Go to the Ligovsky People's House and see. The land I purchased, the building I commissioned, the work I have done for decades now. Yes, I live in luxury. And no, I will not renounce my title or disavow my family, but before you condemn me, you might learn a bit about the woman they call the Red Countess."

With that, Countess Sofia Panina rang a bell, and the butler appeared.

"Our interview is done," she said. "Au revoir, Mademoiselle Malloy."

Ellen slipped a roll and some cheese into her pocket before leaving. Irina would appreciate it.

On the way home after another day at the mansion, Ellen and Irina stopped at a street booth selling American chocolate bars. The price of seven rubles was outlandish, but Ellen bought two of them. She told Irina she had stolen some silver from her former employers and sold it. They agreed that taking from the capitalist class was not theft but simply the procurement of payment owed for centuries of oppression.

"Why did Soso stop writing?" Ellen asked Irina as she bit into the chocolate bar and felt an immediate rush of pleasure. His editorials had taken a conciliatory approach to the Provisional Government. He did not demand that Russia withdraw from the war. This stance drew the ire of Vladimir Lenin, in exile in Switzerland, who began writing screeds he called "Letters from Afar."

"That's easy. Lenin is returning."

Ellen took another bite of chocolate. So, the Germans had finally managed the return of the Bolshevik leader. With Lenin in charge, the Bolsheviks stood a chance of coming out on top. The countess would not be happy when she heard this news.

That night Ellen sat on the bench by the window in the flat she shared with Irina, who was off with some soldier. *The trollop*, Ellen thought with a chuckle.

She gazed out at the swirling snowfall, pondering this strange double life she now led. It had been two years since the *Lusitania* sank beneath her, two years since Hester French fell from a lifeboat into the icy waters, two years of relentless rage. The woman she had loved and who had loved her was never coming back.

She went to her mattress and felt the seam, still there. The treasury bonds safe. She was supposed to give them to the Bolsheviks, but when and to whom? Surely not to Stalin. But Irina had mentioned that Lenin would return soon. Ellen wondered what he was like. He seemed more than a mite curmudgeonly from his writing.

As she crawled into bed, she said her nightly prayer for Hester, and then just as she drifted off to the land of Nod, she had an image of a woman's face. Sofia Panina, blue eyes turning into sky turning into a vast ocean where Ellen floated in a tiny boat.

Chapter 35

Louisa

Francis' eyes burned with excitement as he stuffed papers into his briefcase. Sunlight shined through the dust motes in the air, making everything seem as if it were sprinkled with fairy dust. But there was nothing magical in the way Louisa felt.

"But your heart murmur?" Louisa asked.

"Captain Van Deman has assured me it won't matter. He said he will find a physician who is hard of hearing if he has to. Anyway, I won't be in combat, so they'll make an exception. They're desperate for men like me, apparently."

"Francis, what about your law practice?" She did not ask the real question, which was: What about us? He looked at her and stopped what he was doing. She couldn't hide her feelings.

He took her in his arms. "Louisa, darling, I know you're disappointed. Why don't we get married right away?"

She pulled away from him and shook her head. "A rushed wedding and then set up house only to have you head off to France? No, Dear, we'll wait until you get back and the war is over. Then we'll have a gorgeous wedding, and we'll go to somewhere that isn't war-torn for our honeymoon. And I'll have champagne for breakfast every morning to celebrate that you're alive."

He caressed her shoulder. "You can have champagne for breakfast, lunch, and dinner."

"And caviar?"

He nodded.

She pulled away. She couldn't pretend to be happy for him. Her heart had turned dark and cold, like a shriveled pea inside her chest. "I must go. I promised Suzie I would come over. She's absolutely distraught over Pansy's plans to go to France."

"Of course she is." He looked into her eyes. "Shall we go dancing later tonight?"

"I don't think so, Darling." Louisa pecked him on the cheek and hurried out.

Moving quickly along the street, she noticed banners hanging from street lamps and the façades of buildings showing the stern narrow face of Uncle Sam with his piercing eyes and white goatee, his finger pointing. "I want you," the posters said.

Go to hell, Uncle Sam, Louisa thought.

Suzie thrust a newspaper at Louisa, pointing to a passage on page one. "Look at this."

Louisa read the passage: "According to Germany's wishes, American ships are to be painted like American barber poles and sail along a chalk line drawn across the ocean, otherwise they risked being 'sunk without a trace.'"

Louisa lowered the paper. "That's why she'll be on a Dutch ship, Suzie. They will be safe from German torpedoes."

Suzie wrung her hands. "I can't lose her, Louisa," she said. "I just can't."

"I know, but you have to let her go with your blessing."

Suzie nodded, but her eyes welled with tears.

"Francis is going, too." And then Louisa's tears rushed out as if a pipe had burst.

The two women stood in the cozy parlor and wept in each other's arms.

The next morning Louisa, Suzie, and Pansy rode together in the back of the taxicab, Pansy between the two of them bubbling with excitement. The thick clouds in the sky couldn't diminish her joy.

"You have your passport, don't you?" Suzie asked.

"Yes, Auntie, I have my passport."

"What about the snacks I packed for you?"

"I have them, too. You do know they feed you on a steamship."

Suzie sighed and leaned back. "You're lucky you're in first class, I suppose." She turned to Louisa and asked, "How did you manage that?"

"It was Edith's doing. Pansy's cabin is right next to hers."

"I've never been out of the country before. To think I'd still be in St. Augustine if you two hadn't brought me to live with you in New York City."

Suzie made a sucking sound and muttered something under her breath. They pulled up to the dock. Louisa remembered seeing Ellen off a year earlier. And now Pansy was leaving. So many separations.

They exited the taxicab, and the driver delivered Pansy's trunk to a porter.

"Louisa, yoo hoo!" a voice called out.

Louisa turned and saw Edith Wharton, in her fur coat and big sailboat of a hat, beaming like a light-house. Louisa exhaled in relief. "Suzie, if Edith Wharton is on the ship, you can rest assured, no harm will come to Pansy."

"What makes you say that?" Suzie asked.

"The Germans wouldn't dare."

They hurried over to where Edith stood next to a stack of trunks. Her coat was open, and a long strand of pearls dangled from her neck.

"Mrs. Wharton, this is Pansy, Suzie's grandniece."

"What a lovely young woman." Edith smiled broadly and took Pansy's hand before turning to Suzie." And Suzie, how delightful to see you again. Why, you look wonderful. You haven't aged a bit. Marriage must agree with you."

Suzie nodded. "It does, Mrs. Wharton. Louisa said Pansy will be working in your tuberculosis hospital. Is there any chance she'll catch it?"

Edith looked Pansy up and down. The young woman stood about five feet four inches, but with her perfect posture she looked taller. She exuded confidence and competence. Louisa felt proud even though, admittedly, she had little to do with how Pansy turned out.

"She's young and healthy. I believe she'll be fine. I haven't caught it and I'm there rather frequently. Don't you worry. I'll watch over your niece like a mother hen." The steamship bellowed. Pansy hugged Louisa and Suzie before hurrying after Edith toward the embarkation line.

Louisa put an arm around Suzie's soft shoulders.

"I despise this war," Suzie said.

"So do I." Louisa looked down at the sapphire and gold ring on her finger. As gorgeous as it was, the shiny stone was no match for the tide of history.

Chapter 36

Ellen

Ellen had no intention of following up on Countess Sofia Panina's command to go and take a look at the Ligovsky People's House. And yet she had casually asked Irina about the place, and now here she was on a muddy road far from the comfort of the ballerina's mansion. The area looked like the worst sections of New York with windowless wooden houses, taverns, stables, and factories all jumbled together. She skipped around puddles of melting snow and piles of horse manure and trash. The pungent odor of poverty filled her nostrils.

Ellen couldn't get the countess out of her mind. The woman was rich and pampered and assuaged her guilt by helping the poor, but Ellen couldn't stop thinking of her steely blue eyes and her thin, elegant hands as she poured tea into a porcelain cup. Now, Ellen was on her way to the charitable institution that Sofia Panina had built to "uplift" the Russian people.

Ellen wondered, had she been a wee bit harsh when judging the woman? Perhaps she should write a profile of her, after all. Emma Goldman's anarchist magazine *Mother Earth* might be willing to print it. Or even one of the more mainstream New York women's magazines.

She turned a corner and stopped in astonishment. There was no mistaking the Ligovsky People's House, a three-story brick building with a giant, arched window. It was not an ornate building, but it held a certain dignity like a grand old widow, and stood as a beacon of civilization in the midst of degradation.

Ellen crossed the street and entered through a wrought-iron doorway. Once inside, she found an office and asked to speak to the administrator. A tiny woman with gray hair and smiling eyes emerged from another room.

"I'm Alexandra," she said. "Sofia told me to expect you, Miss Malloy."

"Did she now?" Ellen looked askance. How could the countess have known that Ellen would show up? Such arrogance.

"Come this way." Alexandra beckoned.

Ellen followed the diminutive figure along a wide hallway past a classroom where a group of adults appeared to be learning to read. In another classroom, children played with toys and puzzles. Alexandra turned the corner and headed down another hallway past alabaster statues to an arched doorway, where she stopped and stretched out a hand to display the room. Ellen looked in at a huge theater with chandeliers, plush red seats, and art deco flourishes. Along the side walls were arched alcoves as if they were in a church.

"This is the home of the Mobile-Popular Theater. The company performs both Russian and foreign classics. The director believes that theater unites all the classes," she said, crossing her arms.

"Impressive," Ellen murmured.

Next Alexandra showed her a cozy room where girls were learning how to sew.

"We also teach them mathematics and drawing," Alexandra said, "while the boys learn drafting along with history and geography and such. Are you hungry?"

Ellen's stomach growled. "I am a wee bit puckish, now that you mention it."

"Then let's visit the tea room."

The tea room was large and crowded with workers and their families.

"Is it always like this?" Ellen asked.

"Quite often."

In spite of the food shortages in the rest of the city, the tea room offered biscuits, along with the tea and even sugar.

"We also have a savings bank and an office for legal aid," Alexandra said as they drank their tea and nibbled on the shortbread biscuits.

"All this is Sofia Panina's doing?" Ellen asked.

"Yes. It's rare to meet someone, especially an aristocrat, as selfless as she. She has brought more than just food and literacy to factory workers and peasants. In addition to the theater, we host poetry readings, musical concerts, and dances. One cannot live by bread alone."

"Why do they call her the Red Countess?" Ellen asked.

"Because of this!" Alexandra spread her arms wide. "It's all free."

Ellen gazed around. Sofia Panina had taken her immense wealth and spread it around to the poor. She was a Socialist, at heart.

After they finished their tea, Alexandra took her to a reading room, furnished with comfortable chairs and sofas. Bookshelves lined the walls.

"Does the countess visit often?" Ellen asked Alexandra.

"Oh, yes. Actually, she came more often before the revolution. Now, she is too busy to visit as much as she would like. May I leave you here for a bit? A workman is coming by and I need to give him a work order."

"Certainly."

Ellen looked around and noticed a dark-haired child of about six, staring at the pages of a book. Ellen went over to her.

"Would you like me to read the book to you?"

The girl nodded eagerly, and a little boy who had been playing with a wooden soldier on the floor beside her said, "Me, too."

So, she sat down between the two children and read a story book about a rabbit and a little girl. The feel of the small bodies next to her was as comforting as a warm bath. Her heart grew light. And to think Sofia Panina had made this possible for these children.

She finished the book, and to her surprise the children hugged her.

Alexandra returned. "You can come by anytime, Miss Malloy. We're always looking for volunteers."

"I will come back." Ellen realized she actually meant it.

As she made her way back to the ballerina's mansion along the muddy route, Ellen believed she understood the countess better. The comfort she'd felt reading a book to those two children was deeply satisfying, like having a cool glass of water on a hot day. She imagined the feeling Sofia Panina had as she walked through those brightly lit hallways, hearing the laughter of children and seeing the smiling faces of their parents. *It must be a hundred times as powerful.* The countess had brought hope and joy to thousands of people.

She turned to look at the house once more, realizing that it was only because Sofia's family had been aristocrats who got their immense wealth off the backs of the peasants that she could afford to be so magnanimous. And if the Bolsheviks had their way, the aristocracy would be stripped of it all. Would the Bolsheviks be better stewards? Would they make sure that children had a place to get food and learn how to read? Would they have a chance to show the entire world what justice and equality truly meant? If so, they would make history and she, Ellen Malloy, a girl from the Claddagh, would be part of it, and all her sacrifices would mean something after all.

Chapter 37

Louisa

Louisa put her mother into the taxicab and gave the driver Suzie's address. She felt a welling of gratitude that Anna had found a sense of purpose. When Ellen had been living with them and published her magazine from the parlor, Anna had jumped right in helping with subscriptions and soliciting advertisers. Then all of a sudden, Ellen was gone and the magazine just a memory. Louisa had worried that Anna would regress to her invalid state, but between Suzie's activism and her sewing and alterations business, Anna's "dance card" was full once again.

Just as well, as Carlotta was forever traipsing off somewhere, and Louisa didn't like to leave her mother home alone for long stretches. Instead of worrying about her mother, she now fretted about Carlotta. Louisa could only imagine that, desperate to find something to do with herself, Carlotta had gotten mixed up with that unemployed socialist *poet* she met at the Lenox Club. Not that it was Louisa's business, but she did feel responsible for the young woman.

The phone rang as she returned to the house. It was Nixola, asking to meet at City Hall Park at noon.

Nixola sat on a bench near the statue of her grandfather with her face tilted up to the sun.

"Your skin," Louisa admonished, holding her parasol above her.

"Sunlight is healthy, Louisa. Have a seat." Nixola indicated the other half of the bench.

Louisa sat. "Is this a clandestine meeting, Nixola?"

Nixola shook her head. "Not at all. I just like to visit my grandfather sometimes and let him know how I'm doing."

Louisa gazed up at the statue. The sculptor had portrayed the man as a kindly, curious fellow, his brow wrinkled, a bronze newspaper on his lap. The artist had even taken care to create fringe hanging from the chair that looked as if it might be soft to the touch.

"I understand he's known these days as Nixola Greeley Smith's grandfather," Louisa said.

"Oh, I'll be forgotten someday, but this statue will be here long into the future. People will not forget him." Nixola turned to Louisa. "How would you like a job?"

Louisa's breath caught. A job? She had a job. She was an investigator. *An investigator with no clients.*

"What sort of job?"

"Selling hats." Nixola pursed her lips. "What sort of job do you think, Louisa? A newspaper job, of course."

"Well, I don't suppose you expect me to be a 'newsie,'" Louisa said. "So what sort of newspaper job do you have in mind?"

"The editor of the women's section has gone and gotten herself with child. She can't work any longer. I thought of you."

Louisa sat back. A couple of pigeons squabbled on the walkway in front of her. She kicked out her foot and they flew up in a flurry of feathers.

"The pay is decent," Nixola said. "And the hours aren't as bad as reporting. I almost didn't ask because I know you're getting married…"

Louisa ran her hand over her skirt. She thought of Carlotta's complaints about the price of food.

"The wedding has been delayed due to unforeseen circumstances," Louisa said. "I'd be happy to have a job."

"Sorry to hear about that, but glad you're willing to step up. I'll let the boss man know."

"Just until the war is over," Louisa said. "Then I have plans. Champagne and caviar plans."

Louisa sat in the parlor reading a recent translation of the *Communings with Himself of Marcus Aurelius Antoninus, Emperor of Rome*. She was puzzled by his maxim, "Do not think yourself hurt and you shall remain unhurt." She couldn't help that she felt hurt by Francis' decision to join military intelligence. *How could she simply think herself unhurt?*

The front door opened. A minute or so later, her mother came in, pulling off her gloves.

"You're home reading? Again?" Anna said.

"Yes, Mother. I am." Louisa turned a page. "Why shouldn't I be?"

"I should think you'd be spending every moment you can with your young man." Anna dropped into her overstuffed chair.

Louisa pretended to keep reading. "It hurts too much to see him. I'm having difficulty forgiving him for signing up to be part of this idiotic war."

"So, you're going to sit around and lose yourself in books? At least Suzie is doing something useful. She's working with other Negroes to protest the barbarism going on in the South. She's not moping around like you."

"Mother, you moped around for fifteen years after Father died. Was killed, rather." Louisa gave her mother a pointed look, which Anna ignored.

"Francis Holland is very much alive, dear." Anna paused and then continued, "Louisa, I have never told you what to do, but I think you'll regret not spending time with your fiancé." With that, she rose and went upstairs.

Louisa looked down at the words on the page and tried to read them but nothing made any sense. She gave up and shut the book. Would she regret her behavior? Would she wish that she hadn't shunned Francis before he left for the war? Isn't this just what she had done to Forrest two years ago — gotten so tangled up in her own fear and grief that she lost him to another woman? She and Francis had never even made love. Oh, they had come close, but they'd never lain next to each other, their bodies naked, flesh against flesh. What if he died in France, and they'd never been together?

Her mother was right. She would regret that. Very much.

The next day a huge parade filled Broadway as people cheered the men joining up to fight. A woman in uniform sang "Over There" from a platform and the crowd sang along. America was puffing out its chest and brandishing its sword.

It was almost five o'clock before Louisa climbed the steps to Francis' office. She anticipated the kiss he would give her when they were alone together. She would apologize for her absence and suggest going out for dinner. And then...then she would suggest that they register at a hotel as man and wife. After all, they were engaged now. They could go somewhere discreet.

The secretary was just leaving when Louisa went in. "Hullo, Miss Delafield. Mr. Holland has someone in his office but he said for you to go on in."

"I wonder if he's got an assignment for me," Louisa said.

"Dunno." The secretary gathered her things and left the office.

Louisa heard men's voices as she paused outside his office. She opened the door and saw Captain Van Deman sitting across the desk from Francis. They both rose when she entered.

"Louisa, darling." Francis strode around the desk to take her hand. "You remember Captain Van Deman."

"Certainly. Good evening, Captain." She kept her tone cool.

"Miss Delafield, I was hoping to meet you again," Van Deman said. "Won't you sit down?"

Louisa looked at Francis curiously, wondering what was going on. She sat.

Van Deman got right to it. "Miss Delafield, in addition to the men we will be sending to France, we are also seeking civilian investigators. I understand you have some experience in this realm."

This was not what she expected. The captain leaned forward, elbows on his bony knees. "We pay four dollars a day plus expenses."

Louisa burst out laughing. She knew she was being rude, but she didn't care. First, they were taking her future husband away from her and now offering this insulting sum for her to do intelligence work.

"I know it's not much, Louisa," Francis said. "But you'd be helping your country."

"Is that so? What sorts of assignments would I have?"

"You would be involved in counterintelligence, searching out enemies at home, that sort of thing," Van Deman said.

Not much different from what she had done two years earlier, when she had exposed what the German spies were up to. But she didn't want to work for Captain Van Deman.

She planted her hands on her hips. "Really? The way you did in the Philippines? When I was writing for *The Ladies' Lantern,* we published a letter one of your minions wrote about the 'water cure' you gave your prisoners. Quite gruesome. Your men hold the prisoner down, put some sort of a rod in the mouth and then pour a pail of water in his mouth and nose. Drowning him over and over again until he says what you want to hear."

The major shook his head. "You wouldn't be involved in anything like that." His gaze lowered, betraying his guilt – a guilt that was short-lived. "I understand, however, that you recently interviewed that Russian, Trotsky. A socialist."

She glared at Francis before answering. "I did."

"Well, we need someone like you. Someone for whom doors open, whether it's the highest echelons of society or the dens of anarchists."

Louisa found herself at a loss for words. She wanted nothing to do with this man or his counterintelligence schemes.

"Gentlemen, I already have a job. I will be the editor of the women's desk at *The Evening World.* I'm afraid I must leave now." She headed for the door.

"Louisa," Francis said. But she didn't turn around. She hurried out of the office and down the stairs. He called to her from the top of the stairs, "Louisa!"

She kept going – out into the evening, hurrying along Broadway until she came to one of the new movie palaces. The poster showed a picture of the great vamp Theda Bara in a revealing Egyptian costume. Louisa dug out a dime and went inside. "Cleopatra" would provide a suitable escape from the world of 1917. Soon she would be floating on the Nile.

Chapter 38
Ellen

Thousands gathered at Finland Station to meet Lenin's train. Just before midnight he stepped out of his sealed cabin with Stalin right behind him. It was impossible not to feel the fervor, the excitement that the great man's arrival heralded.

Ellen stood in the back of the crowd with Irina and Molotov. They grinned at each other. He was finally here – the man himself.

"I didn't know Soso was with him," Irina said.

"He met the train at Teryoki on the border with Finland. It won't be long before Soso changes his tune," Molotov predicted. "Wait and see. No more compromises with the Provisional Government."

From the platform Lenin waved to the enthusiastic crowd, Stalin glowering from behind. Lenin wore a Homburg hat and a double-breasted suit and carried an umbrella. He looked like a banker, not the leader of the revolution.

As the band struck up "The Marseillaise," searchlights roved over the crowd, while soldiers and factory workers waved red banners. The new Red Guard – soldiers enlisted as security by the Bolsheviks – accompanied Lenin and Stalin to an armored car. Before getting into the car, Lenin turned to the crowd and proclaimed, "The Provisional Government is lying to you with their promises of land and peace. We will overthrow this lackey government and end the imperialist war once and for all."

Silence spread over the crowd as they absorbed the meaning of his words. Would the Bolsheviks really overthrow the government?

He continued, "The people need peace. The people need bread. The people need land. And *they* give you war and hunger ... We must fight for the socialist revolution, fight to the end, until the complete victory of the proletariat. Long live the revolution!"

In that moment, he owned the crowd. They cheered. They hugged. They kissed.

Ellen, Irina, and Molotov piled into a confiscated motorcar and followed the armored car taking Lenin to the ballerina's mansion, where a giant red flag fluttered over the wall. Irina bounced on the seat in excitement. Lenin got out of the car ahead of them and glanced approvingly at the mansion. Stalin came right behind him and led him inside.

Molotov motioned for them to stay outside. "Wait. Comrade Lenin will give a speech."

As they waited the crowd gathered. The people did not push or shove but stood, gazing up at the wrought-iron balcony. Ellen studied the crowd. She saw no government officials, only factory workers, soldiers, peasants, students, and war widows. These were Lenin's people — the ones the new Provisional Government pretended did not exist. In Lenin's articles he had written that getting rid of the Tsar was not enough. The old system needed to be destroyed entirely and something new built in its place. But could one man accomplish that?

After a few more minutes, Lenin emerged onto the balcony, hands in his pockets.

"Peace! Bread! Land!" he called out. He did not have a deep or resonant voice, but he knew what the people wanted to hear. A resounding cheer erupted. "Hurrah!"

Then to Ellen's surprise, he demanded that soldiers murder their officers and desert the army, that peasants remove the gentry and seize the land, and that workers wrest control of the factories. "You want to get rich? There is money in the banks."

Incendiary talk, Ellen thought, but effective for the starving masses. Soon the crowd was singing, "We will cut their throats! We will disembowel them!"

Such glee, such satisfaction thrummed in the words and the music. Ellen had never fallen for the bloodthirsty rhetoric of the anarchists in New York, but here she felt helpless. If the crowd went on a murdering rampage, she might very well succumb to the power of the mob and follow them. The rage she kept chained in her heart yearned to break free.

When Lenin disappeared back inside, the crowd slowly dispersed. Molotov went inside to meet with Lenin and Stalin, but the women were not invited, so Irina and Ellen took a tram back to their flat in the Vyborg district, Irina bubbling with an infectious excitement.

"Lenin speaks with the tongue of revolution," Irina said. "He will catch the enemy by surprise."

She continued explaining Lenin's strategy, but Ellen was barely listening. She was both horrified and thrilled at the lack of control she had felt in the mob's grip. Her imagination took over, and she saw herself slitting the throat of the enemy — but the enemy's face was that of the Red Countess with the deep blue eyes.

"What are you writing?" Irina asked the next day. "You've been pecking away all day on your English typewriter."

"Just typing some notes. It's nigh impossible to keep the shifting allegiances straight. First, Stalin supports the Provisional Government and so we support them and the war. Then Lenin arrives, and now we're opposing the government and the war. There are Bolsheviks and Mensheviks and God knows what other 'sheviks."

Irina couldn't read English, so Ellen had no concern she would discover the real topic on Ellen's pages — the Red Countess and her People's House. She wasn't sure why she was being secretive, but she had a feeling she should play her cards close to the chest.

"I have to go over to the Winter Palace," Ellen said, taking the paper out of her typewriter and shoving it into a drawer.

"What for?" Irina asked.

Ellen couldn't think of a reason, so she told the truth, though Irina might not like it. "It's my understanding that record numbers of women are joining the army. Figured I might interview one or two of them."

Irina nodded. "Women can be as brutal as any man."

Ellen walked across the bridge and returned to Sofia Panina's office in the Winter Palace. The clerk let her in right away.

Sofia Panina glanced at her and then continued her work. "How may I help you, Comrade Malloy?"

"I've come to apologize. I judged you for circumstances which are outside of your control. I've seen your People's House, and it's most impressive."

"You did judge me, and I felt quite sure that your sentence would be the guillotine."

Ellen wanted to say that she would never dream of harming that beautiful neck but she refrained. In truth, she had not forgotten her vision of slitting the woman's throat – to her shame. "I'd like to continue our interview if possible."

The countess didn't answer right away. After a few minutes of silence, she set down her pen and looked up at Ellen with narrowed eyes. "Let me ask you a question first. Are you on the side of the Bolsheviks?"

Ellen took a deep breath and then lied. "I am here as a neutral observer. But the editors at *Pravda* have given me an office and the use of a typewriter. They are eager to spread the revolution."

Sofia Panina studied her for a long minute. "I'm not sure I believe you are neutral," she said. "However, I am willing to continue our interview. Come to my house again tomorrow night. I promise not to serve you rolls or anything else that might offend you."

"I wouldn't say the rolls offended me…"

The countess smirked. "See you then, Miss Malloy."

The atmosphere in the ballerina's mansion changed almost immediately with Lenin's arrival. The next evening he barged into the *Pravda* office and banged on the desk. They all rushed in to see what the fuss was.

"What the hell have you been writing?" Lenin thundered at Stalin and the other editors. "It's shit!"

Irina slapped a hand over her mouth to keep from laughing while Ellen held her breath and marveled at the way the entire room full of leather-jacketed tough guys quaked in fear. When Lenin was done with his harangue, the men skulked out of the room like dogs with their tails between their legs.

When the editors and writers for *Pravda* met with Stalin in the palace the next morning, his attitude toward the government had indeed shifted.

"Many things are clearer now," Stalin said. "The people want land, but the cowardly Provisional Government insists on honoring commitments made by the Tsar. They say that Lenin is mad, but if he is mad, then he is a mad fox. Together we will win Russia for the Bolsheviks and Russian soldiers will no longer die for the Imperialists."

Lenin was no fox, Ellen thought, he was a lean, hungry lion. Like nearly everyone else, she found herself in his thrall. The next day Ellen took a trip to the telegraph office to send a message to "Olga" in Berlin: *My uncle has arrived. He wants to build a new house. All the brothers agree.*

Chapter 39
Louisa

As the el rocked along the tracks, Louisa looked out the window at the city speeding by. She'd just spent an hour or so in ancient Egypt. What a spectacle *Cleopatra* was. The costumes, the jewelry, the magnificent sets. The handsome and devoted "slave." Louisa had met the actress Theda Bara the previous summer and helped her deal with a blackmail situation. She found it fascinating how different the intelligent, articulate actress was from the double-dealing vamps she played in the movies. The queenly Cleopatra, though still sultry, suited her better than a murderous vamp.

The train car arrived at her station in Harlem, and Louisa exited along with the other passengers. She was no longer in Egypt, but back in her world ,where the new Military Intelligence Division was absconding with the man she was engaged to. She huffed as she descended the platform steps. She felt helpless and didn't like it.

When she turned the corner to her house, she saw a silver Rolls-Royce parked in front of the brownstone.

She peeked in the window of the car. The steering wheel was on the wrong side of the car. She knew only one person who had managed to have a car imported directly from Britain.

She stormed into the house and took off her duster. Her mother was laughing gaily. Louisa peered around the corner and saw him: Reggie Grant sitting on her sofa, a glass of sherry on the table next to him. Carlotta sat in the chair catty-corner to the couch – her expression unreadable.

Louisa stepped inside the room. "What are you doing in my parlor, Reggie?"

"Louisa," Anna said in a loud, cheerful voice, "where have you been hiding this charming man?"

"I haven't been hiding him anywhere," she said. "He lurks in the shadows. He's a British spy who has been trying to convince Wilson to join the Allies in their war against Germany for the past three years. And now he's succeeded."

Anna clapped her hands. "A spy? How exciting!"

"I repeat, why are you here, Reggie?"

Reggie took a sip of the sherry and smacked his lips. "Jolly good sherry."

"I'm glad you like it," Anna said. Louisa was pretty sure Reggie despised sherry.

He set down the glass and looked up at Louisa. "I've come to persuade you to reconsider Captain Van Deman's offer."

"At four dollars a day? I don't think so." Louisa took a crystal glass from the china cabinet and poured herself some sherry.

"My superiors have authorized me to double the pay for you," Reggie said. "I explained to them about the exemplary service you have provided in the past, and they agree you should be compensated accordingly."

Carlotta piped up. "Will your superiors be compensating me for the loss of my looks?" She brushed the dark hair away from her face, revealing the scar from her cheek to her upper lip.

Reggie studied her, his head tilted as if to get a better look. "You have lost nothing in the way of beauty, Carlotta. You are still quite stunning. Only now you have something else as well. Something of the fierceness of your character has been etched on your face. Really, you quite take one's breath away."

Carlotta sat back and stared at him. All three of the women were stunned. Men saw things differently, Louisa realized. Where the women saw a flaw, a man saw an entire story. Carlotta's scar did not obscure her beauty. Instead, somehow it revealed her fire.

"Suppose we take a walk, Reggie," Louisa said. "Good night, Mother. Don't wait up."

"Care to take a ride instead?" Reggie asked once they were outside.

"What choice do I have if I want to find out what this is all about?" Louisa got in the passenger seat of the Rolls while Reggie cranked the engine.

Once inside the motorcar, he said, "As much as I enjoyed your mother's sherry, do you mind if we go somewhere and get a real drink?"

Louisa waved her hand in response. "Reggie, what if I had come into my house with my fiancé and we'd found you cozying up to my mother? How would that look?"

"I wasn't worried about it," he said. "One of my men watched you enter the movie theater alone. How was the movie, by the way?"

She ignored the question. "Why should I take an assignment with Van Deman's Military Intelligence Division?"

"I'll tell you once I've got some gin in me."

He turned onto Broadway and headed toward the lights.

Chapter 40

Ellen

Since Lenin's arrival, Stalin and Molotov were like men with a fever. Not only were they writing editorials for *Pravda*, they were hammering out policies and plotting schemes for subverting the government. They held debates and gave reports. The Bolsheviks had rallies in the ballerina's grand ballroom, demanding armed insurrection. Lenin wavered from full-throated calls for anarchy to conciliatory overtures to the government.

Stalin and Molotov moved into a flat together on the Petrograd side of the Neva. Irina spent most of her evenings with them. As a foreigner, Ellen's role was peripheral and she was not invited to the all-night sessions. Her evenings were free to wander the city. The long brutal winter lifted, and street musicians played balalaikas and domras and accordions for kopeks from the passersby. More and more often she found herself strolling along the banks of the Fontanka where the Red Countess lived.

In the mornings she assembled notes about events as best she could. She translated statements from Stalin. Once a week she sent a brief missive by telegraph to *The New York Call*. She did not take part in the endless meetings, and had not once spoken with Lenin. He seemed unaware of her existence, but she felt his presence whenever he was in the building. A tightness in her throat.

To fill her time, Ellen found reasons to continue her interview with Sofia Panina, who enjoyed talking about her life's work. Eventually, the interviews turned into two-way conversations, and without realizing how it happened, they were on a first-name basis.

Ellen told Sofia about Hester – her charity work, and then her death when the Germans torpedoed the *Lusitania*. She did not reveal the true nature of their relationship but simply said she had been Hester's companion, which the countess probably assumed meant paid companion.

"She must have meant a lot to you," Sofia said.

Ellen nodded, knowing that a part of her reason for wanting to spend time with Sofia sprang out of that lost love.

As they sat in Sofia's study under the stern gazes of family portraits or strolled along the embankment of the Neva River, they often pondered the changing world around them and wondered what difference suffrage for women might achieve. Would the world become a more peaceful place, a more just place? What if every girl could pursue her dreams? What if education were available to all women? What could they accomplish?

Other times, Sofia would be tired and discouraged from the enormous tasks ahead of her. "The orphans!" she bemoaned as they observed a couple of urchins fighting over a potato. "How do we support them? I have access to funds, but in the long run I'm not sure how we manage without some sort of taxation."

"How do you tax people who have nothing?" Ellen asked.

Sofia rubbed her forehead. "I don't know. I must do whatever I can to save as many as I can. I must fight for every kopek to feed and house them. I may not be able to save them all, but if I don't save the ones I can, then I have no purpose in being here."

They sometimes debated the path forward for Russia. Sofia tried to convince Ellen that abolishing the old systems entirely would leave no foundation for any sort of civil society, for democracy, for the rule of law. But Ellen believed, as Lenin espoused, that reform would only provide bread crumbs for a starving populace. Revolution meant upending everything.

From Sofia's balcony one evening, Ellen stared at the blazing colors in the northern sky. Bright enough to read a book.

"It is like a war between dark and light," Sofia said. "Between good and evil. Which side are we on?"

Ellen exhaled and said, "We may never know."

Irina popped her head into the office where Ellen was reading a recent copy of *Mother Earth* that some American anarchists had brought into Russia. Since the revolution, exiles were starting to make their way back home.

"Comrade Lenin wants to see you," she said.

"Me?" Ellen asked. "Why?"

"He wants to give you a medal for your service, Wench." Irina laughed at her own joke.

"You're the one who deserves an honor for *service*, Trollop," Ellen rejoindered.

As Ellen strode down the hallway to the ballerina's boudoir, her heart ramped up a notch. She was finally going to be face-to-face with the man who brought upheaval in his wake. She took a deep breath and opened the door. Lenin sat alone at the desk, writing with an old-fashioned dip pen.

"Comrade Lenin," she said. "You wanted to speak to me?"

He put down his pen and stood up in his pressed suit, hands in his pockets, head tilted as he observed her with eyes deep as canyons. The high forehead added to the impression of a daft genius. She breathed slowly, willing herself to stay placid.

"I know who you are," he said without preamble.

She swallowed. "What do you mean?"

He took a step toward her. "When I was in Cracow, a German spymaster named Nicolai visited me. We talked of many things. At one point, your name came up."

Ellen's breath caught. Nicolai? She looked away quickly and then realized he was watching her reaction, taking it in, assessing her. She returned his gaze. "And what did this man tell you?"

"That you are a spy," Lenin said, his voice cool and matter-of-fact. "He told me he trained you himself."

Her stomach clenched into a hard fist. Anger was better than fear. "He did not train me, but I have met him," she answered.

"Is it true? Are you a spy for the Germans?" He seemed genuinely curious.

She hesitated. How much should she tell? What would he do if she told the truth?

"When we were planning the rising in Ireland, we needed rifles. I went with some members of the Irish Brotherhood to procure weapons from Berlin. But as

you know, the plans failed. The British found the sub-
marine with the rifles and arrested our leaders. When
the British came after me, I escaped back to Germany."

Lenin's tone darkened. "You didn't answer my question."

"I did not come here as a spy. I came here to offer
support to the Bolsheviks. The Germans helped me get
here – as they did you. They want the same thing you
do. They are losing to the Allies, and they want Russia
out of the war."

He scoffed, then turned toward the window and
looked out at the river. As she waited for his response,
she heard soldiers laughing from the hallway. He
turned back to her and crossed his arms, pinning her
with his black eyes.

"Soso says you are useful to us. As an international-
ist, I envision the people's revolution encompassing the
globe."

"As do I, Comrade," she said.

He came close. He radiated the scent of a musty old
lion. His voice grew soft. "Hear me, Tovarisch. If I find
out you have betrayed us, I will turn you over as a spy
to the soldiers who witnessed their brothers slaughtered by the Germans, and it will not be pleasant for
you."

The fear she kept under wraps tapped at the door of
her mind, but she would not let it in.

"Comrade Lenin, I came to Russia of my own free
will. I am on your side. I have seen much oppression
from the capitalist system. This war? Men dying by the
millions all to satisfy the imperial dreams of the mon-
eyed class? I will never betray the people."

Again, he studied her for a long, drawn-out moment.
She felt like a specimen under glass. Then he asked,
"What did Nicolai do to you?"

What had Nicolai done to her? He had found her numb with grief. He had shoved her onto a bed in a flat he had confiscated. He had pulled up her dress, removed her underclothes, and used her like a ragdoll. She had been a virgin, but he hadn't noticed. Then when he was done, he told her she had passed the test. She was suitable to spy for the Germans, and the Germans sent her back to America, where nine months later she gave birth to a girl.

"Nothing." She felt the numbness she always felt when she remembered that night.

The sun broke through the clouds outside and brightened the whole room. Lenin's mood shifted just as dramatically.

"Come with me, Ellen," he said. "Let's take a drive."

"A drive?"

What had happened? Was she suddenly in favor? Or was this some kind of trick? She hesitated but then followed him into the hallway and down the wide polished stairs.

"Get me a car!" Lenin bellowed to one of the lounging soldiers.

A few minutes later they were in the back seat of a confiscated armored car, driving across the bridge to the Vyborg side.

"I know this area, Comrade. Irina and I have a flat here."

"But you spend your days on the Petrograd side." Lenin tapped the driver's shoulder. "Let us out."

The car pulled over and they got out.

"Where are we going?" she asked.

"Around."

Confused, she walked at his side past apartment buildings and down side streets. He hummed a folk song while they strolled into the poor section.

With one hand in his pocket and one gesturing toward the street, Lenin said, "We have no destination. But imagine you are in New York City. What would you see in New York that you do not see here?"

Ellen looked around. She saw a tobacco shop, a cobbler, a newsstand, and the occasional café. Workers, horse-drawn carts, a few motorcars, trams.

"New York has more food vendors…" she said.

"Think, Ellen Malloy. What is missing from these streets?"

At that moment a pregnant woman stumbled past. She was gaunt, practically emaciated, and she limped.

"Children," Ellen suddenly said. "In New York, we have throngs of children. The newspapers call them guttersnipes. They wander the streets in roving bands. I do see some children here. But not in the same numbers."

He nodded in agreement.

"More children have died in Russia since the war than in all the other affected countries together. Children in the cities do not have proper nutrition. In the countryside where they are fleeing the war, out of every 1,000 children, 800 of them die."

Ellen inhaled sharply. How could a country continue to be a nation if its children didn't survive?

"You see, Tovarisch, why we fight," Lenin said. "The children of the workers and the peasants die while the children of the aristocracy and bourgeoisie eat cakes and play under the watchful eyes of their nurses."

"What can you do?" Ellen asked. "What will you do?"

Lenin turned to look at the pregnant woman who had sat down on a bench, resting her head in her hands. He pointed to her.

"Motherhood is the hub of all problems. Each new measure, each law, each practical step in social construction must also be checked against the question of how it will affect the family, whether it worsens or lightens the fate of the mother, whether it improves the position of the child."

As he spoke, Ellen thought about all these months since leaving her own child behind in America, how she had walled off her heart. She'd allowed herself to be dragooned by the British Foreign Office into returning to Germany as a double agent. Then, the Germans sent her here to Petrograd, and she was no longer sure whose side she was on. Certainly not the British, not after what they had done to the Irish rebels. The Americans, perhaps, but didn't the ruling classes there also treat the poor badly?

The wall around her heart crumbled. When she was alive, Hester French, the woman Ellen had loved, cared about one thing — helping poor children. She had gone into the tenements of the Bowery with medicine, food, and toys for the children. She had fought for sanitized milk and health care for pregnant women. Even when she fought for suffrage, she did so to improve the lives of the poor.

Through a fog of feelings, Ellen's murky purpose became clearer. Aside from saving her brother, she had often wondered why she was here, why she had survived the icy waters of the Irish sea after the *Lusitania* sank, why she had given up her own child to a wealthy childless couple. She realized, looking at the pregnant woman, she must do something. Hadn't Sofia Panina bemoaned the plight of Russia's orphans. But how? The answer, of course, was money. She thought of the Scottish Chap and how he had insisted she not deliver the treasury bonds to the Bolsheviks, but he had not kept his word, and how would the Bolsheviks help the children without money?

Lenin touched her arm. "Do you see, Ellen? Do you understand why what we do is important? And you are part of it. Our revolution is for the mothers and the children of the world."

He gazed at her, his dark eyes boring into her, and in that moment she would have done anything for him. She would stand with this crazy Bolshevik who, in spite of his aristocratic background, had a vision of equality and justice that would spread across the world.

"Comrade, there is something I have not told you. I did not want to insult you," she said. "On the train through Finland, I was given a package for you. It was said to be from a man named Parvus."

He looked at her in surprise. "A package for me? From Parvus? What is in it?"

"British Treasury notes. About one million pounds' worth."

Lenin rubbed his goatee. "And why is this an insult?"

"This money comes from the Germans through a capitalist. I thought you might not want to have tainted money."

Lenin smiled. "I will use German money to fund our revolution, and someday the Bolsheviks will fund a revolution in Germany. Let's go and get the treasury bonds."

Some instinct told her to go alone.

"It will take some time," she said. "I will meet you back at the *Pravda* offices."

After the armored car rumbled away with Lenin in it, she found her apartment building and hurried up the steps. She unlocked the door. A picture of Stalin hung over Irina's bed. The only decoration in the room.

Ellen had not checked the mattress since she'd sewn the bonds inside in February. It was now April. She removed the sheet tucked at the bottom of the mattress and felt for the stitches she'd sewn when she stuffed the bonds inside. To her surprise she felt nothing. She pulled up the mattress and looked along the seam. There was the opening but no stitches. She reached her hand into the opening and felt around. The bonds were gone.

She stumbled backward and yanked her hair. What would she tell Lenin? Why had she even mentioned the bonds to him? Then she wondered who could have done this. Irina? No. Irina trusted her, believed in her. Some over-eager member of the Red Guard? They didn't even know she existed, much less that she had treasury bonds hidden in her mattress.

The Scottish Chap was the one person who knew she had the money. She'd told him, fool that she was. And he would have known exactly where to look for it.

She rose from the floor and paced the room. She would have to tell Lenin something. He would become suspicious. He would think she'd been lying. Whatever lie she told, if she didn't have the money to give Lenin, she would lose any standing she had with the Bolsheviks. They could find someone else to translate their ideas to the West.

She stopped her pacing, stared at the blank wall and assessed her situation. She would have to find the Scottish Chap and steal the bonds back. She looked in the bottom drawer of the dresser. At least, he had left the guns she and Irina had stolen from the armory. She took one of them and put it in her purse.

Chapter 41

Louisa

Reggie looked thoughtfully into his Bombay gin and tonic in the lounge at the Ritz-Carlton. "How about we take you out of the frying pan and drop you in the middle of the fire?"

"We? Who's we and what fire do you mean?"

He leaned forward. "I mean, Russia."

"Russia? Are you mad?"

"I've been talking to Van Deman, and it seems that your friends the Murph's have a trip planned to St. Petersburg — or Petrograd as they call it now. However, if the Bolsheviks take over, Russia may back out of the war, which will be disastrous for us. If Germany doesn't have to worry about Russia, they can move all their forces to the Western Front."

Louisa sipped her wine. She did not want to go to Russia.

"Why are the Murphy's going to Russia anyway?"

"A contingent of railroad experts is going to offer advice and supplies to the new Russian government. Wilson wants to implant capitalism there, and the Duma wants to purchase train cars, specifically from Murphy's company. So he's going over to negotiate a deal. It's vital that Russia modernize their rail system or we'll never win this damn war. Right now they can't get food to the cities or to the front."

"I don't love the cold," Louisa said.

"It will be summer when you get there."

"And who will take care of Mother?" she asked, pushing a strand of hair that had loosed itself from her bouffant behind her ear. "Reggie, I simply can't do it."

Reggie lit a cigarette with his gold lighter. Smoke poured from his nostrils. "Too bad. I was hoping you would deliver a message to Ellen for me."

Louisa inhaled sharply at the mention of her friend. "Ellen?"

"Yes, she's smack dab in the middle of Petrograd. The Germans sent her. As you can imagine, they are quite interested in what's going on with the Russians. The whole world wants to know. Will democracy take hold? Will Russia stay in the war?"

Louisa pondered this information. She desperately wanted to see Ellen in the flesh, to make sure she was safe, but travel was perilous with the war going on, and she had just gotten the job offer from Nixola. She couldn't leave now. Besides, if Ellen was working as a spy it might endanger her cover if Louisa suddenly appeared.

"Thank you for the enticing offer, Reggie, but I'll pass."

He sighed. "As you wish."

She decided to leave before Reggie drank much more. His words were slurring a bit, and his hand had fallen onto her knee more often than she liked.

"Where are you going?" he asked.

"Home to pack. Francis and I are going to Connecticut for the weekend." She had only just then decided to forgive him for joining Van Deman's Military Intelligence Division.

His eyes widened. "Are you? That seems rather daring. Why doesn't he just come to your bedroom the way I used to?"

"Because he's not an arrogant ass," Louisa said. She strode out of the bar and hailed a taxicab.

At breakfast the next morning, Carlotta announced to Louisa and Anna, "I got something to tell you."

Oh no, Louisa thought, swallowing her oatmeal. Carlotta was going to marry that socialist poet.

Carlotta leaned forward and said, "I'm joining the police force."

Louisa's jaw dropped. "You're doing what?"

"I've been thinking about it for a while now. I enjoy our investigations, and I feel it's time for me to do it professionally. Policemen are all about joining the army, which leaves openings for us women."

Louisa placed her elbows on the table and leaned forward. "But what about Abe? The man you've been seeing?"

"What about him?"

"I thought you were perhaps getting serious with him?"

"I'm not even twenty years old!" Carlotta frowned. "Ellen never married anyone. You're not married yet. Suzie was at least 60 before she married. Why should I marry and give up my life to take care of some man? Abe is a socialist. He understands women need to make their own way. Besides, he already has a wife."

Anna threw her hands up. "Of course he does."

"But what about your family?" Louisa asked.

"What about them?"

"How will they feel about you joining the police? They are...criminals, after all."

"So's half the police force. I'll be right at home. Look, I love investigating crimes. I've been talking to Martin Malloy about it, and he thinks someday they'll even have lady detectives."

A former prostitute from a Mafia family as a police matron? Louisa shook her head in disbelief. And yet, at least Carlotta was moving forward in her life, unlike Louisa swirling in a whirlpool going nowhere.

Chapter 42

Ellen

Ellen wore the somber but well-made brown dress she had worn as a servant, the kind of clothing that made one invisible to the ruling class.

It had been two months since Ellen had last seen the Scottish Chap at the Hotel Astoria. When she'd gone back to find him, she had discovered that all the foreigners were gone from the hotel, which now mainly housed military officers and cadets. The hotel clerk said that the Scottish Chap had moved into a house on the English Embankment.

She walked along the quiet street to the English residences. The door to the servants' entrance along the side of the house stood open. Cigarette butts lay scattered on the stones outside. She pushed the door, and it swung open. The kitchen had been ransacked. Probably the whole house had been. But she noticed clean dishes beside the sink and a bin with food items – jams and biscuits, things that might arrive in a diplomatic pouch. Someone was still living here.

A deep silence like a living thing met her as she opened the door to the main hallway, and a foul smell hit her nostrils. She put a handkerchief to her nose and walked across the marble floor. The shadow of a man lay on the floor like a discarded coat.

She turned and saw the body hanging over the mahogany banister, from a rope tied to a rail in the staircase. She'd seen so much death by now that she did not feel horror. Instead, her first thought was, what an ingenious way to hang oneself. No bothersome stool to kick away. Just leap over the banister and there you are. Though the face was bloated and a horrid shade of purple, she recognized him. The Scottish Chap. He must have come here when he could no longer stay in the hotel.

Around his neck hung a pig's foot. Pig? Secret police. Spy. Obviously he had not hanged himself. Someone had done it for him. Russians. Possibly soldiers who thought he was a spy?

A Scottish ditty came to her mind: *"Oh, the oak and the ash, and the bonnie apple tree, they're all a-growin' green in my ain countree."* The Scottish Chap's spirit was back in his own country now. She crossed herself and then heard footsteps behind her. Slow. Purposeful. She considered her options. There was no running away. So she turned around.

"Tovarisch," Stalin said.

She thought she might vomit, and not just from the godawful smell. "What are you doing here?"

He kept his voice light. "I followed you. Now I ask you the same question."

"I used to work in this house. As a domestic."

He stepped closer to her, his voice nonchalant. "You worked for a British family? I thought you were wanted by the British."

"Nothing better than hiding in plain sight. Besides, the Foreign Office is not expecting me to show up in Russia. They aren't looking for me here."

Stalin lifted his eyes toward the body of the Scottish Chap, his bare feet pointing toward the ground. "Is this man hanging around, waiting for you? Who was he? A friend of yours? The pig's foot tells me he was a spy. German? But why in a British house?"

Ellen grimaced. "A British spy. He stole some treasury bonds from me. Bonds intended for the Bolsheviks."

Stalin tilted his head in confusion. "Intended for us? From who? Your anarchist friends in New York? No, they don't have money. And why would a spy steal bonds from you?"

He leaned in close to her. She had never felt such menace in her life. He made Nicolai seem like a schoolboy. And yet he usually hid it so well under a veil of charm.

"It was given to me on the train through Finland. From someone named Parvus."

Suddenly Stalin's hand clasped her throat. He ripped her handbag away and threw it across the floor. Had he known she had a gun?

"Parvus? I know who he is. Are you a German spy, woman? What do you think would happen if I delivered you to the Petrograd garrison? You know how they feel about Germans."

Ellen tried to breathe. She waved her arms and tried to signal with her eyes that she needed to speak. He eased the pressure on her throat.

"I have to give the bonds to Comrade Lenin," she squeaked. "He's expecting them."

Stalin released her throat.

She bent over, gasping for breath. When she could speak, she croaked, "The Germans aren't your enemy. They want the Bolsheviks to control the country. I need to look through this man's things."

Stalin gazed around the cavernous hallway. "Let's look together, my Irish friend. If there are no bonds, then you'll be visiting the garrison. They will have much fun with you."

The fear she kept at bay threw off its chains and seized her, but she must not let this wolf see it. She breathed deeply and willed her legs to stop trembling.

Stalin followed her through the downstairs rooms – the dining room, the library and finally the parlor. She looked around the room where she had first met Lady Greystone. Vases and figurines had been smashed. A half-burnt chair from the dining room lay in the fireplace. The animal-skin rugs were missing, but the curtains still hung and the furniture was intact. No suitcases or anything that might have belonged to the Scottish Chap. Ellen took slow, steady breaths.

"Why did you not tell *me* about these treasury bonds?" Stalin asked.

Her fear dissipated. The insecure bastard. She turned to him with an accusatory sneer. "Because you supported the Provisional Government, Comrade. I was waiting for Lenin to arrive."

Stalin grunted. "You knew all along the Germans would get him back to us? You are full of surprises."

She ignored this remark. "The spy might have slept in one of the bedrooms upstairs," she said.

As they walked up the steps toward the second floor, she stared at the rope tied around the bottom of one of the rails.

Upstairs they went from bedroom to bedroom. Each one ransacked, but no suitcases, nothing that belonged to the Scottish Chap. "This is unfortunate for you. Irina will miss her little friend."

"Wait. There's another possibility," Ellen said. "He would be vulnerable here. He might have stayed in the servants' quarters. No one would think to go there. Servants have nothing of value."

She led him to the servants' stairs at the back of the house. As she walked up the steps, she felt his presence lurking behind her. They went from room to room and found nothing in each one. Then she opened the door to the butler's room at the end and heaved a sigh of relief. Stalin pushed past her and saw what she saw: a suitcase on a bench. He threw it open and tossed out clothes onto the floor. Then he stopped and grinned.

The Scottish Chap hadn't even hidden the bonds. Stalin laughed and threw an arm around her shoulders – all malice gone. "You've done well, Tovarisch. Comrade Lenin will appreciate this."

He scooped up the bonds and a flood of regret swallowed her. That money would not be used to help children. It would go into the pockets of thugs like Stalin. She should have given it to Sofia for her People's House, where it would do some good.

Another thought occurred to her. Now that she'd disobeyed the British and helped the Bolsheviks, she might also wind up hanging over a banister.

Chapter 43

Louisa

When Louisa awakened the next morning, the angry voices woke up along with her. She had to stop them somehow. It was time, she realized, for a reckoning with herself. She simply couldn't go on this way – angry and frustrated and helpless.

She rose and performed her morning ablutions, donned her stockings and underclothes and put on the pretty yellow-and-gray serge dress with satin vest that she had purchased last summer, when she'd been flush with money from her first investigation.

She had a quick breakfast of Grape-Nuts with milk, orange juice, and coffee and informed her mother and Carlotta that she was off to visit an old friend. Tucking her copy of Marcus Aurelius into her purse, she grabbed her parasol and left.

When she emerged from the subway into the light of day, she was only a block from her destination – the cemetery at Trinity Church.

"Hello, Papa," she said when she found his grave. "I'm sorry it's been so long since I have visited."

She laid her shawl on the ground and sat down next to her father's grave. She took out her copy of Marcus Aurelius. Her father had loved to read these meditations. So she read aloud, imagining her father smoking his pipe and listening.

In Book One, the Roman emperor recounts the people who contributed to the making of his character. He names his parents, grandparents, a great grandfather, friends, and teachers. After she'd read for twenty minutes or so, she thought of those who had helped in the construction of her own self. Her father, of course, with his gentle and kind spirit and his love of poetry, but also Suzie who had constantly encouraged her to make something of herself, her mother's mother the abolitionist, and her mother who taught her about society. There were ancestors, who had overcome countless obstacles to establish a foothold in the New World. Then recently her friends. Ellen had completely revolutionized Louisa's outlook on the world, not to mention saving her life once or twice. Carlotta and Pansy. Even baby Hester. She couldn't forget Forrest, her first love, who had shown her she was worthy of love.

She let out a sigh. If only she could love Francis Holland the way she had loved Forrest Calloway. She plucked a blade of grass from the ground. It was difficult, perhaps impossible, to give her heart to someone who might be killed in some mad war. But life is the test of your powers, she thought. If ever there was a time to find out who she was, that time was now.

She closed her book and bade her father good-bye. "I won't wait so long next time," she told him. Which was not exactly true, but how was she to know it then?

Chapter 44

Ellen

Spring burst onto the streets of Petrograd like a frolicking lamb. Trees flowered, the river broke through its icy prison, and the people, though hungry as ever, smiled in relief as sunlight danced to the beat of the cracking ice. In spite of the abundant natural beauty, Ellen's mind kept drifting back to the image of the Scottish man hanging like rotting fruit in the great hall of the Greystone house.

Since then Stalin had ignored her, and Lenin said nothing about the treasury bonds, but she assumed he had gotten them from the fact that the Bolsheviks purchased new uniforms for the growing Red Guard.

"Someone has to keep the factories in business," Lenin said when he announced the uniforms.

A few days later, Stalin called her into the *Pravda* office. It was connected to a marble bathroom where he was known to relax in the sunken bathtub late at night, and that's where she found him. She ignored his nakedness.

"What happened to your interview with the Red Countess?" he asked.

"I haven't finished it yet."

He smashed his cigarette into a crystal ashtray. "Did you find out if she would join us?"

Ellen shook her head. "It's not likely, but I will continue to work on it."

"See that you do. I would hate for her to wind up dangling from a staircase." One side of his face curved upward into a smile.

He's bluffing, she thought. Sofia Panina was much too popular among the people to fall victim to the Bolsheviks.

With Stalin's permission, Ellen continued to visit Sofia, and the friendship between them deepened. As they walked arm in arm along the bank of the Neva while Sofia took a break from her work, Ellen wondered whether the countess could ever feel about her the way Hester French had. Simply walking next to the countess was intoxicating. What would it be like to lie next to her naked? To nuzzle against her neck and breathe in the scent of her French soap, to lose herself in the sheets of her hair.

Stop it, she admonished herself, Sofia can't possibly feel that way about you. And yet hope refused to die. The question "what if" lingered in her mind.

One day as they enjoyed a brief respite in the sun, Ellen asked, "Sofia, what happened to your marriage? Divorce isn't common among aristocrats, is it?"

"No, it isn't. I caused quite a scandal," she said with a smile.

"You initiated the divorce? Was he cruel to you?"

Sofia shook her head.

"Then why? Why risk the scorn? Didn't they shun you?"

Sofia laughed bitterly. "Scorn? You mean from society? I was already disillusioned with their boorish behaviors, their greed and vanity, even before my marriage ended. I shall never forget the coronation of Nicholas and Alexandra in Moscow."

"When was that?"

"May of '96. When I witnessed the drunkenness, the affairs right out in the open, and the licentious behavior of the men, I got sick to my stomach. A group of them seized a young prostitute one night. They took turns abusing her. If I hadn't heard her cries, I'm not sure what would have happened. I had to rescue her, a poor rabbit from a pack of hounds. The next day they were at all the parties with their wives, smiling like innocent little cherubs."

Ellen thought of the wealthy men in New York who were known to bid on a girl's virtue. Wealth, power, and abuse could often be found consorting.

"I hope your husband wasn't among the pack," she said.

Sofia brushed away the idea. "No, Sasha would never have forced himself on a woman. In fact, he never had to force himself on anyone. He was charming and ambitious and fun-loving. The first year of my marriage was ecstatic."

"But something happened?"

Sofia slowed her pace. "I discovered that Sasha was not interested in me romantically."

The river glittered in the sunlight.

"Was there someone else?"

"Oh yes, but not another woman. You see, Sasha preferred going to bed with men. He is what we call in Russia a *sodomskii grekh*. Oh, it's common enough. I have even had a relative or two of that persuasion. But I refused to accept it in my marriage. The sight of him disgusted me."

Ellen held her breath. She had not anticipated this. It was all she could do not to pull her arm away and turn and run. If Sofia felt strongly about such inclinations in her husband, how much worse it would be if Ellen had shown her true feelings. She had gotten used to walling in her feelings, but this time the pain felt like a hot coal in her chest. For the first time, she wished she was not the way she was. She wished desperately not to be in love — if that's what it was — with Sofia Panina.

"I'm sorry. I don't like to talk about it," Sofia said. "Let's talk about something more pleasant. Suffrage for women. Isn't it grand to be alive and to be in Russia? How glorious are the changes to come."

"They are indeed, Comrade," Ellen said, forcing a cheerfulness into her voice she did not feel. She must end this friendship. She must make up some excuse and stop seeing the countess, for the only possible ending was heartbreak. She would finish writing the article. She would send it to Louisa in New York, who would find a place to publish it. And she would never see Sofia Panina again.

They had circled the Winter Palace.

"Thank you for walking with me," Sofia said. "I should get back to work."

"I enjoyed it," Ellen said.

As she watched Sofia enter the enormous palace, she felt the hope in her heart finally die. Then she felt something else, a sensation of someone watching her. She turned around but saw no one looking in her direction. She had grown careless, she realized, enamored with a woman so far above her station in life, a woman who would never fall in love with another woman. How could she have been so foolish?

Chapter 45

Louisa

Francis stood on the stoop in front of her wearing a green-corded hat. On his collar was a brass pin marked IP.

"Come in and let's show you off." She put on a false smile.

He entered the parlor, sat down, and pointed to the brass pin. "It stands for Intelligence Police." He grinned. "They're making us all sergeants."

"Very impressive," she said. "Where will you go first?"

"Fort Jay on Governor's Island for one month for training. Then it's off to France." He showed her his gun — a .38-caliber revolver.

"Oh, do be careful," Anna said.

Before their aborted kidnapping, Louisa couldn't imagine Francis shooting anyone, but now she knew he was perfectly capable of taking care of himself should the need arise.

"When will you two be back?" Carlotta asked.

"Tomorrow," Louisa said.

"Tomorrow?" Anna gasped.

"That's right. Tomorrow, Mother. Oh, don't worry, we'll behave," Louisa said and winked at Carlotta, who sniggered.

"Things are certainly different than they were in my day," Anna muttered.

Louisa and Francis took the train from New York to Saybrook Junction in Connecticut. On the way they talked about the future, where to have the wedding, where they might live. They reminisced about their childhoods. They talked about anything except his impending trip to France. Finally they arrived at Essex, where Francis' friend Paul's family owned a shipbuilding company.

They went directly from the train station to the Griswold Inn, a quaint old hotel with a cozy wood-paneled dining room where a fire roared and paintings of ships hung on the walls.

Paul and his wife, Rosalind, had already staked out a table. Louisa immediately liked both of them. True Connecticut Yankees. Proud, down-to-earth, decent people.

Louisa got the clam chowder with potato cakes on the side, and Francis ordered pot roast. As they ate, Rosalind questioned her about her years as a society columnist. Did she really know Teddy Roosevelt? What about the Rockefellers? Yes, and yes. In turn, Louisa asked Rosalind how she and Paul met. Rosalind explained that after her parents had died five years ago, she moved in with an elderly aunt in Saybrook. She was hired as the soprano soloist at the Episcopal church where Paul sang bass.

Paul sang in a deep voice, "I fell in love at first note."

They all laughed.

"Will you be going back to New York tonight?" Paul asked.

"No, we're going back in the morning," Francis said with an innocent look on his face.

"In the morning?" Paul and Rosalind looked from one to the other.

"Well, we are engaged," Francis said under his breath.

Paul grinned and Rosalind giggled. "We didn't wait either," Rosalind said.

Paul tapped a finger on the table. "Look, let's make it official. Francis Holland, do you take this gorgeous woman to be your wife?"

"I do," Francis said.

Then he turned to Louisa. "Louisa Delafield, do you take this poor fool to be your husband?"

Louisa hesitated. The moment felt somehow solemn in spite of their smiles. "I do," she said.

"Then I now pronounce you husband and wife," Paul said. He lifted a hand. "Waiter. A bottle of champagne to celebrate the newlyweds."

Rosalind winked at Louisa, and to her chagrin, Louisa blushed.

When they were finally alone in the hotel room, Louisa realized she did not feel particularly amorous. The thoughts she'd been refusing to think all day crashed in on her. Her throat felt tight and dry.

"Francis, I can't bear the thought of you participating in that awful war," she said, standing at the window, staring out at the swaying masts of sailboats in the harbor. The moon lingered in a field of glitter, but in the back of her mind, she heard the raging voices of the victims of war.

He came close and wrapped his arms around her. "I could never live with myself if I didn't fight for my country."

She smelled his clean, soapy scent, and sank into the warmth of his body. She wanted to feel passion, but the only emotion she could dredge up was fear. What if she allowed herself to love him and then lost him as she had lost her father? And Forrest? And Ellen? It was not too late to back out. She wasn't even sure if she was in love, and if she did not love him, she had to tell him so. It was so clear now. She had thought she wanted to be married, but to marry for the sake of being married would be terribly unfair. She opened her mouth to speak, but then his mouth was closing in on her.

Without her permission a dam burst inside her, washing away her doubts in a torrent of emotion. She reached her arms around his neck and kissed him back, not the way they used to kiss but with a hunger, exploring, tasting, devouring. They kissed for a long time. He pressed her body against the wall, the shaft of his sex stiff against her pelvis, and then his fingers deftly unbuttoned her blouse. She let him undress her, let him admire her naked body in the moonlight. The voices in her head no longer clamored for her attention.

"How beautiful you are," he said. "To think that you'll be my wife."

She laughed. "Will be? Weren't we just married in the restaurant?"

"How could I have forgotten?"

They lay down on the soft bed. He had not had much experience with women, but Francis' instincts and natural gentleness guided him as he kissed each breast and ran his hands down the length of her body. Desire rippled through her.

As his fingers brushed her skin, she touched him, and he quivered. She maneuvered him above her and guided him where he needed to be. She moved under him rhythmically, until he peaked. Then he was breathing hard beside her. A few minutes later, he fell asleep.

She had not reached a climax, but she didn't care. Somehow in the course of the night, she had fallen in love with the man she was to marry. She fell asleep to the sound of his soft snores.

In the morning, he awakened, eager to go again. She stopped him and took his hand.

"You know how you felt last night, Darling?" she asked.

He nodded.

"That's how you can make me feel."

He looked confused. "I didn't know…"

"Here," she said, taking his hand and placing it between her legs.

He caught on quickly. When she arched up in pleasure, he lowered his lips to her breast and his fingers brought her to a pitch. She moaned in delirious pleasure. He entered her, and for a moment all was oblivion as their bodies moved like dancers. The explosion came, and they collapsed onto the feather mattress, holding each other.

"I didn't know it could be like that," he said.

"Neither did I."

Chapter 46

Ellen

It had been three weeks since Ellen had stopped visiting the countess, so she was surprised to look up from her desk and see Sofia Panina standing there.

"What a surprise, my lady," Ellen said. "How can I help you?"

Sofia gazed around the room – the gold wallpaper, the elaborate moldings, the mahogany furnishings. "So, Ellen, you are part of the Bolshevik propaganda machine, after all."

"I told you they gave me space to work. But 'tis a cause I believe in," Ellen admitted. "The Provisional Government has done nothing to meet the demands of the peasants and the workers."

"I am not here to argue politics," Sofia said. "I want you to meet some friends of mine."

"Is it far?"

"My driver will take us."

Ellen followed Sofia outside and got into the back of a Fiat with velvet seats. The Russians had been so busy with the war that they were far behind the rest of the world when it came to car production except for armored cars, but Sofia had obviously managed to hold onto her imported motorcar.

"Where are we going?"

"The Smolny Institute. I'd like you to see the girls who have been left behind so you can tell me whether or not they deserve their fate. It seems that even the most moderate of our revolutionaries believes anyone connected with the old regime has no place in the new Russia. But these girls are not to blame."

Ah, Ellen thought, remembering their first conversation when she had disparaged the daughters of the aristocrats. Sofia Panina could hold onto a grudge.

They drove through the city and pulled in front of yet another grand building with arches on the lower level and huge classical columns on the next level. One more temple to opulence. They passed an elaborate garden that had not yet gone to seed and arrived at a blue-domed building tucked next to the main building.

"This used to be a convent before becoming a school. Now the first floor has been taken over by the Petrograd Soviets," Sofia told Ellen as they entered the building. "Try to ignore the trash."

Soldiers had placed desks in the dark cavernous hallway where they sat and played cards. A few of them made obscene gestures or whistled loudly when the women passed, but most ignored them. Sofia led Ellen through the hallway into an enormous ballroom with colonnades and silver candelabra. It now served as a mess hall for the soldiers with long wooden tables and wooden benches. Next, they walked through a giant kitchen where a vat of cabbage soup boiled.

"This way," Sofia said, pointing to a staircase.

On the second floor, Sofia opened the door into a dormitory. Ellen gazed around. A group of half a dozen girls in linen dresses sat on beds while a woman stood in the center and read to them in what sounded like Latin.

The girls looked up startled when Sofia and Ellen approached. They were mostly teenagers, but there were also a few younger pigtailed girls.

"Countess, how kind of you to come by," the teacher said.

Sofia kissed her on both cheeks and then turned to face the girls.

"Hello, girls. This is a friend of mine. Her name is Ellen Malloy, and she used to live in America." The girls looked confused, as if they could not imagine such an exotic place and couldn't fathom why such a thing would matter. They made Ellen think of a litter of abandoned puppies.

"Where are my parents?" one of the girls asked.

"I'm afraid I don't know," Sofia said.

Another girl, who looked to be about 11, piped up. "My mama says I can't go home because there is no home to go to. Factory workers live in our house. She says they want to put Papa in jail." She hesitated and then admitted, "I'm scared."

"Don't be." Sofia put her arms around the girl. "I'm sure your parents will find somewhere to live. The government is not putting people in jail." She turned to Ellen. "Let's go meet a princess, Ellen. Another wicked old aristocrat."

Ellen understood what Sofia was trying to do. She was trying to humanize these people, and she was succeeding. All Ellen saw in this dormitory were frightened girls who had lost everything they'd ever known.

They walked through the dormitory down the hall, up another staircase and into an opulent room with a huge canopied bed.

"This was the apartment of Emperor Alexander the First's mistress," Sofia said. She pointed to a table with strange carvings on the legs. "The empire style, they were fascinated with all things Egypt. You are looking at the dust of centuries."

The past felt like a living presence, as if some tempestuous beauty might emerge from the walls and demand diamonds. A green light shone through the lime trees outside, creating the feeling of being inside an emerald. At a desk sat an old woman with white hair.

"Princess Golitsyna, this is Ellen Malloy."

The woman shrank from Ellen in fear.

"Don't worry. She won't hurt you."

Tears flowed down the woman's face. "Is it time?"

"I'm afraid so," Sofia said. "The Soviet of Workers plans to use the entire building for their headquarters."

Ellen looked at Sofia in shock. She had not realized they were on an errand to evict the inhabitants of the Smolny Institute. "Is that true?"

"Of course it is." Sofia's expression was taut. "Comrade Lenin's orders."

"But where will we go?" the old princess asked.

"We will take the girls to the Hotel Europe. The manager has agreed to house them while I find families to take them in if I can't find their own. You should go to your family, Princess."

"What family? I have no one." Tears crawled down the old woman's face.

"You have a cousin in the country. I spoke to him. His family will take care of you." Sofia handed her a handkerchief.

Ellen and Sofia watched as the princess, the teacher, and the girls packed what they could carry. As they left, the soldiers jeered at them, making obscene gestures or spitting on the floor. Ellen thought it would be impossible to feel pity for the pampered offspring of the aristocracy, who had done so much to oppress the peasants, or for the children of the merchants and factory owners who had profited so handsomely off the labor of underpaid workers. But these girls were young and helpless, caught in the web of history. They knew nothing of the evils the Tsarist system had wrought. They were lambs, forced to wander a world of wolves.

Ellen offered to walk back to the *Pravda* office so that Sofia could ferry the girls to the hotel. Sofia put a hand gently on Ellen's arm.

"Miss Malloy, would you like to come to my house for dinner Friday night?" Sofia asked.

Ellen couldn't decline the invitation. She was in love with Sofia, and yet Sofia could only see her as a friend. Ellen would have to satisfy herself with kindness while longing for something more.

Chapter 47

Louisa

Louisa stood at the Battery and watched the ferry chug across the water toward Governor's Island. Francis would not be coming back. After his training, he was to go straight from Fort Jay onto a ship that would take him to France. She desperately hoped the ship would not be torpedoed by a German U-boat.

She could see the island from where she stood. He would be so close and yet completely unreachable. She wished she hadn't fallen in love with him. Part of her soul had been wrenched away. She turned and walked toward the terminal, dragging her heart with her. Through the terminal to the street to hail a taxicab. When she reached the curb, a motorcar pulled up in front of her. It was a Rolls-Royce.

The driver looked up at her and smiled.

She shook her head. "For heaven's sake, Reggie. What do you want now?"

He got out and led her by the elbow to the other side of the car. "I'll tell you on the way."

"On the way where?"

"To Fort Totten."

She looked at him in utter confusion. "In Queens? Why?"

"I want you to meet someone."

She got in the passenger seat. She didn't know what Reggie was up to, but at least it was a distraction from the pain of separation from Francis.

"So he's gone, is he?" Reggie said, flinging a cigarette butt out the window.

"Do you know what I discovered, Reggie?" She glared at him. "Sex is so much better when you actually love the other person."

Reggie's lips tightened into a thin line. "I wouldn't know."

"Really?" Louisa said. "Not even with the woman you married?"

"Louisa, I enjoy your company immensely when you're not being mad at me, and I admire you as well. And I truly enjoyed our romps. But if you must know, when it comes to sex, women are a means to an end."

Louisa felt as if he'd slapped her. What an awful thing to say. Then she thought, how terribly sad for him. "Explain, please."

"Marrying my wife was a means to becoming an aristocrat. Thanks to her I have a fortune and a country estate in the Staffordshire moorlands."

"And me?" Louisa was curious.

"You have been helpful in my work a number of times, as you know. Besides, you're fun."

"Well, I feel sorry for you."

"Don't," he said drily. "I have a purpose, which is nothing short of saving the British Empire. And I advise you to find your purpose as well. It's the only thing that will save you from inevitable heartbreak."

She gazed at his handsome face, the strong jawline, the planes of his cheekbones. She remembered a story he once told about a collision he'd had in a ship where he was the captain. "A total of 35 men lost their lives," he had said. The accident still haunted him.

She sighed. "Very well then, Reggie. Tell me why we are going to Fort Totten and about this someone you want me to meet."

As Reggie drove north on Second Avenue and crossed the Queensboro bridge, he explained the situation. "Captain Van Deman has discovered a German spy enlisted in the U.S. army."

"That doesn't surprise me," Louisa said. "There are hundreds of thousands of German-Americans in the United States."

"Well, I'm not sure he's a German spy. He admits he was recruited as a spy for Germany, but says he escaped from them, and he wants to serve the United States. What's more, Van Deman didn't actually find him. The German man came to us, and I believe he might genuinely want to help."

"Then what's the problem? And why are we going to Fort Totten?"

"Van Deman has him squirreled away there, and I'm worried he might employ some of his more suspect means of interrogation."

Louisa remembered the letter she had found in *The Ladies' Lantern* about the interrogation technique invented by Van Deman in the Philippines — simulating drowning to make men talk. She shuddered. "Dear God, I hope not."

"I have persuaded Van Deman to let you speak to the man."

"Why me?"

"Obviously, you're a skilled interviewer. Also, the man is a baron. And I think he'd respond more readily to a woman from the upper classes."

"I'm rather poor these days, Reggie."

"Class is not about money, and you know that. It's about breeding. Besides you don't dress like a poor woman."

She looked down at the pale green silk suit she'd worn to see Francis off, which sent her thinking of Francis again and how her heart ached. "What will I do?" she muttered to herself.

Reggie heard her. "You will do your duty to your country and to humanity, Louisa Delafield."

"By going to Russia? While I would love to see Ellen, I have a good job offer and I want no part of this war."

Reggie cleared his throat. "The other thing is that I want someone to make sure the Murphys are safe. They're taking the child with them."

"They're taking Hester?"

Reggie nodded and glanced over at her, watching her from under his blond eyebrows.

They drove through Queens and up into the country along the shore before finally reaching the gates of the fort. Reggie drove along the bay past rows of brick barracks and then parked the Rolls outside a stone storage house.

"This way," he said and led her along a walkway to a stone tunnel. She peered in and could see all the way down the tunnel to the bottom. She assumed that made it easier to watch out for enemies. While Louisa did not suffer from claustrophobia, she was glad to emerge from the other end of the tunnel into the daylight.

A granite and blue stone battery jutted into the water. Several soldiers stood along the top of the battlement. A tall man came toward them. It was Captain Van Deman.

"Miss Delafield, thank you so much for coming," he said.

"Where is the baron?" she asked.

"This way," he said. He led her down to the bottom floor of the battlement. Their footsteps echoed on the stones as they walked along the vaulted corridor. "What a marvelous construction," Louisa said, gazing up at the wide stone arches. It felt like a Roman fortress.

"It was originally designed by Robert E. Lee before he became a traitor," Van Deman said. "He was quite an engineer, you know."

Louisa wondered where they were going and where in particular the baron was being held.

"Captain Van Deman, just what do you expect me to find out from this man?" she asked.

"I don't know. Talk to him, find out if he has any secrets. Get inside his head if you can."

Louisa suddenly had an unpleasant suspicion. "I do hope you don't expect me to do anything besides talk to the man."

The captain's head tilted in confusion and then he understood her meaning. "Of course, nothing sordid, Miss Delafield. I wouldn't dream of it. Right over here."

He led them out of the battlement to a row of storage rooms. He unlocked a door and opened it.

"Hullo there," he said. "Come on out."

A man emerged from the dark room and blinked in the sunlight. He had curly blond hair peeking out from a jaunty straw boater. He wore a bow tie and a light-weight jacket. He looked as though he'd been interrupted during a stroll along the Danube.

"You kept him in a dark hole?" Louisa said, incredulously.

"Not for very long," Van Deman said.

"Long enough." The man dusted off his trousers.

"Good afternoon, Baron," Louisa said. "My name is Louisa Delafield." She turned toward Van Deman. "Captain, I would like to speak to the baron privately. Somewhere comfortable, if you don't mind."

"How about on a rowboat?" Reggie interjected. He had been silent since they'd come down to the battlement.

"A boat?" Louisa asked.

"There's one right over there." Reggie pointed down past the battlement. He turned to the German. "You can row a boat, can't you, old boy?"

"I am quite a strong rower, as a matter of fact." She heard the trace of his German accent.

Louisa was skeptical, but the water lay flat as a slightly wrinkled sheet.

"Let's go, sir," she said, opening her parasol and heading toward the rocky beach with the baron following.

She got in the bow of the boat and the baron took up the oars. Reggie and Van Deman gave the little boat a good shove, and soon they were on the water. The baron's strong arms rowed away from the shore.

"It's good to be out of that dank little cell."

"Captain Van Deman had no business putting you in there," she said. "I'm so sorry."

He shrugged. "It is understandable. But why did he choose a fine lady such as yourself to speak with me?"

"Frankly, I'm here to learn your story, Baron."

"Please call me Erich. Titles are a silly affectation."

Louisa laughed. "Tell that to New York's socialite mothers. They're more than willing to sell a daughter to get one."

He grimaced and shook his head. Then he cleared his throat and leaned forward. His skin glowed a pale gold color in the sunlight. He had held up well in his secret life.

"What do you want to know, Miss Delafield?"

She exhaled. The boat had been a good choice. The water smoothed over any rough spots in the conversation. "Tell me about your youth. Where did you grow up?"

"I grew up in Vienna. Have you ever been?"

"No."

"It's quite lovely, though I didn't appreciate it as I should have."

"I've heard it called the city of music. Do you like music?" she asked, letting her fingers dangle in the water.

His eyes brightened. "Oh yes. My favorite composer is Mahler. Do you like Mahler?"

"Of course," she said, and smiled. What a pleasant man. "So, tell me, how did a cultured young man from Vienna wind up sitting in a dank little hole in Queens, New York?"

"Long before the war began, I was a lieutenant in an elite German regiment. But I drank and gambled and ended up embezzling casino money.

"Dissolution seems to be a common fate for well-off young men," Louisa mused. "How did you get out of your trouble?"

He tilted the oars out of the water and let the boat float in the current. "I promised to make myself available to the Secret Service, and so they let me off the hook. In Charlottenburg, I received my training as an army and naval spy."

"What sort of training?" she asked.

"Cryptology mainly. But also...assassination, poisons, that sort of thing. When I learned that war was inevitable, I tried to leave the Secret Service. I didn't want to become an assassin. But they threatened to kill me and then ordered me to England. So I went, and once there I took the first available ship to the United States."

"Why?"

"I was not in favor of this war," he said. "When the Kaiser insisted on invading Belgium, I wept. I knew in my very soul he was starting a global nightmare. So I came here."

"Why? If you were against the war, why did you enlist in the American army?"

"America was neutral at the time, and it was a good place to hide. Now, I understand that Germany has forced America into the war with its threats of U-boat attacks."

"That and the Zimmerman telegram."

"An incredibly stupid move. I was angry with Germany. I still am." He took up the oars again and rowed near the shore out of the strong current.

Louisa thought of the angry voices she'd been hearing. Even now on the placid water, she heard their low murmur.

"Erich, how is the U.S. military to know if you are telling the truth? How do they know you aren't still in cahoots with the Germans?"

"Because your Captain Van Deman did not find me. I found him. I sent an SOS signal, which can mean Secret Order Service as well as the distress signal Save

Our Souls. Now that the U.S. has a military intelligence division, I realized I could be of some assistance."

The oars splashed gently against the water, and the sunlight felt soft and caressing.

"Why would you work for American intelligence if you hated it so much when you were working for the Germans?" she asked.

"For one thing, I am not German. I am Austrian. Perhaps you noticed how many German spies have been executed in London. I didn't want any part of that shoddy operation. As soon as I landed on American soil, I felt that I was where I belonged. I have read every word of the American constitution. Have you?"

"Not in years."

"It is an astounding document. It grants rights to ordinary people. These titles. Baron! Ha. What an absurdity. I want to be judged on my own terms. Yes, I drank and gambled because I felt I was entitled to behave that way."

"Erich, what can you tell me to convince Captain Van Deman that you are sincere?"

He set down the oars, leaned his elbows on his knees and gazed out at the water. "I wasn't active in German intelligence very long. I did learn the code they use to transmit international messages."

"The British have already broken the code," Louisa said.

"Well, there was one thing that happened in London just before I left. Before he was executed, a spy named Ludovico stole some British Treasury Bonds. They were never recovered."

"Do you know where they are?" she asked.

"A businessman named Parvus got his hands on them. His idea was to fund a revolution in ..."

The shot that rang out was so loud, Louisa jolted from her seat and dropped her parasol into the water. The baron fell headfirst into the boat with a groan. On his back, blood bubbled from a small hole.

Chapter 48

Ellen

Ellen generally left the ballerina's palace before the nightly revels began, but she'd gotten caught up writing an article about rebellion at the front from a soldier, a member of the 2nd Guard Infantry, she'd been able to interview. The soldier was dismissive of Kerensky's efforts to rouse the troops, calling him "bourgeois," and telling that half his company refused to go to his rally. In fact, some of them simply walked away from the front and that's how the thin-faced soldier with red-webbed eyes wound up lounging in the garden, drinking wine and telling her his story. Ellen knew she was only getting one side of the story, but this was the side that Stalin wanted her to share with the outside world.

"I prefer to fight against the bourgeois than against the Germans," the man said and ground out his cigarette with his boot.

Ellen went to her desk upstairs to put the story together along with some other reports from the front. She was not a fast writer or a fast typist. She had to search for words, but she could accurately record the quotes, and piece together the background story from other sources. When she finally looked up from her typewriter, the sky had gone dusky. The days had grown long and she figured it was close to 9 o'clock. Irina leaned in the doorway and said, "The trams aren't working. You may as well stay and have some fun, Tovarisch."

Fun? Ellen had seen the aftermath of the nightly parties, bottles everywhere, men and women passed out on couches. Blood and vomit and rotting food on the floor. It looked like utter debauchery.

"Come on," Irina said.

Ellen had an aversion to this sort of thing – drunken men who would grab and grope at anyone they could lay their hands on. But with the abundance of half-naked women streaming in, she felt she might be safe from them in her trousers, leather jacket, and cap. If she were going to support this revolution, she might as well see all aspects of it. She followed Irina through the malachite doors into the grand salon, where a band played dance music on the ballerina's grand piano with its silver gesso work.

Ellen took a silver flagon of wine and found a chair underneath a silk hanging. She sipped slowly and watched the revelers. They danced with wine-mad feet. They fell against walls, ripping down tapestries. A man and woman fornicated upright in one of the corners. Irina came by every once in a while and exhorted her to get up and dance, but Ellen shook her head.

"I wonder about you sometimes." Irina leaned close, shouting above the music. "Do you even like men?"

Ellen snorted. "I don't have time for them. I am too busy delivering the glorious revolution to the rest of the world."

Irina waved a hand at her and plunged back into the dancers.

And then gunfire.

A woman dancing not ten feet from Ellen arched her back, slinging wine from her flagon, before slumping to the floor, blood spilling from a hole in her back. A man nearby yelped and leapt about, blood spurting from his leg. Ellen's head swiveled to the window. The glass had been shattered. The men stopped dancing. They yelled and cursed and drew their weapons. The next thing she knew, about a dozen of them were at the windows firing into the night while others dragged the dead woman out. A couple of the women tended to the man who had been shot in the leg but to no avail. The bullet must have hit an artery because he bled to death in a matter of minutes.

As soon as the bodies were gone, the band struck up another tune, and the dancing began anew. Ellen shook her head. Life had so little value in this new Russia. She slipped out of the room, kicking broken bottles out of her way, and went upstairs to find a spare couch to go to sleep. What sort of revolution was this, she wondered, that cared so little for humanity. But she knew. She knew this riotous behavior was the result of centuries of chains. Now that the chains were off, insanity reigned. The Bolsheviks would have to exert some sort of control if they ever wanted to rule an actual civilization.

The next day she dropped her article off at the post office. It would get to *The Call* eventually, but it was too long to send in a telegram. She was tired, but she had agreed to have dinner with Sofia at her house, and she wasn't about to turn down an opportunity for a good meal even if being with the unattainable countess would break her heart.

The butler showed Ellen into the study. Sofia wore a red jacket with gold fringe and a navy blue skirt.

"You look like you're ready to march to the front," Ellen said. "But I fear things aren't going so well there."

"No, they aren't, but Kerensky is doing what he can."

As they nibbled on herring, pickled beets, cheese and caviar, Sofia told her about finding the families for most of the girls from the Smolny. A few had been placed with other families outside the city.

"Something else is bothering you," Ellen said.

Sofia nodded. "Ellen, I have come to regard you as a friend. I worry that you are blind to the true nature of Vladimir Lenin and his henchmen."

"I value your friendship as well," Ellen said. "But who can argue with 'bread, land, and peace'?"

Sofia shook her head. "I have read Lenin's ideas. He believes in sowing hate, revulsion, and scorn toward those who disagree with him. Those are his words, not mine. This will not end well if they get into power."

In spite of the carnage she witnessed on a daily basis, Ellen had the hopeful sense that the entire world was on the verge of a new beginning. "You worry too much. To get power Lenin will have to compromise with more moderate forces. He speaks a tough game, but ultimately cooler heads are sure to prevail."

Sofia exhaled and brushed a stray strand of hair from her face. "That's why I invited you over tonight. To tell you I have resigned from the ministry. I need to get away from the city for a while. I'm going to my estate at Marfino for the summer."

This was a surprise. "Your estate?"

"Yes, believe it or not, I still have an estate."

Not for long, Ellen thought. The Soviets were reclaiming all the land for the peasants – and killing gentry in the process. In spite of everything that had happened and all she had seen, Sofia Panina lived in a fantasy world where her wealth protected her from harm.

"Are you sure that's wise?" she asked.

Sofia placed her hand on top of Ellen's, which was resting on the balcony railing. "The peasants on my estate are very well treated. They are happy. Do you know I have even sent some of their children to university? The ones who want to go and who show promise."

Ellen said nothing. She did not tell Sofia she knew one of those whom she sent to university. Irina felt no gratitude, no love for the mistress of her parents.

In Ellen's mind, she saw the Scottish Chap hanging from the baluster in the Greystone house, his feet pointing to the ground as if he were a dancer caught in midair. "Please, be careful, Sofia."

A few days later, Ellen sat down on a park bench outside the telegraph office to read Captain Boehm's message: "E. Thank you for delivering gift. Stay in touch with yr sister. She can get into trouble. Love – Olga."

Of course, he had known about the treasury bonds, the "gift." And he wanted her to continue sending anti-war articles to the American publications. Anything to stoke unrest in their new enemy.

She looked at the telegram and reread the sentence: "Stay in touch with yr sister." If she had a sister in her life, it was Louisa. She wished she could talk to her, to tell her about the revolution, about Sofia, and to ask about little Hester. She gazed at the canal next to the telegraph office and thought of the long walks she and Louisa took along the various New York rivers. She wondered if Louisa was near water now, and if she ever thought of Ellen.

Chapter 49

Louisa

Louisa, Reggie, and Captain Van Deman sat in silence in the comfortable parlor of the officers' quarters in a huge brick castle on the hill. Louisa wore a borrowed officer's jacket since she had used her linen blouse to stanch the baron's gunshot wound while Reggie swam out to the boat. They had not been far from the shore, and once Reggie got them to the rocky beach, Van Deman had summoned his soldiers to carry the baron to a car and drive him to the "castle."

A soldier strode into the parlor and whispered something to Van Deman, who cleared his throat and announced. "They found the shooter. Unfortunately, he did not give himself up and now he's dead."

Louisa rose and went to the window to gaze out at the long green lawn. "At least we know Erich was telling the truth. They wouldn't have tried to kill him if he was one of them. I believe he sincerely wants to help the Allies."

Van Deman crowed, "You've been most helpful, Miss Delafield. A real feather in our proverbial cap. He's just the sort of man we need."

"If he lives," Reggie said in his desultory fashion.

Louisa's stomach ached, and she found herself making a bargain with God, an entity she believed probably didn't care a whit about human affairs. *Let him live and I'll do what you ask.*

Thirty minutes later, the doctor emerged from one of the officers' rooms. "He'll make it. He needs about a week of bed rest, but there's no infection and no internal damage."

Louisa said a silent prayer of gratitude.

"I'd like to see him," Louisa said.

"Go right ahead," the doctor said.

She went into the room where the baron lay in an army bed. "Miss Delafield, you're still here?"

She placed her hand on his. "I couldn't leave without knowing you would be all right. I'm so sorry you were shot."

"I'll be fine. Now I can join the Military Intelligence Division. I believe I can do some good."

"Captain Van Deman seems to think so, too," she said in an encouraging voice.

He yawned and then apologized. "The doctor gave me something to help me sleep, and I don't know if I can keep my eyes open..."

"Please don't worry," she said. He was already out. She sat in the chair next to the bed and watched him. There was something noble in his features, and she didn't think it had anything to do with his bloodline. He had resolved to do what he could to help America win the war. Just as Francis had been resolved. Ellen was in Russia doing her part, whatever that was. Carlotta had a purpose now, protecting the citizens of New

York. Even Anna had a role to play, helping Suzie and her activist friends protest lynching. Louisa was the only one floundering about, searching for some elusive happiness.

On the way back to Manhattan, she told Reggie what Erich had said about the stolen British treasury bonds.

"Interesting," he said. "I wonder if Ellen knows anything about it. If only I could contact her..."

He glanced over at her.

She gazed out the window at the ruffled waters of the Sound. "What about my pay?"

Reggie's voice was hopeful. "Pay?"

She sighed and turned to face him. "For leaving my family and going to Russia."

He grinned. "I'll see if we can bump it up. Hazardous duty and all that. I'll also make sure your mother is taken care of."

She couldn't quite fathom what she had agreed to. She'd been so adamant, and now for some reason she couldn't imagine not going. Maybe it was the bargain she'd made with whatever passed for God these days. "What is your message to Ellen?"

Reggie's jaw jutted forward. "First of all, our contact with her seems to be missing. You should ask if she knows what happened to the poor chap. Find out if she knows anything about those stolen treasury bonds. Also, she's been wanting proof that her family is alive and well in New York. You can provide that for her."

He pulled the news article she had written about the citizenship ceremony from his jacket pocket and dropped it on her lap. Ellen's family. She must be worried sick, Louisa thought. That settled the matter. What kind of friend would she be if she didn't go to Ellen and reassure her that her family was safe?

After dinner Louisa informed Carlotta and her mother she would be going to Russia and she had no idea how long she would be gone. She glanced at her mother, worried who would take care of her.

"I can take care of myself," Anna said, reading her mind. "We'll hire a girl to come clean. Carlotta's useless as a maid anyway."

"I'll still live here even once I'm working," Carlotta added.

Anna tilted her head. "Why are you going to Russia?"

"I'm going with the Murphys as a companion for Katherine and also to help with Hester. My main reason is to find Ellen, make sure she's all right, and let her know her family is safe."

Anna took a deep breath. "Then you must go. I've been worried sick about her."

Louisa's eyes widened. "Mother, I didn't know you cared."

"You don't know a lot of things about me."

"I suppose you're right. You've always been a bit of an enigma."

Carlotta chuckled. "I don't know what enigma means, but Mrs. Delafield and I will be just fine, Louisa. Your mama can stay with Suzie when I'm off being a policewoman, arresting criminals and the like."

"That's right," Anna agreed. "Suzie enjoys having me around."

All the obstacles had fallen away.

"I suppose there's nothing stopping me." Gingin wove her lithe body around Louisa's ankles. "Oh, but what about the cat?"

Carlotta scooped up the small ginger cat. "Gingin likes me. She'll be fine. She's a cat. We're very adaptable, we kitties." She scratched the creature behind the ears, and Gingin purred loudly.

As Louisa rode in the back of the taxicab to the *Evening World* to tell Nixola in person she would not be able to take the women's editorial position after all, the sense of dread that had been hanging over her lifted and dissipated. In the western sky, the sun broke through the cloud cover, shooting crepuscular rays toward the horizon. She'd been avoiding the call to her duty, afraid of losing the people in her life, afraid of missing out on some illusory idea of happiness. As she gazed out the window at the thronging streets of the city, the shoppers hurrying along the sidewalks, the panhandlers begging for pennies, the schemers, the desperate, and the hopeful, she understood the only way to silence the furious voices in her head was to join them.

Chapter 50

Ellen

As May crept into June, Ellen and Irina spent more and more time at the ballerina's palace. With Sofia gone, Ellen had no reason to wander off to the Winter Palace or to the mansion on Fontanka Street. She spent her days in the small former guest room that she and Irina used as an office. There she read newspapers — foreign newspapers when she could get them, right-wing Russian newspapers, socialist pamphlets, and Bolshevik papers. A story in one of the London papers caught her attention: "American Railmen on Way to Russia."

The article said that President Woodrow Wilson hoped to democratize Russia and implant capitalism there. Under Alexander Kerensky's regime, "the first wave of American technicians will arrive to revamp and run the vast Trans-Siberian Railway. The European allies, in concert with Kerensky, have agreed to establish the American-run Russian Railway Service."

The Bolsheviks would not be happy about Americans coming over to "implement capitalism." On the other hand, were the trains to actually run efficiently, were goods able to reach the city, then perhaps some of the creeping despair would lift. Everywhere she went, Ellen saw furrowed faces and haunted eyes, women with faces bloated and blue, children fighting over hard, black biscuits. How long could people continue to hope in the face of such deprivation?

Irina came in the room, sat down, and propped her boots up on the desk. She lit a cigarette and asked, "Where has your lady friend gone?"

Ellen averted her eyes. "You mean the Red Countess? She's hardly a friend."

"Don't be coy, Tovarisch. I saw you two walking arm-in-arm along the Neva."

Ellen was taken aback. Had Irina been spying on her? Of course she had. Irina may be her friend, but she wouldn't tolerate any perceived betrayal of the Bolsheviks.

Ellen cleared her throat. "It was an act. Comrade Stalin asked me to try to convince the countess to leave the Provisional Government and join with us. He wants her money for the cause. But she has already resigned from the government and left the city."

Irina sneered. "Isn't it nice she can leave the city whenever she feels like it? She's no revolutionary. She's bourgeois to the bone. Gone to Marfino, I assume?"

Ellen nodded. She didn't wish to talk about the countess any longer.

Irina stood up, walked over to the window. "Soso doesn't need her dirty money. When the time comes, we will take everything she has. Her car, her clothes, her mansion on the Fontanka. She has no right to any of it. Let her learn how to work."

Irina's scorn was justified, Ellen knew. Why did one woman get to own so much for the mere fact of having been born? And yet, Sofia somehow lived up to the responsibility of every advantage she'd been given. Not that Ellen would dare utter such blasphemy in the temple of Bolshevism.

She picked up the newspaper to distract herself and continued reading, "President of the Steel Car Company, John Murphy and his family will be among the visitors to Russia to help the Duma rehabilitate Russia's rail system with new equipment." Ellen dropped the paper, her mouth agape. His family?

"What is it?" Irina asked.

Ellen stammered. What could she say? Not the truth. Not that her child's adoptive father was coming to Russia and bringing *his family*. "I...I just remembered, Soso told me to try to get an article about Russian women and their rights in one of the British socialist papers, and here I've been lollygagging about."

Irina smirked. "Aren't you the lazy thing? You should be flogged in public."

Ellen forced a chuckle and stuck a piece of paper in her typewriter, but all she could think about was the possibility of seeing her daughter once more. Her heart fluttered, the barricades inside it crumbling into dust. For this moment nothing else – not the countess, not the Bolsheviks, not even the revolution – mattered.

With all the commotion of the revolution, Ellen had often been too tired to whisper her nighttime prayer of protection for Hester, but as her fingers mechanically typed, another prayer sang in her heart: *St. Christopher, protector and guide, watch over my little girl as she travels. Guard her from accidents, dangers, and hazards. May Your presence be with her through every mile, granting peace, courage, and vigilance throughout this journey. Amen.*

Author's Note

This story was initially inspired by a seven-page, single-spaced, typed letter that my grandfather, John MacEnulty Sr., vice president of the Pressed Steel Car Company, wrote to the president of that company. My grandfather and grandmother and their five-year-old daughter, Katherine, were in Petrograd when the February revolution occurred. My grandfather concluded that it was a fairly peaceful revolution that would most likely result in a free and democratic Russia. They left before things took a less democratic turn, but his eyewitness description of those events was gripping enough. I have held onto this letter for most of my life, knowing that someday it would be the inspiration for a book.

The other inspiration for the story was the development of MID – the division of military intelligence founded by Captain Ralph Van Deman with the help (allegedly) of the novelist Edith Wharton. According to the book *World War I and the Origins of Military Intelligence* by James L. Gilbert (The Scarecrow Press, 2012), prior to the United States' entrance into World War I, there was no "permanent intelligence element" within the War Department. Van Deman tried to get the attention of his superiors to organize military intelligence efforts, with little success. He wrote: "No amount of talking or argument could change the Chief of Staff's opinion, and after two or three interviews he became exasperated and ordered the writer to cease his efforts with the organization of a military information service." On April 30 when Van Deman conferred with Secretary of War Baker, that attitude changed and MID was born.

As with any historical period, the sources I found are full of contradictions. Did Edith Wharton help Van Deman accomplish his goal as was rumored? Was she even in the U.S. at the time? With the help of conjecture and imagination, I decided she was and she did. As for events in Russia, according to a *New Yorker* article, Stalin was not present at the arrival of Lenin's train. But according to the book *Young Stalin* by Simon Sebag Montefiore, he went into the train car and left with Lenin. As for the idea that Ellen brought money from the Germans to support the Bolshevik revolution, this was based on accusations that were made by the Provisional Government specifically against Lenin. In the West, this version was believed to be true while the Soviets dismissed it as pure fabrication. The actual truth seems to lie somewhere between.

From the Carl Beck Papers in Russian and East European:

Studies found that the initial accusations by the Provisional Government were most likely unfounded: "This conclusion does not necessarily eliminate the possibility that Parvus may have supplied funds to the

Bolsheviks by different channels. There is some probability, for instance, that funds reached the Bolsheviks through Parvus' intelligence agents. ... The documents of the German Foreign Ministry indicate that substantial funds were allocated to support Bolshevik anti-war activities in 1917. But since the present research disproves the generally accepted view of how the assistance reached the Bolshevik organization (that is, through Fürstenberg-Kozlowski-Sumenson's business), it appears more likely that the Germans used other intermediaries than the banking system. There is documentation of at least one occasion on which a significant sum of money was delivered to the Bolsheviks through other channels." (Lyandres, No. 1106)

The year 1917 in Petrograd was absolutely chaotic. Since this is historical fiction and not history, I have omitted several key figures and events because I worried the history would overwhelm the stories of Louisa and Ellen. I deliberately did not go into the many different political factions and omitted certain incidents.

Books I found useful in my research include *Reilly: Ace of Spies* and *Memoirs of a British Agent* by Robin Bruce Lockhart; *Caught in the Revolution: Witness to the Fall of Imperial Russia* by Helen Rappaport; *Petrograd, 1917: Witnesses to the Russian Revolution; Molotov: A Biography* by D. Watson; and *Trotsky in New York, 1917: A Radical on the Eve of Revolution* by Kenneth D. Ackerman

Some of the characters depicted in this novel are real people (Sofia Panina, Ralph Van Deman, Edith Wharton, Lenin, Stalin, Trotsky, Molotov). I learned so much about Sofia Panina's life from the fascinating book *Citizen Countess* by Adele Lindenmeyr. Some are fictional characters inspired by real people (Reggie

Grant, the Scottish Chap, Irina, Lady Greystone, Lulu, and the baron). The Murphys have always been stand-ins for my grandparents, whom I unfortunately never met. Louisa and Ellen and their friends and family are fictional, of course, but they feel real to me.

While you're waiting for the next installment in the series, I hope you'll check out my stand-alone historical novel *Cinnamon Girl* (Livingston Press, 2023), an award-winning coming-of-age novel set in 1970 and inspired by my own experiences as a teenager in 1970. In 2027, *The Woman with the Wicked Face*, a novel inspired by the life of Theda Bara, will be released by Histria Books.

To keep abreast of my books and appearances, please sign up for my newsletter at trishmacenulty.com.

Acknowledgments

No writer is an island, at least none that I know. Thanks to my dear friends Pamela Ball and Kathleen Laufenberg for setting me on the right path with this book. I didn't always want to take their advice, but turns out, of course, they were right. Much thanks as well to my "histfic gals," Gina Edwards and Melody Harris, who prodded my revisions. Finally, thanks to my fellow writers in the Historical Fiction Collective (Gail, Pamela, Carrie, Shirley, Sue Ann, Kerry, and Micah), who are always willing to give helpful feedback and provide moral support. As always, without my husband and business partner, Joe Straub, this book wouldn't exist.

The Delafield & Malloy Investigations

If you liked *The Furies of Winter*, enjoy the other **DELAFIELD & MALLOY INVESTIGATIONS**

Book 1, The Whispering Women: A pair of female sleuths dig into 1913 New York's elite, and its dark underbelly!

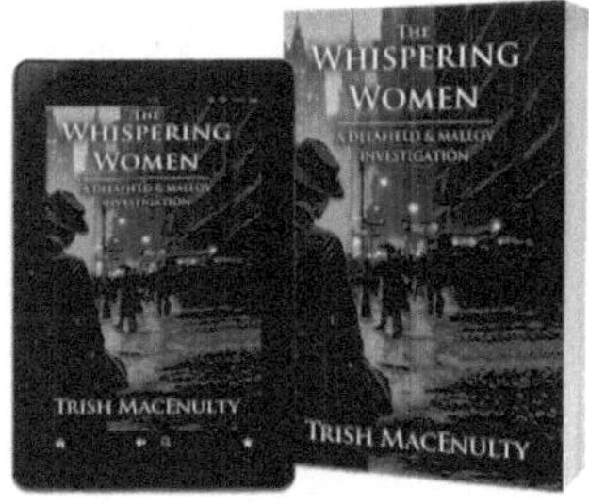

Book 2, The Butterfly Cage: Buffalo Bill, the Prince of Monaco, panic attacks, and a mysterious string of abductions to Panama!

Book 3, The Burning Bride: Dynamite-wielding anarchists, hungry alligators, a raging fire, and Louisa and Ellen's wayward hearts!

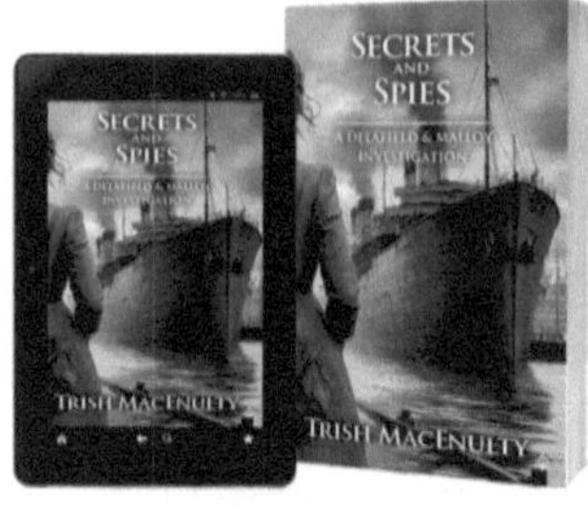

Book 4, Secrets and Spies: Subterfuge, deception, German saboteurs, and the sinking of the Lusitania!

Book 5, The Ladies' Lantern: Murders on Broadway, Ellen's new magazine and new baby, and her brother's battle with the Irish against the British oppressors!

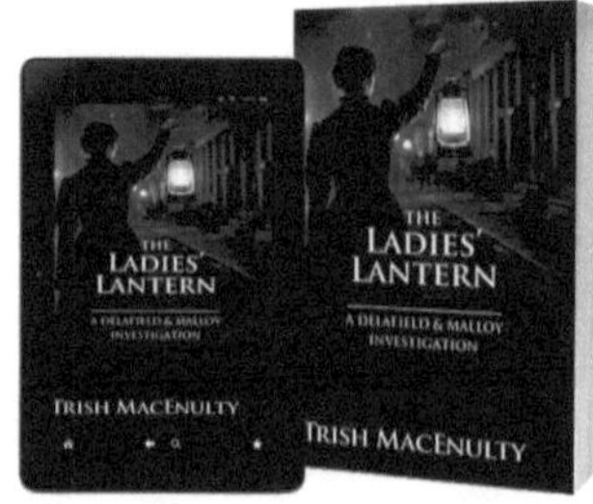

About the Author

Trish MacEnulty has been a journalist and a professor of journalism and English; she writes historical fiction, literary short stories, and memoirs. She earned degrees from the University of Florida and Florida State University, where her passion for deep research and historical accuracy was cultivated. Through her association with the Historical Novel Society, she is a regular contributor to the *Historical Novels Review*. For 20 years, she lived in Charlotte, North Carolina, where she was a Professor of English at Johnson & Wales University, teaching writing and film classes. She now lives in Florida and teaches journalism.

www.ingramcontent.com/pod-product-compliance
Lightning Source LLC
Chambersburg PA
CBHW032216050726
47591CB00001B/143